ARCTIC FIRE

THE FIRE AND ICE SERIES, BOOK 2

ERICA STEVENS

Inferno (Book 4)

Phoenix Rising (Book 5)

The Ravening Series

Ravenous (Book 1)

Taken Over (Book 2)

Reclamation (Book 3)

The Survivor Chronicles

Book 1: The Upheaval

Book 2: The Divide

Book 3: The Forsaken

Book 4: The Risen

Books written under the pen name
Brenda K. Davies

The Alliance Series

Eternally Bound (Book 1)

Hell on Earth Series

Hell on Earth (Book 1)

Coming August 2017

The Road to Hell Series

Good Intentions (Book 1)

Carved (Book 2)

The Road (Book 3)

Into Hell (Book 4)

The Vampire Awakenings Series

Awakened (Book 1)

Destined (Book 2)

Untamed (Book 3)

Enraptured (Book 4)

Undone (Book 5)

Fractured (Book 6)

Historical Romance

A Stolen Heart

Special thanks to all the fans. Love you all!

CHAPTER ONE

"You know Clint is going to be pissed at me for letting you stay in here after hours."

Julian shrugged at Quinn's words. He draped his arm around the back of the chair as he leaned back to watch her wipe off one of the last tables. "Don't care," he replied.

She shot him a look as she tucked her rag into her apron and stepped away from the table. That look guaranteed she wouldn't be as cuddly tonight as she had been last night, but he was willing to have her annoyed with him if it meant keeping her safe.

Plus, he couldn't deny he liked watching her as she worked. She had her chocolate-colored hair pulled into a ponytail that accentuated the angles of her face. The faint scar running from her right temple to her eyebrow, and the one running from her bottom lip to beneath her chin, were more visible with her hair back, something deliberate on her part.

She saw her scars as displaying to the world what she felt were her sins for killing her uncle when she was first turned into a vampire. It didn't matter that her uncle would have died anyway or that she'd had no control over her actions. She wore those scars to punish herself for that night. He saw her scars as her battle wounds; ones she should be proud to wear as they marked her as the warrior she was.

He would love her if her entire face were covered in scars. She wasn't beautiful in the delicate, classical sense, but with her honeyed eyes, proudly pointed chin, pert nose, and high cheekbones, he found her to be more beautiful and alluring than anyone he'd ever known. He also couldn't deny he enjoyed watching her trim, athletic body as she glided from one table to another. Her ass fit nicely in her formfitting, black pants that hugged her thighs.

Yep, he could definitely get used to watching this, even if he had to endure the daggers she kept sending his way as she worked. He'd offered to help and received a snap of the towel in response, which was fine by him. He was a beer drinking, blue jeans kind of guy, but manual labor wasn't something he'd done much of since becoming a vampire.

"You'll care when I get evicted from my apartment, and you're out on the street," she said with a huff.

He gave her a wicked smile that caused her to stop scrubbing at the table. The color flushing her porcelain skin told him his smile had affected her even as she narrowed her eyes at him and thrust her chin out. "Then you'll just have to stay at the motel, in my room, with me."

Her full mouth pursed. "I'd get my own room."

"I'd be more than willing to share," he replied with a wink.

"I'm not."

"Come now, Dewdrop, you would enjoy yourself."

∼

OH, Quinn had no doubt she would thoroughly enjoy herself with him. Looking at him was enough to make her insides turn to goo; what his mouth and hands could do to her was an entirely different ballgame. The worst part was that the conceited ass was also one of the most considerate, kind, and irresistible men she'd ever encountered.

She still felt like a teen in the early stages of puppy love, and couldn't help but smile every time she recalled their date last night. The picnic on her roof had been perfect; *he'd* been perfect, which was something she'd never believed possible, given how arrogant he could be and how many times she'd considered giving him a solid punch in the nose.

She'd completely lost her heart to him last night. The realization didn't make her feel like running through fields of grass while singing; instead, it chilled her to the center of her core. She loved this cocky, brutal, killer of a man, who was vastly more experienced with the world and women, more than she'd ever dreamed possible. She was petrified that loving him would cause her to lose him like she'd lost everyone else she'd loved in her life.

Dropping her rag on the table, she planted her hands on her hips. "Perhaps I wouldn't enjoy myself."

One of his black eyebrows quirked up. "Is that a challenge?"

It was a lie, they both knew it, but she refused to be swayed by those ice-blue eyes and entirely delectable mouth —a mouth she knew could make her forget her own name. "No, it's not. It's simply a possibility."

He grinned arrogantly as he leaned toward her. "No, that is *not* a possibility, and I think it is definitely a challenge. Believe me, Quinn, I'll make sure you enjoy yourself *very* much."

Her toes curled so deeply into her black boots, she felt

like she'd bore a hole through the soles. If she had a heart-beat, it probably would've beat straight out of her chest. Instead, she thrust her shoulders back as his gaze did a hungry perusal of her body that made her tempted to jump on him. She didn't know how someone could infuriate and arouse her so much at once, but Julian had somehow perfected the art of it.

She opened her mouth to answer him when she heard the knob on the door turn. "Crap," she muttered. Her annoyance over Julian's refusal to leave had distracted her from locking the door. "I'm sorry," she called to whoever stood beyond the door. "But we're closed."

She took a step toward the door with the intention of locking it. Julian came out of his seat so fast, she didn't see him move until he stood before her. Quinn took an abrupt step back from him; her eyes darted toward the door as it opened and four men stepped into the bar. Their distinct lack of heartbeats told her immediately they were vampires.

Her heart plummeted as she realized she'd been discovered. Her hands subtly fell to the stakes tucked into the holsters at her waist. The vampires never looked at her; immediately, their red eyes latched onto Julian.

"If it isn't Julian, the betrayer of our kind. I thought it was you when we spotted you from outside," one of them murmured while two of the others grinned. The fourth vampire cracked his knuckles, as if readying to fight.

The chiseled muscles in Julian's back rippled; the icy blue of his eyes became a fiery red. "You boys are asking for more trouble than you can handle," he growled.

"Oh, I doubt that," the first speaker replied.

Quinn went to step out from behind Julian, but he held his arm out, pushing her back. "Stay out of this."

"Like hell!" she retorted.

Julian's shoulders hunched when the vampires gave her a leering grin. The sound that came out of his chest made the hair on her nape stand straight up. He grabbed hold of her hands, pulling them away from the weapons at her waist.

"You're to stay out of this." She glared at him. "I mean it, Quinn. Stay out of this."

"You should probably listen to him, Quinn," one of the intruders snickered.

Her eyes shot to the mouthy intruder; she glowered at him as her fingers itched to throw one of her stakes right between his eyes. Julian pushed her back further. "I can *fight*," she hissed at him. "Better than most."

"Not this time," he said as he pulled a stake from the holster at her waist. "They're mine, and I won't take the chance of you getting hurt."

She snorted in disdain. "That's not—"

"Stay out of this!" he snapped at her.

Quinn's teeth grated together so forcefully she could hear them scraping against each other. He'd never yelled at her before. It infuriated her at the same time she worried about why these vampires had him so on edge. What was it about these vamps that had him treating her like she was the useless little woman who should be baking cookies? He'd always respected her ability to fight.

Her eyes slid back to the intruding vamps. If the two of them fought side by side, these vamps would be easy to take down, but if he was hell-bent on being a chauvinistic ass, who was she to argue? "They're all yours," she said and stepped away from him. His features softened in relief. "And I hope they kick your ass."

She only half meant it, but he deserved the ass whooping. His eyes sparkled; he grinned at her before spinning away to face the vampires charging at him. Julian fisted his hands and smashed them into the back of a vamp who wrapped his arms around his waist and propelled him backward.

Quinn's hand instinctively went to one of her stakes again, but she stopped herself from removing it from the holster. *Screw him*, she thought. He thinks he's so big and bad; let him deal with these guys on his own. She really did hope he got staked, maybe not through the heart, but a good shot to somewhere that wouldn't kill him might deflate his ego a little.

Bang!

Quinn winced as the barstool crashed off Julian's back and splintered into a dozen tiny pieces. The broken shards clattered and rattled as they exploded through the air and bounced off the walls. Clint was going to lose his mind if he found out another stool had somehow been broken.

She tried to remember if there were any extra stools in the basement, but she couldn't recall off the top of her head. She hoped so; she had no idea how she would explain *this* to Clint. There were only so many stools she could "trip over and break," and there wasn't enough super glue in the world to put that one back together.

Oh well, I'll figure it out later.

Grabbing hold of one of the chairs in the poolroom, she turned it toward the main barroom and settled in to watch the fight. She leaned the back of the chair against the wall before pulling a package of peanut butter cups from her apron pocket. Mountain Dew and peanut butter cups were her left-over vices from her human years, and the reason why Julian sometimes called her Dewdrop.

The fresh scent of chocolate and peanut butter tickled her nostrils when she tore open the wrapper. The smell did nothing to prick her appetite, but it was still tempting and comfortingly familiar.

Julian swore loudly and drove the palm of his hand up and into the nose of a vampire lunging at him. The coppery scent of blood filling the air from the vamp's shattered nose did what the candy had not. Hunger immediately rolled through her stomach; she pushed it aside as she continued to unwrap her sweet treat.

Julian snarled when a vampire leapt onto his back, putting him into a chokehold that did nothing but piss him off. Reeling backward, he slammed the vamp into the wall. The glass mirrors, with numerous beer logos etched into them, rattled against the wall. The Budweiser clock with the prancing Clydesdales swung back and forth like a pendulum, threatening to fall at any second.

"Hey, watch the merchandise!" she yelled at Julian. "If you break that clock, *I'm* going to kick your ass!"

Julian's eyes flashed angrily toward her as he flipped the vamp over his back and onto the floor. Holding the vamp's neck, he kept him pinned to the ground as he spoke to her, "I could do without the commentary from the peanut gallery!"

Quinn rolled the peanut butter cup wrapper in her hand and shoved it into her pocket as Julian drove the stake through the vampire's heart. "You know us delicate little females, we can't get our hands dirty, but we sure do like to gab," she blithely replied.

His scowl deepened, but before he could say anything, another vampire lunged at him. The vamp wrapped his arms around Julian's waist and knocked him onto the floor. *That had to have tickled, and not in a good way.* Quinn nibbled at the ridged chocolate edge, making a circle around the cup as she watched the melee before her.

She had to admit, watching him fight caused butterflies to flit through her stomach. He was so strong and powerful, and she loved the way those thick muscles rippled as he moved. She had to fight the urge to lick her lips. The impulse had nothing to do with the chocolate lingering on her mouth and everything to do with the way he heaved that one across the floor with barely a flick of his wrist. He'd barely broken a sweat; the others looked as though they'd gone ten rounds with Mike Tyson.

The vamps had still barely looked at her as all of their concentration remained focused on Julian. Julian and his friends had been so concerned about vampires finding her, they'd forgotten Julian had pissed off more than a few in his lengthy life, and with his attitude, they'd all take a chance to spill some of his blood.

She didn't blame them.

Leisurely, she pulled the chocolate top off the peanut butter cup after she finished eating the sides. *He deserves a good smack upside the head.* Just as she thought it, one of the vamps landed a solid blow to his temple. Julian drove his fist through the vamp's chest. Blood dripped from between his fingers when he tore the heart free and crushed it in his hand. The vamp's lifeless body slumped to the floor as another one cracked a table on Julian's back.

She winced again. He'd pissed her off with his high-handed behavior, but she didn't like seeing him injured in any way, even if she would like to be the one beating on him right now.

She liked that he wanted to protect her, but she didn't have to have a watchdog by her side at all times, and she definitely didn't like being kept out of a fight. She'd survived eighteen years in hiding with her family and six years as a vampire on her own. She would survive whatever the world threw at her next.

Quinn turned the cup over and pulled off the bottom layer of chocolate as Julian took another punch to a place no man should be hit. *Good thing vampires can't reproduce.* His face flushed red; he doubled over as he covered his nuts. *Kind of like shutting the barn door after the horse is out.*

As one of the vamps grabbed a broken stool leg from the ground, she half rose out of her chair, prepared to kill him if it became necessary. Julian may have pissed her off, but she wouldn't stand by and let him die because he'd turned into a macho man for some reason tonight. Julian swung an uppercut that shot the vamp's head back and sent him flying into the bar. The vamp shook his head before launching back to his feet.

"Hey! Watch the glasses!" Quinn protested before sliding back into her chair.

Julian's eyes were the color of fire when they met hers. Both his arms shot out at the same time, crashing through the chests of the vampires lunging toward him. With a vicious curse, he ripped their hearts from their chests and stomped them into the ground.

Quinn rolled the remaining peanut butter into a ball and popped it in her mouth before rising to her feet and wiping her hands on her apron. Julian wiped his hands down the front of his blood-splattered, body-hugging, midnight blue shirt. The cut of his shirt showed off his broad shoulders and chiseled stomach.

"Did you enjoy the show?" he inquired.

"Immensely." She opened the closet door beside the bathroom and pulled out the cleaning supplies. "You deserved it. Besides, I thought women shouldn't be fighting or whatever crazy idea was going through your mind tonight."

"They almost castrated me," he muttered as he stared woefully at his groin.

She held the steam mop out to him. "And you deserved it for pushing me to the side like that. Those spermies don't work anyway."

His hand wrapped around the plastic handle of the steam mop. His white-blond hair hung against the corner of an eye as blue as the arctic ice. His broad cheekbones, square jaw, and magnificent features made her stomach do summer-saults; her deadened heart gave a little leap when her gaze fell to his mouth.

Stop it, she scolded herself. *You can't be thinking about kissing him when you should be yelling at him.*

"Everything else still works, something you're going to learn one of these days," he replied.

Her mouth went completely dry at his words; she felt she should be pissed about the confidence behind his statement, but how could she be when it was the truth? She intended to learn every inch of his firm body, when she was ready. Most likely, it would be someday soon, when he wasn't acting like such an asshat. It took all she had to sniff at him before turning away.

"Admit it, that just got you all hot and bothered," he coaxed.

She forced herself to scowl at him over her shoulder, even though she loved the playfulness in his eyes. He was right, but she'd never admit it. "You're incorrigible."

"And proud of it. I did all the work with these guys, and you expect me to clean up the mess?"

"They were only here because of *you*. I'm pretty sure their exact words after walking into the bar were, 'If it isn't Julian, the betrayer of our kind.' Last I checked, that's not *my* name."

"Women, you all have minds like a steel trap when it comes to things we don't want you to remember," he muttered.

She planted her hands on her hips as she glared at him. "It sounds like you're speaking from experience with a *lot* of women."

Realizing he'd stepped into a steaming pile of shit, his mouth clamped shut. Quinn bit her inner lip to keep from laughing as he placed the mop against the wall and bent to lift one of the bodies over his shoulder. She walked over to one of the others.

"I'd prefer it if you'd let me take them," he said to her.

"And I'd prefer it if you'd stop trying to coddle me, but you won't."

He grabbed hold of her hand when she bent to grab the man's arm. "I'm not coddling you," he said quietly, his eyes burning into hers. The paler blue band encircling his pupils darkened in color. The turquoise flecks in that band danced in the light.

She released the dead man's hand and stood. "You can't keep treating me like a child. I've survived bigger threats before—"

"No, you haven't."

"Yes, I have. I spent my entire life in hiding from Hunters, Guardians, The Commission, and vampires. Now, I only have the vampires to worry about; I think those are much better odds."

His gaze never wavered from hers. "*Desperate* vampires who believe you could be their only hope at regaining the power they once enjoyed. There is *nothing* more lethal than a desperate vamp."

She despised that damn prophecy the vampires were spreading about her. She wasn't anyone's savior, and she especially wasn't the vampires' savior. She may be a vampire, but it hadn't been by choice. Having been born a half-vampire and a Hunter, she'd had enough vampire blood within her to undergo the change on the night she and her family were attacked and killed by vamps.

"These guys seemed pretty desperate, and there's not much left to them," she said with a wave at the bodies.

A muscle in his jaw jumped. "Vampires en masse, Quinn. What if a horde of them comes at us?"

"Then we will fight them, but there has never been a horde of vampires searching for me. They have no idea where I am, what I look like, or that I'm with you."

"That doesn't mean they couldn't find out."

She threw her hands up in the air. "We will deal with it then! But I can't have you constantly prowling around me like an irritable bear ready to lash out at anyone who comes too close. It's exhausting!"

"I couldn't stand it if something were to happen to you." Damn him, he could always make her melt, even when she was trying to get her tirade on. "What if you had used your ability to drain the life from one of them while fighting, and one of the others took off before we could stop him? He could have told everyone he came across about you. The vampires would then know exactly where you are and what you look like."

"I understand, but you have to ease up. I'm a fighter, and if you try to take that away from me, I'm only going to end up resenting you for it. And you *definitely* cannot order me around like that again, or I may stake you myself. If you want to be with me, then we are going to be equals. If you don't want to be with me, then tell me to go sit in the corner again. It will be a surefire way for whatever this is between us to come to a halt."

His head lifted; the smile quirking his mouth didn't light his eyes. Strain radiated from his compressed lips and the lines that etched his mouth. "Anything for you."

The rest of her ire faded away with those words. There had been many women in his past, most of whom he barely remembered, but those three words were the complete truth. He cared for her, she knew that, and he had no idea how to handle it. That was something she completely understood as she felt the same way, but she wouldn't be locked away or ordered about by him.

She forced a smile as she bent to grab the dead vamp's hand again. "Next time, I promise to help if they try to castrate you."

A bark of laughter erupted from him. "I'd appreciate that." He pulled out his cellphone and hit a button. Lifting it to his ear, he juggled the dead guy on his shoulder as he held the phone. "Come to the bar," he said in a clipped tone before hanging up and sliding the phone into his pocket. "Do you mind waiting here for Chris?" he asked her.

Quinn shook her head and dropped the dead hand yet again. The thumping sound it made on the wood floor made her cringe. "No."

He nodded before turning and heading for the kitchen doors down the hall. Her heart swelled when she realized this was his first concession to her request. He never would have left her alone here just hours ago.

She grabbed a trash bag and began to clean up the mess while she waited for Chris and whomever else he brought with him to arrive.

CHAPTER TWO

JULIAN FORCED himself to keep putting one foot in front of the other, out of the bar and across the desert. The idea of leaving Quinn alone and unprotected made him want to kill the vamp draped over his shoulder all over again. Thankfully, these vamps had come for him, but if they'd heard the prophecy and realized she was the vampire of the prophecy, they would have gone for her too.

She was tough; he knew it. She was one of the toughest women he'd ever met, but she could be killed. He could lose her. His hands tightened on the dead man, the wintry night air blew through his hair and over his skin as he raced across the desert toward an outcropping of rocks.

Dumping the body behind the rocks, he turned and fled back across the shifting sand toward the bar. He heard voices when he entered through the kitchen and walked toward the bar. Quinn, Chris, Zach, and Melissa were inside, working to clean up the mess. Just two years ago, the idea of being in a room with three Hunters, four if he counted Quinn, would have delighted him as he planned to tear the throats out of every one of them. Now he considered them amongst his best friends, minus Zach.

Created by twisted humans, known as The Commission, the Hunters had been forged by a series of experiments that had tortured many humans and vampires before a line was created of humans who shared the vampire's attributes and would be able to fight them. Most of the Hunter line had been wiped out years ago, during The Slaughter unleashed by the Elder vampires, but he now worked with them to help find what remained of the scattered survivors.

Julian's eyes went to Quinn, his shoulders relaxed as he drank in the sight of her. Her honey-hued eyes gleamed in the dim light filtering from the lamp over the bar. She stood, her lithe body moving with easy grace as she bent and picked up another dead vamp.

Mine, he thought as he watched her move. He'd yet to tell her he loved her, but he did. He wanted to mark her as his, to feast on her blood and body, and make it clear to everyone she was off limits to anyone but him. The idea she was his mate had been growing inside him with every passing minute. He'd tried to deny it, tried to brush it off and not acknowledge it, but the truth of it niggled at his mind, refusing to be denied.

And if he didn't back off and give her some space, he would drive her away.

Clenching his hands, he fought against the impulse to toss her over his shoulder and drag her all the way to Antarctica if that was what it took to keep her safe. She'd be pissed; he'd be miserable in the cold snow and ice, but it wouldn't matter if it kept her alive and away from anyone who could associate her with the newest vampire prophecy.

He could still clearly hear Seanix's words to Quinn in his head... *"The prophecy is spreading through the vampire*

*community like wildfire. Whoever finds you is going to have
a lot of power to force those to do their will."* The memory
of those words caused a chill to press against his neck.

Then Seanix had actually revealed the prophecy, and
Julian had known it could only be about Quinn. *"A vampire,
not born of vampire blood, will burn like the sun the life from
anyone she touches. If used correctly, she will become our
greatest ally, our savior."*

Our greatest ally and savior. The younger, disorganized
and scattered vamps would latch onto those words. The
nonexistent promise within the vague prophecy would have
the vampires still floundering, since most of the Elders were
killed while scrambling to find her. They were trying to seize
hold of something stable, and they would see Quinn as their
chance to reclaim their old life. He'd tear the throat out of
anyone who so much as left a scratch on her, never mind
trying to take her and bend her to their will.

"If you're going to kill everyone who doesn't like you, a
lot of bodies are going to add up," Chris said to him.

Chris wiped the back of his arm across his forehead as he
stood up from where he'd been tossing broken barstool bits
into a trash can. His shaggy, sandy-blond hair clung to the
sheen of sweat beading across his brow. Amusement filled
his sapphire eyes when he smiled at Julian.

"They started it," Julian replied.

"I'm sure they had a good reason," Melissa said as she
dumped a heart into the trash bag Quinn held open for her.

"Funny," he muttered.

The grin Melissa flashed him caused her onyx eyes to
sparkle. She'd pulled her short black hair into a small ponytail that fell against her neck and emphasized her olive
complexion and the refined features of her Egyptian
heritage. Behind her, her sort of boyfriend, Zach, lifted

another heart from the floor using only his thumb and index finger. Zach's upper lip curled in revulsion, he held the heart away from him like it was a tiger ready to bite. He already didn't exactly like Zach, but seeing this squeamish side of him caused Julian to shake his head.

"You can do better," he said to Melissa.

She glanced over at Zach and bit on her bottom lip to keep from laughing. "He's not used to your tendency of leaving insides on the outside. Besides, we're not really together." Julian gave her a questioning look; she lifted a delicate shoulder. "Some things just don't work out."

"I'll kill him for you."

"They didn't work out on *my* part. The chemistry wasn't there, you know?"

"I do."

His gaze slid to Quinn. There had been many women in his past, and he could say the exact same thing about most of them, but he could never say it about her. She challenged him, stood up to him, and he desired her in a way he'd never desired another; loved her in a way he'd never known possible until her. He'd loved in the past, deeply, but never with every bit of himself like he did with her.

"I'll still kill him if you'd like," he offered, only half-kidding.

"Thanks for the offer, but no. Sometimes things are just…" She frowned as her words trailed off. "Just not what you were expecting."

"I understand."

"You would understand, perhaps better than anyone." Her gaze flickered to Chris before she turned away and lifted another broken stool leg from the floor.

Julian studied her for a minute, but he had a feeling that was all she was going to say on the subject right now. She was suddenly very focused on the pieces of splintered wood she picked off the floor.

"That heart's not going to bite you, Zachariah," he said to Zach. "I already killed it for you."

Zach lifted his head to scowl at him. "It's just Zach," he said for probably the hundredth time. Julian had no idea why he kept bothering to correct him; he had to realize by now it was useless.

Zach placed the heart into the trash bag and wiped his hands on the rag Quinn handed him. His dark-blond hair stood in spikes around his head; his brown eyes were red-rimmed from lack of sleep. Zach was the newest Hunter they'd discovered shortly before arriving in this Arizona town. Neither he nor Chris got any bad vibes from the young, surfer-looking kid, but Julian still didn't like him.

However, that wasn't saying much as there were few people he did like.

Walking across the room, Julian lifted another body and heaved it over his shoulder. As if determined to prove he wasn't squeamish, Zach came alongside Julian, grabbed the arms of another, and lifted the body up. Julian caught a glimpse of the tree of life tattoo on the inside of the young Hunter's right wrist when he swung the body over his shoulder.

Chris grabbed hold of the last body and draped it around his shoulders. One of the dead guy's hands fell down to slap him across the nose with a thwack. "I really hate our heritage sometimes," he muttered.

Julian laughed as he turned toward the swinging kitchen doors. *Don't look back; don't tell her to be careful.*

Despite telling himself not to, he couldn't stop himself from pausing at the doorway to take one last look at Quinn as she tied off the trash bag and dropped it on the floor. He hurried through the kitchen and back across the desert. He left Zach and Chris in his dust as he raced over to the boulders again and threw the new body on top of the other one. When the sun came up, it would burn away the remains, erasing all evidence the bodies had even been there. Chris and Zach caught up with him and added their bodies to the heap.

Stepping back, his gaze scanned the shifting sand and dunes rolling out before him. Cactuses and rocks dotted the landscape, his eyes picked out the different hues of oranges and reds swirling throughout. In the distance, he saw a coyote hunting amongst the rocks, searching for its prey.

The idea of hunting caused his fangs to tingle. He'd killed tonight. He'd unleashed some of the brutality he kept so restrained within him, but he hadn't fed. The scent of all the blood and the rush of the kill had made him ravenous. He could go now, give Quinn more of the freedom and space she'd asked for, but he was already itching to be at her side again, and she would most likely have to feed too.

Turning on his heel, he ran back across the desert and back into the bar. He paused before the swinging kitchen doors when he heard Quinn and Melissa giggling. "I can't believe you ate a peanut butter cup while he fought off four vamps," Melissa said.

"He deserved it, with his caveman attitude," Quinn replied.

"Aw, he doesn't know how to handle what he feels for you, and at least he hasn't hit you over the head with a club."

"Yet!"

The sound of Quinn's heartwarming laughter melted his irritation over the two of them talking about him. He shoved his way through the swinging doors and into the main part of the bar. They both stopped speaking as they looked up at him.

"I don't have a club, but I could always get one if you'd like," he said to Quinn.

Melissa chuckled and turned her head away. Quinn brushed back a strand of her that had worked free of her ponytail as she grinned at him. He wasn't surprised she felt no shame over getting caught talking about him.

"Just you try it," she retorted.

"Try what?" Chris asked as he shoved his way through the kitchen doors.

"Nothing," Julian said.

He grabbed the trash bag from the floor and carried it across the desert to dump the contents on top of the bodies. They would also turn to ash with the first rays of the sun.

CHAPTER THREE

QUINN LEANED BACK in the tub and rested her head against the little pillow she'd bought for her baths. She stretched up her toes to turn the hot water on again, letting a fresh wave of heat pour into the basin.

They should have fed before coming back to her apartment, but Julian had wanted to wash off the blood coating his skin and change into some clean clothes. While he was showering, she'd decided that after this night a quick soak in the tub was too tempting to resist. As soon as he was done and out of her bathroom, she'd told him she was taking a bath and would be out shortly, before slipping by him. She could get at least half an hour in the water and still do some hunting before the sun rose.

She scooped up two handfuls of the thick bubbles floating on the surface. She blew the bubbles away, unable to suppress a smile as they floated through the air to stick against her white tiled wall. Her apartment may be small, but the tub was large and she'd taken advantage of it since she'd moved in there.

As a vampire, her throbbing feet and back eased faster than a human's, but it was still a little bit of heaven to sink into her scented, hot water as often as she could. Tonight she'd used her lavender and peppermint bath salts to relax and rejuvenate.

She lifted another handful of bubbles and blew them at the wall. A knock on the door drew her head around. "What?"

"You've been in there for a while," Julian called to her.

"It's called relaxing!"

She could picture him standing on the other side, his arms folded across his chest as he stared at the door. "I thought you planned to feed tonight."

"I do. Give me a few more minutes."

"What?"

"Just give me a couple more minutes!" she called over the hot water flowing into the tub.

"What?"

Quinn slid her foot up and turned the water off. "I'll be out soon!"

"What did you say?"

Sighing in exasperation, Quinn slid down so only her shoulders were out of the hot water. She made sure the bubbles covered her body before yelling at him again. "Come in!"

The door opened to reveal Julian leaning in the doorway, his arms folded over his chest just as she'd known they would be. His nearly white-blond hair was darker in color due to his shower. He'd chosen not to put a shirt back on, which was something she both appreciated and disliked as her eyes raked over his magnificent form and chiseled abs. Her gaze finally settled on the black tattoo of an angel weeping on his right bicep.

She slid further into her bubbles and scowled at him. "You could hear me fine," she accused.

His mouth curved into a smile as his gaze slid over the bubbles. "This was too tempting to resist."

"You could have waited until I got out, like any respectable gentleman would do."

"Those are two words I've never been called before."

"Respectable and gentleman?"

"Exactly."

She shook her head and brushed back a piece of hair that fell free from the bun she'd piled on top of her head. "What am I going to do with you?"

"I know what I'd like you to do with me." He stepped further into the bathroom, sniffing at the air as he moved. "Smells fantastic."

He moved around her, but didn't come close enough to see anything. Her shoulders relaxing, she tipped her head back against the pillow as he stopped near her sink. He grasped the edge as he leaned against it.

"Maybe I should start calling you Bubbles," he said with a smile.

"That's a stripper name."

"I wouldn't turn you down if you offered to dance for me. I have dollar bills, and I'd be more than willing to hand out some hundreds too."

For some reason, that caused her to laugh. Sliding her foot toward the hot water tap again, she froze when his eyes latched onto her exposed leg. Passion radiated from his eyes as he watched the water and bubbles slide over her skin. His hands clenched on her sink so hard she feared he might rip it from the wall. She couldn't tear her eyes away from the ravenous look on his face as her body quivered.

Knowing she had to do something to break the tension

before he pulled her from this tub, she turned the water on again and slid her leg back into the water. "There's your strip tease," she said through the constriction of her throat.

"Worth it."

Extending her toe up again, she turned the water back off. The nearly white band around his pupil turned red as he followed every movement she made with a predatory expression. "Julian."

His head tilted to the side when his ice-blue eyes met hers again. He released her sink and brought his hands before him. "Need me to go, Dewdrop?"

No! Yes! No! The words bashed around in her head like a bat trapped in a belfry. She wanted to touch and feel him so badly, yet she knew she wasn't ready for what that progression in their relationship would mean. She didn't know if she was ready to have sex for the first time. He already had her heart, would she ever be able to survive the loss of him if he had her body too? There were too many enemies out there hunting them both to believe everything would be okay for any length of time.

Walking over, he kept his eyes on her face as he knelt beside her and brushed back her damp hair. He leaned forward and kissed her lips. "Maybe we could blow some of these bubbles out of the way or something?" he suggested.

The teasing glint in his eyes eased some of her tension as she chuckled. "Let's not."

He kissed her forehead and leaned back on his heels. "Take your time."

A sense of loss slid over her when he rose and walked over to the doorway. "I thought you were hungry," she said, unwilling to have him leave already.

He glanced at her over his shoulder. "I am, but if you

move some of those bubbles aside, I'll be able to wait a little longer."

She shook her head and sank lower in the tub. "I like my bubbles."

Turning to face her, he rested his hand high on the door jam and leaned against it. "One day, I'm going to climb in there with you and pop every last one of them."

Her toes curled at the idea and the promise of his words. "I'll get out now." She lifted her fingers through the bubbles to give him a little wave. "Now shoo, before I give you a zap that will make that punch you took to the nuts earlier seem like fun. I'll make it not work for a week."

His smile faded away. "Can you do that?"

"I'd be willing to find out," she teased.

He glanced at his crotch, then shook his head as he turned away from her. "We're taking hand jobs off the table," she heard him mutter before closing the door behind him.

Quinn laughed and rose from the tub. She grabbed the towel dangling from the hook and wrapped it around herself before stepping out. Her need to feed hadn't been pressing before she climbed into the tub, but she found herself starving. She just wasn't sure if blood would be enough to satisfy the urges clamoring through her body right then.

Her resistance to him was melting away; it was only a matter of time before she gave into him completely. She smiled at the realization.

∿

JULIAN RELEASED the coyote and sat back on his heels. His gaze drifted over to Quinn as she fed on the coyote she'd caught. The silvery rays of the moon falling over her caused her hair to glisten. Her eyes opened; their golden color shone in the light as she gave the coyote a pat before sending it unsteadily into the night.

Rising to her feet, she wiped the sand from her knees and brushed back her hair. He continued to watch as she wiped the sand from her ass before turning to face him. Her head tilted to the side when she caught him. "Do I have blood on me or something?" she asked.

He rose to his feet and dusted the sand off his clothes. "No blood."

"Good, can't spill any," she said with a laugh. She looked toward the sky as it brightened in the distance. "We have to go."

"We do."

He broke into a brisk run through the desert with her at his side. He moved so she was ahead of him as they sprinted through the shadows and rocks obscuring their approach to the back of her apartment building. They broke into a leisurely jog, appearing to be nothing more than two people out for a run before the sun came up. So what if most people would be in bed after a night of work? Humans were used to the oddities of other humans and often wrote off or ignored the strange and unexplainable.

The rays of the sun hit his back as he pulled the back door open. He stood over her, using his body to block her from the beams. He could tolerate them; she wouldn't be able to. Closing the door behind him, he stayed close to her back as he followed her up the stairs and waited while she unlocked her apartment.

Slipping in behind her, Julian made his way over to the window and pulled down the slat on the blind to look out at the motel. Luther sat in a chair at the corner of the building, flipping through one of his numerous books. Behind him,

Chris poked his head out of his room before striding down the wooden walkway toward his Guardian. As a Guardian, Luther was entirely human, but he had vast knowledge of the Hunter line and trained them to fight vamps. Luther had adopted and raised Melissa after her family was killed in The Slaughter. He'd discovered Chris and his best friend, Cassie, years later and had started their Hunter training.

He glanced over at Quinn as she unzipped one of her knee-high, black leather boots and dropped it on the floor. She pulled out the stakes hidden within her boot, set them aside, and then unstrapped the one wrapped around her calf. He couldn't help but smile as he watched her take off her other boot and more weapons before pulling free the stakes strapped to her waist.

They'd only gone out to the desert for an hour, and she'd prepared herself for war. It was one of the many things he'd come to love about her. One of these days, he'd work up the courage to tell her that.

"I'm going to speak with Luther," he said as he released the blind.

She looked up at him from behind her curtain of brown hair. "It's light out."

"I can move through it," he said. Walking over, he rested his hands on the couch behind her. "You'll be safe here now that it's daytime."

Her gaze went to the window before coming back to him. "It can't wait until later? When *you'll* be safer?"

"I'll only be exposed for half a minute at most. I can tolerate that." He'd been working hard to increase his tolerance to sunlight by gradually exposing himself to it; that short amount of time would barely affect him.

He bent to press a kiss against her forehead. Her hands squeezed his wrists before she released him. He didn't want to leave her, but Luther had talked to some of his Guardian friends to try to learn something new about the prophecy. He'd been hoping to hear back from them soon.

Reluctantly pulling away from her, Julian walked to the door. "Make sure to lock it behind me."

"I will."

She walked over to the door as he slipped out. He remained in the hallway until he heard the locks slide into place. Turning away, he strode down the poorly lit and dingy hall of Quinn's apartment building. The smells of cooking bacon and eggs filled his nostrils. The couple at the end of the hall was fighting again, and the one in the apartment to his right was doing his daily routine of waking and baking with his pot.

Julian ran down the stairs and shoved the door open. The early morning sun spilled over him, heating his skin as he ran across the street toward the motel. Luther looked up at him as he jogged by and into the shade of Chris's room. Chris glanced away from a rerun of "Married With Children."

"Privacy," he said around a mouthful of potato chips.

"You're the last person who should ever talk about privacy," Julian replied as he moved to the window. He pushed the curtain aside and peered up at Quinn's shaded windows. "Are you seriously eating chips at seven thirty in the morning?"

"Breakfast of champions." Chris wiped some of the crumbs from the front of his shirt. "And are you seriously questioning *my* eating practices, blood boy?"

"Christopher-"

"Yeah, yeah, I know. You stopped being a boy before you became a vampire."

Julian shot him a look as Luther strolled into the room

and placed his books onto one of the tables. "Have you managed to learn anything new about the prophecy?" Julian inquired.

Luther lifted his glasses and rubbed at the bridge of his nose. "There's nothing left for me to discover. I've tapped the few Guardians I trust; no one has heard anything. If we're going to learn anything more, it's going to have to come from the vampire community. They're the only ones who can tell us what they're planning, how many of them believe the prophecy, and how many want to do something about it. Infiltrating them is the only way we'll learn anything."

"And there's no way to do that," Julian said. "We saw how vampires react to my presence last night."

"Some of them would welcome you back amongst them." Chris set the bag of chips on the nightstand as he swung his legs out of the bed. "You are an Elder after all."

At over five hundred and seventy-six vamp years, he was one of the only two Elders left. Any vampire who managed to survive to five hundred was considered an Elder. Their speed, strength, and other inherent vampire abilities increased at that age, as well as whatever ability they'd acquired upon becoming a vamp. Julian's psychometry, the ability to learn things about others from touching them or an object they'd touched, had nearly doubled upon becoming an Elder. It was why he often kept it shut off. The flood of images from his surroundings was distracting and tedious.

"To go back amongst the vampires and earn their trust, I would have to kill again in order to prove my loyalty to them," Julian said. "I'd also have to leave Quinn here, unprotected."

"You had me convinced it was a bad idea once you said

killing again," Chris said. "I feel like that wouldn't be the wisest of choices."

"No, it wouldn't." Especially when the need to kill was always just beneath the surface, lurking within him. Quinn helped to calm the hunger and the urge, but if he ever gave in again, he didn't know if he'd be able to bring himself back. For her, he believed he could bring himself back from the darkness within him. However, she may be able to forgive him if he returned to being a murderer, but she'd never forgive herself if he killed innocents in order to keep her safe. He rubbed at his temples as he paced away from the window.

Melissa entered the room; her brows drew together as she watched him. "What's going on?"

Chris filled her in when she sat on the bed beside him. "Definitely not a good idea," she agreed.

Julian stopped pacing and pulled the curtain back to check on Quinn again. Not for the first time, he realized the vampires had to be organized and *ruled*. These confused and angry vamps were more dangerous than if they were united under a general guideline, as they had been when the Elders were alive. Granted, the Elders had pretty much let them have free rein to do whatever they pleased as long as they kept the vampire species a secret, but there had been rules, and there had been rulers they'd listened to and respected.

These stupid vampires didn't realize that most prophecies were so arbitrary they could be taken one of a thousand ways. It was like the man who wished to be wealthy, and the next day his entire family died in a plane crash and he collected their life insurance. He'd gotten his wish but had suffered greatly in the end.

The prophecy stated that, if used correctly, Quinn could be their greatest ally and savior. Many of them probably believed she would be on their side, or they'd be able to bend her to their will. They didn't stop to think that if they pissed her off enough, she might destroy them all. He was sure some had questioned how a vampire not born of vampire blood could even exist, but most probably hadn't. He doubted any of them had considered the possibility she may be part Hunter and would fight them every step of the way.

How could he possibly go about trying to get the vampires to fall in line? How could he bring some stability back into the vampire world without crossing a line he'd vowed never to cross again? How did he do it without pushing Quinn away and ruining what was growing between them?

He had no answers for those questions, only a growing headache.

"We'll figure something out," Melissa said.

"Yeah." He had a feeling the battle would be coming to them soon, and they were not ready for it. His gaze slid back to Quinn's window. The driving urge to get back to her had him walking toward the door before he realized he was moving.

"I'll see you later," he said and slipped outside.

Higher in the sky, the sun burned his skin as he sprinted across the road to Quinn's apartment building. He ran up the stairs and nodded hello to the kid who liked to wake and bake as they passed in the hall. Julian's eyes rolled when the kid flashed him a peace sign.

"Don't like Dusty?"

He hadn't realized Quinn was standing in the hall with a cat in her arms until she'd spoken. Whenever that cat escaped its apartment, it would sit outside Quinn's door, crying until someone finally opened it. He'd suggested tossing the cat outside last time it had gotten loose, but she'd insisted on returning it.

"Mittens escaped again," he stated.

"She did." Quinn walked down the hall and knocked on the door of apartment six. The door cracked open an inch. Quinn handed the marmalade cat through the door to the elderly woman who kept stranger hours then they did as vampires. The woman took the cat and closed the door without so much as a thanks.

"Three years ago, I'd have eaten her rude ass. Mothball scent and possible dusty veins be damned," Julian muttered as they walked away.

Quinn shot him a censuring look, but the corner of her lips quirked in a smile as she stepped into her apartment. "So what's your problem with Dusty? He's harmless enough."

Julian closed the door and threw the locks. "That kid never would have survived the sixties. I was immortal, and *I* barely escaped them alive. I spent a good chunk of the decade high or tripping my balls off, but I did love Woodstock. It was a hedonistic indulgence of music, sex, and blood."

Quinn blinked at him, her mouth opened then closed again before she shook her head.

"What?" he inquired.

"Sometimes I forget how much older you are than me, and how much more of this world you've experienced."

"And you forget how brutal I once was."

Her forehead furrowed. "No, there's no hiding what you're capable of. I don't want you to either. It's just your talk of feeding on flower children, twenty-some-odd years before I was born. It can be a little disconcerting."

He grinned at her as he approached. Resting his hands on her hips, he backed her toward her bedroom. "None of those flower children were as cute as you, and they definitely didn't smell as good."

"You're an ass," she told him.

"I am."

"What did Luther have to say?"

"He's discovered nothing new."

She bit her bottom lip. "I didn't think he would." She focused on him again and leaned up to press a kiss against his cheek. "And I'm exhausted." Before he could stop her, she spun out of his grasp and sauntered toward her bedroom.

"One of these days, you're going to let me in there."

"Today's not that day," she shot over her shoulder with a saucy smile that made his deadened heart lurch before she closed the door.

CHAPTER FOUR

JULIAN YAWNED and stretched out on the couch he'd bought to replace Quinn's old one. Rolling over, he propped his head on his hand as he listened to her moving around behind her closed bedroom door. Rising to his feet, he walked over to the blinds. He pulled them up and stepped into the rays of the sun hanging on the horizon.

His skin heated, his flesh reddened, but he tipped his head back and savored the warmth pouring over him. He could still only tolerate small amounts of time within the sun's rays, but it was much more than he could have withstood two years ago. He ground his teeth together, refusing to move as his skin blistered and peeled.

Finally, unable to take it anymore, he stepped away from the window and lowered the blinds before Quinn emerged from her room. He turned to find her leaning in the doorway, her wet hair waving about her face, her golden eyes filled with yearning as she stared at the blind-covered window. Her gaze drifted to him, and she flinched at the sores marring his bare chest and face.

"You stayed in it too long," she chastised as she stepped away from the door.

Stopping before him, her hands hovered over his flesh. His body tensed as his eyes remained locked on her raised palms. He didn't care how much it would sting; all he wanted was for her to touch him. Taking hold of her hands, he pressed them against his chest. The heat of her palms warmed him more than the rays of the sun ever could.

She tried to pull her hands away, but he kept hold of them. "It must hurt," she protested.

"No," he grated through his teeth. "I want to feel you."

Her head tilted back; her eyes became molten gold as she searched his face. Lowering his head, he rested his forehead against hers and inhaled the cucumber scent of the shampoo she used. He wrapped his hand around her neck, his thumb stroking her nape. He closed his eyes as the feel and scent of her engulfed him.

"Julian."

Her fingers curled into his flesh before she tried to pull them back again. He kept her tight against him, unwilling to break the connection. Her eyes searched his chest. He glanced down to find the blisters had faded, though his skin still looked as if he'd fallen asleep on a Florida beach in August.

"It doesn't hurt," he assured her.

He could feel the sizzling arc of her power as she instinctively swayed toward him. The draw of his life force wasn't an unpleasant sensation, as she gave and took from him in equal measure. The loss of control over her ability signaled her growing desire for him more than the darkening of her eyes or the increased scent of her arousal.

With a low growl, he bent his head to hers and took hold of her mouth. His arm latched around her waist, drawing her flush against him as his tongue brushed over her lips. Her mouth parted to his questing touch, allowing his tongue to slide in to taste her. Her tongue met his with eager thrusts that threatened to unravel all his restraint.

Walking her backward, he pressed her against the wall and braced his leg between her thighs when they began to shake. Her fangs lengthened against his lips, one of the sharp points puncturing his flesh. *Harder*, he almost groaned against her mouth, but he held the word back. He so badly craved her blood and to have his tasted in return, but he had to proceed carefully with her, or she might become frightened and bolt.

His hands ran over her ribcage, lifting her loose t-shirt up so his fingers could run over her silken skin. Her arms slipped around his neck as her tongue continued to entwine with his in hungry thrusts. Pushing her shirt up higher, he broke the kiss so he could drink in the sight of her exposed skin.

Her lips were swollen; her eyes dazed when they met his. He watched the subtle nuances of her face while he leisurely explored her body with his hands. The ebb and flow of her power increased as her head fell back. His gaze latched onto her neck and the enticing vein running just beneath the surface.

He'd never experienced such a driving need to mark someone, to taste them, like he did with her. Brushing back the strands of her hair, his eyes remained latched on her vein. Saliva rushed into his mouth as his fangs thrummed with the urge to be buried in her flesh. They'd both fed well only hours ago, but he was suddenly *ravenous*.

"Julian," she whispered.

He tore his gaze away from the vein and back to her flushed face. His fingers traced over her cheeks, then across her swollen lips. He ran his thumb over her full bottom lip before bending his head to kiss her again. "I want all of you, Quinn," he murmured against her mouth.

Her fingers dug deeper into his chest as her hips arched against his. "I'm not sure I'm ready for this."

The ebb and flow of his life force between them caused his skin to prickle as it became electrified by her incredible ability to drain the life from someone but also give it back. A Soul Master, Luther had called her. In all of his many years, Julian had never encountered someone like her.

"Should we go on another date?" His lips brushed against her mouth as he spoke. "I'll take you anywhere you want."

Goose bumps broke out on her flesh as his other hand continued its caress of her ribcage. She smiled sensuously at him. "Even someplace cold?"

She knew he hated the cold, but he'd take her anywhere she asked him to, especially if it was somewhere remote where no one would think to look for them, much less find them. "Anywhere," he told her.

Her head tilted to the side, her eyes dancing with merriment as she watched him. "Paris?"

"I'll book the ship tomorrow and climb the Eiffel Tower for you."

"You're just trying to get me out of this town." He shrugged as his fingers slid over the bottom edge of her lacy, black bra. She grabbed hold of his hand, pressing it flat against her. "There are vampires all over this world. We'll be no safer in Paris or Moscow than we are here."

"Maybe not." He kissed her nose before moving his lips to her ear. "But a trip to Paris must equal at least ten dates and would have to get me bonus points."

She laughed as she pushed at his shoulder. "You're a horndog."

"And you love it."

"I do." Her husky voice made his body quicken as his fingers continued to explore her bra. "But I also love getting paid. So if you don't mind, I have to get ready for work."

She ducked beneath his arm with a laugh and darted into her bedroom. Her door closed with a click. He couldn't help but smile as he stared at the closed door. She had him more wound up than he'd ever been before, but little did she know how much he enjoyed the chase she led him on.

CHAPTER FIVE

QUINN SET her tray full of empty glasses on the bar and turned to place them in the dishwasher before filling her order. Clint's was packed tonight. Even for a Friday, the crowd was larger than usual. Probably because Hawtie's strip club was closed for the week to undergo some renovations and repairs.

It may be early February outside, but with so many people in the bar, it felt like July. Using her forearm, she wiped the sweat from her brow before shoving the glasses into the dishwasher. When she was done, she closed the door to the machine and stood to survey the bar again. The normal mix of bikers, cowboys, young college kids, Native Americans, and Mexicans filled the bar as well as more women than normal, which was making the men a lot happier and a lot louder than they normally were.

Her gaze found Julian amongst the crowd. It was easy to spot him in the mix as his natural vampire magnetism drew people toward him, even as their human instincts told them he was a predator. An extremely good-looking, unable-toignore predator, who was watching the crowd with a look of part disdain and part boredom.

Sensing her stare, he lifted his head to gaze at her. A sensuous smile curved his mouth, a mouth that could do delicious and wicked things, and that was only with his kiss. She shut off fantasies of what else his mouth could do before she shattered one of the clean glasses she'd pulled from the rack overhead.

"Can I get a PBR?" some guy asked as he leaned over the bar.

Quinn tore her attention away from Julian and focused on the man before her. "Sorry, we're out."

The man smiled as he tapped his fingers on the bar, his eyes raking leisurely over her. Like Julian, her inherent vampire abilities lured them to her. A lascivious look filled his eyes when he leaned closer. "So what can you get me, sweetheart?"

A punch in the face, she thought, but forced herself to smile at him. *Bills to pay,* became the mantra on repeat in her head. "You can see the beers on tap," she replied and gestured toward the half a dozen taps lined up along the bar. "Pick your poison."

"What if my poison is you?" he inquired.

Quinn couldn't help but snort at his response. Resting her elbows on the bar, she smiled at him. "Believe me, *sweetheart*, you'd prefer poison to me."

"Oh, I doubt that." He inched his fingers closer to hers as his smile grew.

"I don't," Julian grumbled from behind him.

The man's eyebrows drew together. His hand fell to the gun at his side as he spun to face Julian. "Who do you think you are?" the man demanded.

Julian rested his hand on the bar as he leaned closer to

the man. The man was two inches taller than he was and had a good thirty pounds on him, but the look on Julian's face would have made a lion tuck tail and run. "I think I'm the man who will break every one of your fingers if they move another centimeter closer to her," Julian replied.

The man glanced over at her. "I, ah… I gotta go," the man stammered out, apparently deciding she wasn't worth not being able to use his hands for a while.

Quinn shook her head as she turned her attention to Julian. "I told you, don't scare off my tips."

The thunderous expression on his face eased when he turned his attention to her. "You have to agree he was pathetic."

"Maybe so, but he pays my bills, not you."

"Ah, but I do so much more for you," he replied with a wink.

Her entire body turned to Jell-O, but she still forced herself to lift her chin. She had no idea how to respond to that. She was, thankfully, saved from having to reply when Clint walked by with a case of beer.

"Back off, Draco Malfoy," Clint tossed over his shoulder to Julian and dropped the case on the bar.

Julian had to snatch his hand back to avoid having the case dropped on it. Quinn couldn't hold back her laughter as Clint pulled open the box and pulled out some beer bottles. Bushy gray hair poked out from under Clint's baseball cap; his brown eyes twinkled merrily as he stored the beer in the coolers.

Clint had started calling Julian by the name of anyone extremely blond the minute they'd met. Quinn had begun to suspect Clint was actually googling people, as he had yet to call Julian by the same name twice. She'd never known there were so many popular blonds in existence, but she had a feeling she'd be learning more of them soon.

She gave Julian's hand a pat before turning away from him to finish filling her order. She placed some mugs and a pitcher of beer on her tray and lifted it. Expertly weaving her way through the crowd, she arrived at a table with a couple of women who worked at Hawtie's seated around it.

"Thanks."

Quinn recognized the woman who spoke as the bartender from Hawtie's. She'd dyed her hair purple since the last time Quinn had seen her, but her pumpkin-colored contacts were still in.

"You're welcome."

Turning away from the table, she twirled the tray in her hands as she made her way through the crowd toward one of her tables near the door. She almost felt like whistling as she spun the tray around. Sure, there were God only knew how many vampires searching for her and there was some crazy-ass prophecy about her, but for the first time in years, she actually felt happy again.

Then, she felt guilty for feeling happy in the same building where Angie had died. Her smile slid away and the tray stopped spinning in her hands as a pang of sadness stabbed her heart. Angie hadn't known every detail of Quinn's life. Julian was the only one who knew her most gruesome secret about having killed her dying uncle upon turning, but Angie had been her friend.

Stepping up to a table, she smiled at the group of college students gathered around it. "Same as last round?" she asked them as she stacked their empty mugs on her tray.

"Sounds good," one of the men replied.

Quinn was about to lift her tray from the table when the front door opened and a male vampire stepped inside. She could only stand and stare as the world lurched out from under her. She thought she was going to fall over, but she remained unmoving.

Memories of death and brutality assailed her as the bar around her faded away. She found herself in the home she'd fled six years ago. Under the influence of this vampire's ability to control minds, her cousin Barry had opened the door to him. Barry had invited his death and those of his loved ones into their home that night. Her mind replayed the echoing screams as their blood streaked the walls and pictures of her home.

Unable to hold her tray up, it fell onto the table with a clatter. The students jumped back on their stools to avoid the toppling glasses. Quinn's legs shook as a scream rose inside her and strangled in her throat. The scream was so full of anguish and fury it would have made a banshee cower. Her nails dug into her palms as she tried to rein in the warring emotions tearing through her.

The man's gaze slid past her to the crowd beyond. Then his shoulders straightened and his gaze came back to her. His eyes widened until they were about to pop out of his head. Quinn felt as if someone had kicked her in the gut as she stared into his blue-green eyes. Fangs sliding free, she took a step toward him.

The man's gaze raked her. The smile spreading across his mouth caused her blood to boil. Lunging away from the table, heedless of those around her, she shoved herself through the crowd straight toward him. She didn't care who witnessed it; she'd rip this vampire's throat out with her bare hands when she got a hold of him. Before she could reach him, he fled out the door.

"No!" she gasped and burst free of the crowd.

She raced across the few remaining feet to the door and

smashed into it. She didn't feel the chill in the air. Her feet barely hit the stairs as she ran down them and into the parking lot. At the corner of the building, she saw a flash of coattails as the vampire she pursued vanished into an alley.

As she raced across the parking lot, her only thoughts were of digging her hands into his flesh and tearing it apart while she drained the life from his miserable body. Rage tasted bitter on her tongue, or maybe that was her desire to sink her fangs deep into this monster's neck.

Just as he had once done to her.

JULIAN RESTED his elbow on the bar as he surveyed the crowd. He glanced at the clock on the wall, urging the time to go faster so he could get Quinn out of here and back to her apartment. He wouldn't mind picking up where they'd left off earlier, and he didn't think she'd put up much of an argument.

Chris and Melissa sat at a table near the poolroom. Lou, a young Guardian in training, was sitting with them. Luther and Zach hadn't arrived yet. Quinn flipped the tray in her hands as she walked through his line of vision. He surveyed the crowd again, but the main barroom and the poolroom were full of people with heartbeats. No matter how many vampires there were, no vampire would be foolish enough to attack her in this crowd.

Julian tapped his fingers on the bar. Quinn stopped at a table, a smile on her face as she spoke with the young kids gathered around it. Chris rose from his seat and disappeared into the poolroom. He returned a minute later with a pool stick and lifted it toward Julian to let him know it was their turn to play.

Julian rose from his seat and stepped away from the bar. He froze when Quinn began to shove her way through the crowd, oblivious to those in her path. Julian's eyes shot toward the door as it closed seconds before she crashed into it. He opened his mouth to shout at her to stop, but she'd already disappeared from view.

Julian leapt away from the bar and rushed through the crowd behind her. It took everything he had not to ruthlessly shove everyone out of his way, but he managed to keep himself restrained enough not to reveal to every person in this bar they were in the presence of something more than human.

A snarl tore from him when a couple danced into his way. It had been two years since he'd killed a human, but he nearly broke their necks in frustration. Only seconds had passed since she'd gone out the door, but it felt like hours as time seemed to crawl. She was out of his sight, and something or someone had drawn her out the door.

He'd strangle her when he got his hands on her, but first he had to find her.

Just as Julian reached the door, Zach was stepping through it into the bar. He took a step back when he spotted Julian and shoved the door open again. "She went around the back of the building," he said.

Julian raced down the steps and hurried around the corner of the building. Ahead of him, he spotted Luther running through the desert in pursuit of Quinn. There was no way the middle-aged Guardian would be able to keep up with her.

"Where did she go?" he demanded when he easily overtook Luther.

Luther pointed ahead of him. "That way."

Julian poured on the speed, racing across the sand as it

shifted and slid beneath his feet. The small sliver of moon spilling across the sand lit the way as he ran up the side of one dune and down the other.

He almost bellowed her name across the open desert, but he had a feeling stealth was best right then. Racing over another dune, he finally spotted Quinn in the sand below him facing off against a man with a distinct lack of a heartbeat. The vampire's ankle-length duster swirled around his calves as he moved. She was more careless than he'd ever seen her before as she charged heedlessly toward the vampire. The vamp raised his arm and backhanded her across the face, causing her to stagger to the side.

Unable to suppress a roar, Julian plunged down the dune toward them. Quinn spun around, a stake in her hand as she went at the man with a ferociousness that had the vamp dodging back to avoid her crazed swings. Leaping to the side, the vamp smashed his arm on top of hers when she lurched awkwardly at the spot where he'd been standing. The vamp swung a punch at her, but she dodged to the side in time to avoid the blow.

The vampire's head shot toward him when Julian bellowed again. The man backpedaled in the sand. Quinn lunged at him, swinging the stake in an arch that sliced across the vamp's chest. The blow tore his skin open and blood spilled free to stain his shirt. Quinn lunged at him again, but the vamp managed to dart to the side.

Pulling his arm back, he swung it at Quinn as her forward momentum caused her to run past him. The blow hit her so forcefully that it caused her head to snap around with a loud crack. Red burst across Julian's vision when Quinn landed face down in the sand. The vampire looked from her to him before he turned and fled across the desert.

Bloodlust pulsed through Julian. He'd make the vamp

pay in the most excruciating and innovative ways for striking Quinn. His fangs pulsed with his hunger for blood, but he pulled to an abrupt halt next to Quinn, as she lay unmoving in the sand. No matter how badly he wanted to catch and destroy the vampire fleeing across the desert, he couldn't leave her.

Kneeling at her side, his hands shook as he turned her over. "Quinn?"

Her arms fell across the sand. The spill of her dark hair sprawled around her, her eyes remaining closed. His fingers trembled as he brushed aside the sand and hair sticking to her cheeks and forehead.

"Come on, Dewdrop, wake up," he urged.

He ran his hands over her still body as he searched for an injury other than the dusky bruise high on her left temple. His fangs pressed against his inner lip as he stared at her. He took a minute to steady himself against the rage simmering within him before sliding his hands under her. Lifting her into his arms, he cradled her limp form protectively against his chest. He didn't look at her as he ran. He was halfway back to town when he encountered Melissa, Chris, and Zach running after them.

"What happened?" Melissa demanded.

"She chased a vampire into the desert," Julian grated through his teeth and pulled Quinn closer against him. The sweet scent of her filled his nostrils. What had she been thinking? He trembled as the image of her falling in the sand slithered through his mind. "I'm taking her to her place. Tell Clint she got sick or something and meet me there."

Melissa turned and ran back toward the bar while Chris and Zach followed him toward her apartment building.

CHAPTER SIX

WHO WAS BEATING on her head like it was a freaking snare drum?

"Ugh," she groaned, when attempting to move her head turned it into a full-blown death metal beat in her head.

"Quinn." Cool fingers brushed over her cheeks and temple. She recognized Julian's voice, but she couldn't bring herself to open her eyes yet.

"My head," she muttered.

A cool cloth was draped over her forehead, and a sigh escaped her when some of the pounding eased. His fingers were back on her face. The feel of them so light against her skin did more to ease her pain than the cold cloth on her brow had. Finally feeling brave enough to open her eyes, she lifted her lids to peer at him.

He leaned over her, his striking eyes searching hers as he caressed her face. His lips were pinched, and lines etched the corners of his mouth and eyes. "Quinn," he breathed.

She forced herself to smile in an attempt to ease some of his torment. "What happened?"

"You took off after a vampire," he bit out.

Memories of what had occurred assaulted her. On her feet in an instant, she swayed as the movement caused her to feel as if someone had fired off an M-80 inside her head. Taking a step to the side, she braced herself as the world lurched beneath her feet. Julian grabbed hold of her arms, but she shook him off.

"Where is the vampire?" she demanded.

"He got away."

"We have to find him."

"Quinn—"

She spun toward him. "Now, we have to find him *now!*"

"We will, but the sun is coming up soon, and there's nothing we can do during the day," he said in a calming tone that only made her more agitated.

"You don't understand. It was *him!* That was the bastard who murdered me and helped to kill my family."

His hands clamped on her arms as the color drained from his face. The silence was so complete in the room that she could hear the beat of someone's music floating across the night. "He'll know then," Julian said.

"Know what?"

"That you weren't born of vampire blood. If he knows about the prophecy, he'll put two and two together. We have to leave this town."

"No! This is the closest I've been to him in six years. I'm not leaving here without killing him. I don't care what you say, or what he may or may not know about me. I'm going to *destroy* him."

Julian's eyes turned crimson. He lifted her arms and pulled her closer so her palms pressed against his chest. "I will do whatever it takes to keep you alive, including dragging you out of this town kicking and screaming."

Her chin rose as her eyes narrowed on him. "He destroyed my life. I will not walk away from him, and I will not leave my friends unprotected if he decides to come back with a pack of vampires. If you take me from here, I will try to escape from you every chance I get. When I finally succeed, and I will, I'll make it so you *never* find me again. He has no idea how I turned," she continued as the red blazed hotter in his eyes. "For all he knows, one of his cohorts could have given me their blood when he wasn't looking."

Julian shook his head. "He won't think that."

"You have no idea what he thinks. He now knows I work at Clint's. He'll most likely assume I've established some kind of a life in this town. I've spent my entire life hiding. I refuse to do it anymore."

He released her so suddenly, she took a startled step away from him. Pacing toward the kitchen, he ran his hand through his hair as he stalked. She hadn't realized all the others were in her small apartment until he moved out of her way to reveal them gathered by the door.

Luther's pale-gray eyes were intent on her behind the lenses of his Lennon style glasses. His salt and pepper hair was slightly disheveled and damp. She knew he'd tried to follow her when she'd left the bar, but she'd been too focused on hunting her killer to acknowledge him. He lifted his glasses and rubbed his nose as he bowed his head.

Lou stood beside him, his tawny-brown eyes flitting between her and Julian. He had his hands folded before him and his thin shoulders hunched forward. The ends of his brown hair curled against the collar of his alligator shirt. He looked younger than his eighteen years, yet he had an air of wisdom about him that made him appear far older.

"I should have killed him," Julian muttered.

Turning to face him, Quinn folded her arms over her chest. "He's mine."

Chris and Melissa both sighed; Zach took a step closer to the door when Julian spun to glower at her. "He's far older than you! Look at what he did to you!" he shouted.

She didn't want to think about it; it made her head pound all over again. She'd gone against all of her training. Wrath had fueled her attack, not reason, and it had nearly gotten her killed. She wouldn't make the same mistake again.

"I wasn't prepared for the shock of seeing him or the anger and memories his arrival brought with it. I'll be better prepared for him next time."

Julian stopped before her. She tilted her chin up to meet his fiery eyes, determined not to back down. She simply couldn't; there was too much on the line right now.

"Not prepared?" he said and rested his hand against the holster on her hip. "You have more weapons strapped to you than anyone I know."

"I didn't expect to come face to face with the man who tortured me and left me for dead while I was at work tonight. Excuse me if it threw me off my game a little."

"And it will be easier the next time you see him?"

"I don't care if it's ten times harder! I'm going to drain every ounce of life from that man before I tear his throat out."

Julian lifted an eyebrow at her vehemence, his mouth actually quirking in a smile. She fought the urge to scream and kick him in the shin. She had no idea why he was looking at her like that when seconds before he'd appeared to want to choke her.

"Leash the fangs, Dewdrop."

Her nails dug into her palms as she glowered at him. "I'm not leaving."

"I don't think she should leave," Luther interjected.

Julian's smile vanished as he turned toward the Guardian. "And why is that?" he demanded.

"For one, our departure from this town will leave it vulnerable. Also, if this vampire has heard the prophecy, he may not know it involves Quinn. Running from here could confirm it to him. He knows what she looks like. He will spread the word. We can make a stand in this town. If we run, we'll never know when they might catch up with us. If we stay here, he may not believe Quinn is the vampire of the prophecy. She won't be able to reveal what she can do until we know he's going to die. Unless you revealed it tonight?"

"I never got a chance to use my ability on him," Quinn replied to Luther's questioning look.

"And if he comes back here with a group of vamps?" Julian demanded.

"Yet another reason not to leave this town unprotected. Did you recognize him?" Luther inquired of Julian.

"No."

"Then he probably doesn't know who you are either, or that you're an Elder. He certainly doesn't know there's also three Hunters in this town. I bet his interest in Quinn just became a lot more intense now that he knows she's a vampire. He's going to try to satisfy his curiosity about her, and we'll be able to get him when he does."

"Clint and Hawtie are the only friends I've had for years. I can't turn my back on them," she said.

Julian bit out an explosive curse before swinging away from her and pacing over to the kitchen once more. She could feel his hunger and need to destroy radiating from him. "Julian—" she started.

He held his hand up before glancing at the window. "I have to feed."

"The sun will be up soon," she protested.

"I'll be back before then. Stay with her," he commanded the others. "Don't forget that vampire was able to get into Quinn's house and at her family because he has the ability to control minds. Don't go outside until it's daytime, and no one goes anywhere by themselves anymore."

Lou scrambled to get out of Julian's way as he strode toward the door. He didn't look back before slipping outside. They stared at the closed door before the others all turned to look at her. "He'll be okay," she said. "He has to calm down a little bit."

"Yeah," Melissa agreed.

Quinn ran a hand over her face. "Clint must think I lost my mind or something tonight."

"I told him you got sick and had to go home," Melissa replied.

"Or he's going to think I'm pregnant," she said with a half-hearted laugh. She slumped tiredly onto the couch and dropped her still-throbbing head into her hands.

JULIAN PROWLED THROUGH THE DESERT, going from one animal to the next as he tried to ease his need to murder with a glut of blood. What he really wanted was to sink his fangs into someone's neck and tear out their throat. In the two years since he'd stopped killing, the urge to murder and destroy had never been as strong as it was now.

None of the animal blood was going to be good enough tonight. It would never satisfy his need for death the way actually killing someone would. The wind howled across the open land as he stood amongst the shifting sand, staring at the homes across the way. Curtains and blinds shaded the windows; some had sparkly decorations hanging from the windows that reflected the night-lights within the rooms. There were so many unsuspecting people within those homes, sleeping soundly, unaware of the predator lurking in their backyard.

He could so easily walk up to one of those homes, manipulate an invite from someone within, and destroy them before they realized what they'd invited into their home. The prospect was entirely too tempting for his liking.

You're a better man now, he reminded himself, but the reminder was doing little good right then.

Killing someone was not the answer to his problems. It wouldn't make Quinn any more willing to leave this town. It wouldn't destroy the vampire who had tortured and unknowingly turned her, but damn if it didn't sound like one of the most pleasing ideas he'd had in a while.

His fangs tingled. He ground his teeth together as he stared at the shadowed windows. *Just slip inside and feel a little better. Unleash the monster within that's been begging to be free since it was caged. Lose yourself in murder and death by indulging in the blood of the innocents.*

It had been two years since he'd fed from a human, but he could clearly recall the taste of human blood; could still feel the warmth of it as it flooded his mouth and slid down his throat. The thrill of power and excitement it had given him as his victims struggled and screamed in his arms was something he could never forget. Those screams…

A smile curved his mouth at the memories. Those screams had filled many of his nights and had made him feel alive in a way he hadn't felt in centuries. Then he'd met Cassie and his love for her had made him feel alive in a different way. It had made him realize he could be, and wanted to be, a better man. He'd always known Cassie was

Devon's and could never be his, but he'd still wanted to be better for her, and he was.

Now he had Quinn. He wanted to be a good man for her, like she deserved, but he would do whatever it took, no matter how merciless and horrific, to keep her safe. She made him feel more alive than he'd ever felt and made him love in a way he hadn't imagined possible. Even when he'd been human, he'd never felt as alive as he did when he was holding her, touching her.

And he could lose her. So many things out there were trying to tear them apart. He never knew where the next threat might come from.

I could walk into one of those homes, shut out the world for a few hours, and lose everything I've worked to achieve.

A light came on in one of the homes. He remained where he was as the sky turned pink in the distance. He should take shelter soon, but he couldn't tear himself away as the thrill of the hunt and the kill pulsed within his body.

He couldn't return to Quinn like this, not when he was so close to losing complete control of himself. She could soothe the beast within him, but he wasn't in the mood to be calmed.

Instead of taking shelter or returning to Quinn, he flexed his fingers again as he walked toward the house.

CHAPTER SEVEN

QUINN LIFTED her head when she heard the lock sliding free and watched as Julian stepped into her apartment. Placing her can of Mountain Dew down, she launched to her feet as he stepped inside and closed the door. His skin was puckered and red; parts of his shirt were actually charred. While she wanted to shake some sense into him for taking off like that, the wildness of his crimson eyes and the harshness of his chiseled features made her heart ache.

"Where have you been?" she demanded.

His gaze flashed around the room. "Where is everyone?"

"I told them to go after the sun rose. He couldn't come at me now that it's daylight, and I preferred to be alone."

His eyes focused on her briefly before sliding away again. "You *never* should have been left alone."

"Nothing could possibly happen during the daytime," she replied impatiently.

"He can control minds. That means he can use a human to do his bidding, and they can walk about in the day."

She hadn't considered that. She'd been desperate to be

alone, desperate for him to return to her. "Oh," she said dully.

He *finally* focused on her. "Yeah, oh."

She planted her hands on her hips. "You left too, you know."

"I shouldn't have."

"Where have you been? The sun came up *two* hours ago."

His powerful body moved with the grace of a predator as he came toward her. "Out."

"Out?" she parroted, but she had no idea how to respond to his flippant reply. "You fed."

"I did."

Despite the burns on him, his skin shone with vitality and power. He radiated an aura of barely leashed violence that caused her fight or flight instinct to rear to life, even though she knew she had nothing to fear with him.

Most would have been afraid of what he could do; it only made her love him more. He would never hurt her, but there was something different about him right then. Something within him was extremely volatile, and all his attention was focused on her.

"You were caught out in the sun. Why didn't you come back sooner?" she asked when he stopped before her.

"I had some things to take care of."

Despite her misgivings about his current state of mind, she instinctively leaned closer. Yearning slipped through her body, making her stomach clench. Unable to stop herself, she wrapped her hands around his forearms to steady herself.

Beneath her touch, his powerful muscles rippled. Her hands slid over his skin and the bristly blond hairs covering his arms. She barely managed to suppress a moan from the shivers of delight the contact elicited in her.

"I wish you'd come back sooner," she breathed.

"So do I." Her head tilted back to take him in. His face was unreadable as he watched her, his full mouth compressed into a thin line. "You somehow make everything better, Quinn. You make me feel like a man and not a monster."

"You're not a monster." She raised her hand and pressed her fingers against his cheek. He flinched as if her words and touch distressed him. Confusion swirled through her. She had no idea what had happened tonight, but he felt distant from her.

She went to withdraw her hand, but he clasped hold of it and pressed it against his face. "You have no idea what goes through my mind about you, and what I'd like to do to you. No idea about the cravings for blood and death that are my constant companion. The need I feel to sink into the oblivion the blood can bring me is a temptation that follows me everywhere. You'd run screaming into the night if you knew the half of it."

Quinn swallowed heavily, but she kept her hand pressed against his cheek as she rested her other hand on his chest. "I'd never run from you," she whispered. "There is nothing you could do that would make me turn from you."

The circles around his pupils burned with fire. "What if I returned to killing humans?"

She closed her eyes and rested her head on his chest as she tried to think through his words. "I couldn't be with you." A knife pierced her insides and sliced them apart as she spoke the words, but she couldn't lie to him. "But I wouldn't turn against you."

"You'd try to save me."

She lifted her head to look at him. "You don't need saving, Julian. You will be who you will be, and it will be your choice to make, but no matter what you do, I will love you."

She'd been fighting back those last words for weeks. She'd been certain saying them would spell doom for them, as it had for the others she'd loved or gotten close to over the years. Now, she realized her life had always been precarious, it always would be, but he *had* to know how she felt.

If something were to happen to either one of them, and she hadn't told him she loved him, she would never forgive herself. She sensed he needed to hear the words now, more than ever. He may not feel the same way about her, she may have just opened herself up to a world of hurt, but she would never take them back.

His eyes sparked, and a tremor shook his hands. Anguish flitted across his face before he wrapped his hand around the back of her head and dragged her against his chest. "I'm not sure I deserve that love," he said in a voice hoarse with emotion.

"I am."

He groaned low in his throat before threading his fingers through her hair and tenderly pulling her head back. His eyes were their beautiful blue color again as he searched her face. "I love you too, Quinn. More than I ever dreamed possible; more than I ever realized I could."

Before she could respond, he bent his head and kissed her with a hunger so desperate it caused her knees to give out. The arm he snaked around her waist kept her from going down completely. He lifted her off her feet as his tongue slid between her lips. Hot and heady, his tongue stroked in and out of her mouth in thrusts that she met eagerly.

No reason, not anymore, she realized when her hands wrapped around his neck. The lingering taste of the coppery blood on his lips and tongue from his hunt aroused her further. Her hips arched instinctively into his. The rumble of pleasure he emitted over the friction the action caused between their bodies made her do it again. Excitement and need pulsed through her, drowning her within their consuming depths.

She felt out of control as her hands ran over the corded muscles of his back. Her body moved of its own volition against him, rocking as it begged for more. She hadn't realized he'd carried her into the bedroom until she felt the mattress against her back, and he was coming down on top of her.

Too fast. Not fast enough. Have to have more.

Her thoughts became a tangled mess. She stopped thinking completely when he pulled the bottom of her shirt up to expose her flesh. Given what had happened in the last few hours, his powerful hands caressed her far more gently than she'd believed possible when he'd first returned to her apartment.

She didn't stiffen when his fingers brushed over the scar high up in the middle of her stomach, as she would have only a month ago. That scar was just one of the places where the vampire who had walked into Clint's last night had pinned her to the floor with his knives before feeding on her.

Julian knew her history; he knew her scars were her constant reminder of the atrocity she'd committed upon turning. He didn't pity her or condemn her for them, and he never would. He understood why she'd never allowed the scars to heal and had reopened them for years before they'd finally stopped healing on their own.

It only made her love him more.

Nudging her thighs apart, he settled himself between them. Breaking the kiss, his eyes searched hers as he stared at her. "Tell me if you want me to stop."

"Please don't," she whispered.

His eyes blazed a fiery red before he pulled his ruined shirt over his head and threw it aside. She hungrily drank in the eye-popping marvel that was his body. Delicious, lickable, and hot, were all words that fell far short of what he truly was. Her fingers trailed over the chiseled ridges of his abs as her body quickened with excitement. Moving higher over him, she traced over his tattoo. He was beautiful and ruthless enough to make the angels weep.

Her fingers trembled on his body. She'd never get enough of touching him, of looking at him. She'd never get enough of *him*.

"Say it again," he grated.

Her gaze flew up to his crimson-colored eyes. She didn't have to ask what; she knew what he wanted from her. "I love you."

His eyes closed, and his head tilted back as if he were in extreme ecstasy. When his eyes came back to hers, they were the color of the Mediterranean Sea as they shimmered with passion. His hands slid under her shirt, dragging it leisurely up her body before tugging it over her head. His eyes burned with yearning as he drank her in, but he took his time running his hands over her belly and up her ribcage before sliding around to unclasp her bra. He tossed it aside and sat back to drink her in before bending to her once more.

His mouth took hold of hers again as he pulled her closer. The feel and smell of him, the sensation of his body sliding over hers encompassed her whole world. Beyond this room, nothing else existed.

She bit into her bottom lip when his body took complete possession of hers. She fought back tears as her hands dug into his back. He stilled above her as his mouth pressed against her ear. "I'll stop."

The roughness of his voice against her ear made her shudder. She turned her face into his sweat slickened neck. "No," she whispered. "Don't."

"The pain will fade," he promised.

She kept her mouth pressed against his neck as he remained unmoving within her. His scent enveloped her; the enticing aroma of his blood transfixed her, causing her fangs to lengthen. He groaned when she scraped them against his flesh. "Do it!" he commanded.

Quinn didn't have to be told twice. She'd longed to taste his blood, craved it almost as much as she'd craved to know the feeling of his complete possession of her body. Her fangs sank deep, releasing a hot wash of blood into her mouth. His body pushed deeper into hers. Something within her shifted and changed; her mind opened to his as pathways she'd never known existed unwound before her.

His pleasure engulfed her, and his need for her beat against her mind. Tears spilled freely down her cheeks. She was unable to stop them as his love for her poured into her mind. The amount of love he felt for her was consuming and beautiful in its purity. He'd lay his life down for her in an instant and destroy anyone who harmed her without hesitation.

She'd never doubt or question how he felt about her again as she saw herself the way he saw her—proud, strong, defiant, a warrior he found more beautiful than anyone he'd ever known. A small part of her had believed Cassie still would have been his first choice, if he could have had her. She knew now, he wouldn't trade her for anyone, ever. She was his everything.

Beneath the love he felt for her, she also brushed against the barely leashed brutality residing within him. His desire to kill and gorge on blood slid through her mind. It was a constant battle for him, far more of one than she'd ever experienced. She was the only one who could calm him when he was on the verge of going over again. She could also so easily push him over that edge. Until he'd met her, his control had been more stable; now he felt far more volatile because of his need to keep her safe.

Warmth enveloped her as she bit deeper. "That's it," he murmured as his tongue swirled over her ear, and his body moved within hers. "*Mine.*"

Something within her completely fractured at the word and the overwhelming sensations pounding against her. It was too much pleasure all at once; she couldn't handle it. She wanted to withdraw, but at the same time she wanted more and more of him.

Her power surged up within her. It was beyond her control as it sparked across her fingers to illuminate his pale skin. She almost screamed at the sensation of his fangs pressing against her neck. His arms beside her head shook as he kept himself restrained from tasting her.

Unwilling to release her grasp on his vein, she wrapped her hand around the back of his head and pressed him closer against her neck in invitation. A sound of possession rumbled through his chest seconds before his fangs slid into her flesh. She cried out in ecstasy as he hungrily feasted upon her. She poured all of her love into him as more pathways unfolded between their minds to envelope her.

Her power exploded out of her before she could stop it, but it didn't launch him off the bed or drain him of his life. No, this burst did something she'd never experienced before or had ever known it could do.

For the space of ten heartbeats, she actually heard a heart *beat*. She fell back, a gasp escaping her when she released her hold on his vein. His fangs retracted, and his dazed eyes met hers as his heart gave one more lumbering beat before going still again.

His mouth hung open as his gaze went to his chest. She lifted a hand to press it over his heart. "What was that?" she breathed.

His glazed eyes cleared when they met hers again. A smile curved his mouth. "A miracle, like you."

She stared up at him wordlessly before he reclaimed her mouth and began to move within her once more, pushing her closer and closer to the edge of something she didn't fully understand but longed for. Her head fell back, a cry escaped her when the pressure that had been building within her splintered apart. Waves of ecstasy crashed through her body as he drove into her once more before following her over the edge.

CHAPTER EIGHT

QUINN SAT on the couch behind where Julian stood as she strapped her stakes to her calves. Luther, Lou, and Zach stood by her door. She could hear Chris in her kitchen, pulling a package of peanut butter cups from the fridge before popping the top on a can of her Dew. He'd eat all of her chocolate stash if she left him in there for too long. Melissa sat beside her on the couch, watching as Quinn armed herself.

"For a vamp, you sure are comfortable being strapped with things that can kill you," Melissa commented.

Quinn tugged on her boot and zipped up the side. "Hunter too," she reminded her. "I've been comfortable with this stuff since I could walk."

"Oh, the toddler years. Most people babyproof, we were vampproofed."

Quinn laughed as she tugged on her other boot. "And you're still alive because of it," Luther said from the door.

Turning on the couch, Melissa draped her arm across the back. "And I thank you for that," she assured him.

"We're going to have to stay together from now on," Julian said, bringing them all back to the reason why they were here. "Since the vamp who attacked Quinn can control minds, we can't take the chance of him getting a hold of someone and bending them to his will. From now on, we'll stay in groups of twos and threes. At all times."

"What if he's already gotten hold of someone?" Chris asked from the doorway of the kitchen. Quinn's eyes focused on the *bag* of peanut butter cups in his hand. She'd purposely put that one in the oven to keep it hidden from him. Sensing her stare, Chris looked over at her and grinned.

I will not hit him, she told herself. Still, she couldn't help but smile over the fact he felt comfortable enough around her to brave her annoyance with him. She'd have to find better hiding spots for her treats if they all agreed to what Julian was about to propose.

"He seemed as surprised to see me as I was him," Quinn said as she rose to her feet.

"He could have faked that," Zach said.

"He could have, but I don't think so."

"If he did, one of us could be under his control right now," Melissa said.

Luther lifted his glasses to peer around the room before rubbing at his nose and settling them back into place. "But since we have no way of knowing if that's true, we're going to have to trust each other."

"Isn't there some kind of vamp test?" Chris asked.

"No," Julian replied.

"Would Devon be able to tell?"

Julian shook his head. "The only thing Devon could do is take control of all of your minds himself, in order to make sure none of you went against him."

"Thanks, but no on that one," Chris said and shoved a

peanut butter cup into his mouth. Quinn stalked over and snatched the bag away from him. "Aw, come on!"

Opening the stove, she threw the bag inside it. She supposed it hadn't been such a great hiding spot to begin with; she never used the stove, so of course he would think to look there. "I think you've had enough."

"Someone never taught you how to share," he replied with a smile that had her reaching back in and pulling out two more chocolates for him. His sapphire eyes twinkled when he took them from her hand. "You vamps, all bark and no bite."

A burst of laughter escaped her as she slipped past him and into her living room. "I'll bite him for you, if you'd like," Julian offered. "I don't think anyone here would say he hasn't deserved it at least once."

"Feeling the love," Chris replied as he popped another peanut butter cup in his mouth.

"Thanks, but no," Quinn said to Julian.

He held his hand out to her, and a quiver of pleasure raced up her spine when she took hold of it and stepped against his side. Her body instinctively pressed closer to his. His thumb stroked the back of her hand.

"Since I know no one here wants to be under anyone's control, and I think we can agree we don't want Devon and Cassie involved in this, we're going to have to watch out for each other," Julian said.

"Could you touch us to learn if he has taken control of one of our minds?" Lou asked Julian.

"I could try, but he most likely would command you to forget any encounter you had with him, especially if he knows who I am."

"Wouldn't there be something on our skin from him if we had contact with him?" Chris asked.

"He doesn't have to touch you to take control of your mind."

"I'd still feel a little better if you tried," Lou said and held his arm out to him.

Julian walked around the room, taking hold of everyone's hands. Images of their lives flashed through his mind, but he saw nothing involving the vampire from last night. He shook his head before returning to her side. "There's nothing there."

"Can he take us in a group?" Lou asked.

"No, he's much stronger than the last vamp we came across with this ability, but the only vamp I know who can take control of more than one mind at a time is Devon, and he's an Elder," Julian replied. "This vamp can't be older than two or three hundred, I'm guessing from the little I've seen of him, and that's not old enough. If he gets you separately, he can take control of you and keep control, but he couldn't take an entire group at once."

Chris wiped his fingers on his jeans and leaned against the doorframe of the kitchen. "What if we're in a group and he's hiding somewhere, could he take over the mind of one without the others noticing?"

"That's a possibility," Luther replied. "But we're all trained to know when a vamp is present, to look for signs of something unusual. We're much stronger in a group than separated."

"We are," Julian confirmed. "And you'll be much safer here than in the motel. He can enter any of those rooms at any time. Before the sun sets, you should move in here."

They all glanced around her cramped apartment. There was barely room for the sofa, TV, and milk crate coffee table, never mind five more people, but there was little other choice. "Where?" Zach asked.

"Wherever you can find room. It's not going to be pleasant for any of us, but it's better than the alternative," Julian replied.

Zach ran a hand through his hair. "Can't argue with that."

"We should get moving then," Melissa said. "We'll see you at the bar?"

"I'm going to walk Quinn over. I'll meet you at the motel after," Julian told her.

Quinn watched as they all filed out her door before following. She stepped into the hall and locked the door behind Julian and her. Together, they walked down the hall. Dusty was coming up the stairs when they reached them.

"Hey, Quinn-o," Dusty greeted and flashed the peace sign at Julian.

Quinn bit back a laugh as Julian shook his head at him. "I'm going to have some friends staying with me, Dusty," she told him.

"The same peeps I've been seeing a lot around here lately?"

"Those are the ones."

"The black-haired girl single?"

"Sorry, but no." It was better she broke Dusty's heart with a lie now than have him chasing after Melissa while she was staying here.

"Oh well, she probably couldn't handle all this anyway," he said and gestured at his skinny body.

Julian looked at Dusty as if he'd sprouted a third eye. "We have to go." She grabbed Julian's arm and propelled him down the stairs before he could say something to hurt Dusty's feelings. Dusty was a little strange, but she liked him.

~

"ARE you sure you're feeling better?" Clint asked as she tied her apron around her waist.

Despite having come face to face last night with the man who had ended her life as a human, she felt like she was walking on clouds. Every time she recalled what had transpired between Julian and her earlier, she couldn't stop herself from smiling. She half-worried she'd become like one of those Disney characters and burst into song at any second. Unlike Snow White, her singing voice would chase off every animal in a ten-mile radius.

"Much better," she replied. "It must have been one of those twelve-hour bugs or maybe food poisoning."

Clint chewed on his gum as he eyed her skeptically. "Never heard of a twelve-hour bug before. Don't need you puking on the customers."

"I'll make sure to take it outside again," she assured him.

"Fine," he relented. He'd turned away from her when Julian stepped into the bar with Chris and Melissa. "I hope you're not the one who got her sick, Hulk Hogan," Clint said as he walked by Julian.

Julian did a double take before a thunderous expression crossed his face, and he glared at Clint's retreating back. Melissa and Chris burst into laughter; Quinn had to bite her lip to keep from laughing aloud.

"One of these days," Julian growled.

"You'll what?" Quinn asked as she grabbed her tray from the table.

Julian shook his head. "I might flash my fangs and go all red-eyed on him in order to make him piss himself."

"He'd probably just shoot you," Chris choked out. "And then I'd laugh more."

Julian gave him the finger before walking over to kiss her cheek. "Are you okay?"

"As okay as I was the last six times you asked me," she assured him as she rested her hand on the black stubble lining his jaw. "I have no regrets."

He settled his hands on her hips and shook them a little. "Just checking."

She gave him a quick kiss before reluctantly stepping away from him. The place was already beginning to fill up. Quinn kept her attention on the front door as she took orders and worked her way through the crowd with ease. She didn't think the vamp would return so soon, but she hadn't expected him to appear last night either. After work, she planned to search the surrounding desert for him, but until then, she had rent to pay.

The laughter of the barroom, the smell of alcohol, and the clink of the pool balls were all familiar sounds that comforted her as she worked. She stopped at the table where Julian, Melissa, and Chris were sitting. Luther, Lou, and Zach had recently joined them. "What can I get for you?" she asked as she pulled her pen from behind her ear.

Before they could respond, a wash of red and blue lights spilling through the plate glass window at the front of the bar drew her attention to the road. Everyone in the bar quieted as first one and then another police cruiser sped by. Their sirens echoed through the night, shaking the glass with their forlorn wails.

Quinn stepped closer to the window and craned her head to peer out. All the patrons who had seen the cruisers go by approached the window to see where they were going. Ed and Beverly Johnson were the only two full-time cops in town. They rarely worked nights, and the married couple was most often in the same cruiser when they were at work. The last time she'd seen them go to a call at the same time was when the bar was shot up and Angie had been killed.

The five part-time deputies on the force mostly drove one of the three police motorcycles at the station. Occasionally, they would be in one of the cruisers. It could be one of the part-timers, instead of the Johnson's, driving one of those patrol cars now, but for some reason, Quinn didn't think so.

The ghostly hand of impending doom slid over her back, causing the hair on her nape to rise. Someone opened the bar door and stepped onto the porch outside. The splash of red and blue lights continued to play over the street and window, but she couldn't see the cars anymore.

Murmurs ran through the crowd. Shoving her pad into her pocket, Quinn walked over to the open door and stepped outside. At the end of the road, both of the cruisers were parked.

She frowned as she watched the Johnson's approach the house with their guns at the ready. Most of the calls in this town were bar fights that couldn't be handled by the bar employees themselves, some cats in trees, and the rare domestic abuse. She'd never seen Bev or Ed with their hands near their weapons before.

A middle-aged woman stood on the porch of the house; she gestured frantically for the couple to hurry up. With her superior hearing, Quinn heard the woman talking, but she was sobbing too hard for her to be able to make out the words. People pressed closer around her, and some made their way down the steps toward the dirt parking lot.

"They're at the Kemp's place," someone behind her commented.

"That can't be good." Quinn hadn't realized Hawtie stood beside her until she'd spoken.

In the flashing lights, Hawtie's deep-auburn hair was a vibrant shade of red. Her red lips were pursed, her creamy complexion illuminated.

"No, it can't," Clint said from beside Hawtie. With Clint's barely five-five height and Hawtie standing at six-foot, the top of Clint's head just made it past Hawtie's breasts as he wrapped his arm around her waist.

The whispers of the crowd picked up. More people filed into the parking lot and a few made their way down the road as Bev and Ed disappeared inside the house. Ed reemerged a minute later. He grabbed hold of the porch railing and threw up over the side. Such a spectacle probably would have brought laughter from the patrons of the bar on any other occasion; now it only increased the concerned voices surrounding her.

Bev strode past Ed. She jogged down the steps of the house and over to the police cruiser. She sat in the driver's seat, talking with someone over the microphone before grabbing something and heading back toward the house. Her husband wiped his mouth before joining her to spread out the yellow crime scene tape around the perimeter of the home.

"Oh God," Quinn breathed. She pressed her palm against her mouth as she watched the home being taped off.

She felt the pulse of Julian's power before he stepped against her back. Her stomach turned sickly, but even though Melissa had told Clint she'd gotten sick last night, as a vampire, she didn't throw up. Right now, she really wished she did; it might make her feel a little better. Tilting her head back, she looked at Julian. No emotion flickered over his features as he watched the scene unfold.

"We should find out what happened," Luther said from beside Julian.

Quinn gestured at the crowd gathering in front of the Kemp's house. "We'll know soon enough. Word travels fast in this town."

"Come on," Clint said and nudged her elbow. "Whatever has happened, we can't do anything about it. Best to get back to work."

Quinn nodded, but she had a hard time tearing her attention away from the house at the end of the road.

CHAPTER NINE

"THEY WERE MURDERED."

Quinn lifted her head as Carlie Jean whispered this to her. C.J., as she preferred to be called, was a pretty redhead with deep-brown eyes and a freckled, round face that would forever make her look years younger than she was. Her five-foot height and slender figure also made her appear more like she was twelve than the actual twenty-two she was.

C.J. had worked at the bar part-time for a year now, but after Angie's death, she'd been promoted to full-time. She was a friendly girl, but the fact she always had her eyes on Julian and had taken Angie's position, made it difficult for Quinn to like her.

"They're saying it was brutal too, sadistic. Well, I mean you saw Ed puke right?" C.J. continued with an enthusiasm that made Quinn wonder about her.

However, she supposed if someone hadn't grown up around blood and death and hadn't experienced a traumatic event of their own, it might all be a little fascinating, especially in this small town. It made Quinn's skin crawl as memories of the night her family had been murdered swelled toward the surface.

"I did," Quinn said. "Did they say how they were killed?"

C.J. shook her head. "Not sure if they know yet, but I'm sure they will soon."

Quinn rubbed at the bridge of her nose. Her head throbbed. If there was ever a night she could go home sick, tonight was it.

"What is going on in this town? First Angie..." Quinn's head shot up at C.J.'s words. "Oops, sorry," she said hastily. "But we've had more murders in the past month than in twenty years."

"Yeah," Quinn murmured, her eyes going back to the massive glass window. The red and blue strobes had been turned off. Three black, unmarked cars were also parked outside the Kemp's now. The men inside had climbed out and joined Ed and Bev an hour ago. She assumed they were crime scene technicians or detectives from the state, but she wasn't sure. She'd watched the new arrivals with the rest of the bar, but hadn't gone outside again. "It's horrible."

Gathering her tray, she went to lift it, but her hand trembled too bad to get it off the counter. Quinn flexed her hand as she willed it to stop shaking. No matter how badly she tried, she couldn't rid herself of the feeling that her killer was also the one who'd killed the Kemps. That it was somehow *her* fault they were dead.

That poor family. She didn't know them well, they didn't come to Clint's, but they'd seemed happy enough the few times she'd seen them.

She lifted the tray again, her hand was steadier, but she had to carry it with both hands. The bar had cleared out considerably since the first cruiser had gone by. A good chunk of the crowd was still outside the Kemp's house; the rest had gone home.

Maybe one of them had been the killer. She doubted it, but what did she know anymore?

If the vampire who had killed her had done this to the Kemp's, it meant he'd already started to take out his vengeance on the residents in town.

She didn't know how to find out if it had been a vampire attack on the Kemp's or not. Unless...

Her gaze slid to Julian sitting at the table with the others. An air of wariness surrounded him as he kept his head bent and his hands clasped around the mug before him. With his ability of psychometry, he'd be able to see what the police had seen at the crime scene. He would be able to tell what had caused the murders if he could touch something of the Kemps.

Or even better, she thought eagerly. *He may be able to tell who did it!*

The idea of forcing him to witness such a thing caused a pit to form in her stomach. What if it hadn't been a vampire and he was forced to witness something terrible he never would have had to experience otherwise? Maybe it had been a murder-suicide type of thing over there. No, she decided, there was no way she would ask him to do such a thing.

She placed the tray on a table of subdued bikers and handed out their drinks. They gave her a brief nod of thanks before turning their attention back to the window. The men and women may not be able to see much from here, but they remained riveted.

Turning away, she walked over to where Julian and the others sat. "C.J. said the Kemp's were murdered," she said quietly.

Julian folded his arms over his chest and leaned back in

his chair. His eyes glittered like ice shards as they slid to the window. She had no idea what he was thinking or what had him looking so exhausted with shadows lining his eyes. She rested her hand on his arm; his hand fell over the top of hers, but she couldn't shake the feeling he didn't really see her right then.

"I'm sure there will be a lot of rumors in the beginning," Luther said. "That's why we're going to have to find out what really happened. If it was a vampire or human who caused the deaths."

"And how do you plan to do that?" Zach inquired.

"Well, he plans to use me, Zachariah," Julian replied as he released her hand and casually took a sip of his beer.

Zach shot him a look, but wisely refrained from the usual correction of his name. Julian had become completely still as he sat with his gaze pinned on Luther.

"It is the best chance we have," Luther replied.

"I don't see us being able to get anywhere near the bodies, so it will have to be something they touched while being murdered," Julian continued.

"You can get memories from a dead body?" Melissa inquired.

"They are inanimate objects."

Those last two words made Quinn rub at her arms when a chill ran through her. She had withheld from asking Julian to do this, but Luther had none of the same reservations that she did. She scowled at the Guardian, but Luther kept his attention focused on Julian as he pretended not to notice her.

"I don't think they'll be able to handle the bodies here. This town isn't exactly set up for that kind of police work. They might take them over to Yuma," Quinn said. "They'd be better equipped to handle it over there."

"Which means I have to get into that house," Julian said.

Quinn's gaze went back to the door as more flashing lights sped down the street, ambulances this time, probably to carry the bodies wherever they'd be going. She turned away from the vehicles, unwilling to watch anymore.

Julian rose to his feet and walked stiffly toward the window. Watching his back, she began to think it was more than the murders and the arrival of her killer that had him so tense and distant, but she had no idea what else it could be.

~

"SHH!" Julian hissed from ahead of her when Chris kicked the side of a lawn chair on the back patio. The clinking sound of the metal chair legs skittering across the patio set her teeth on edge.

"Sorry," Chris muttered.

Her gaze slid over the patio and neighboring homes. She scanned the houses, but all of their lights remained off and she didn't see anyone amongst the sprawling desert behind the Kemp's home. Everyone in this town had been on high alert after what had occurred last night. She'd half-expected them to all still be awake, afraid to go to sleep now that they *knew* a killer walked amongst them.

Multiple killers, if she included the group with her.

Julian had wanted to enter the house last night, while the memories were still fresh, but the police hadn't finished doing whatever they had to do until mid-morning. Now at two o'clock in the morning, they were slinking through the shadows of the Kemp's porch to their back door. She had no idea what possible excuse they could use if they were caught doing this, so she hoped someone else had one.

Julian stopped at the back door and rested his hand on the knob. He tried to turn it, but the knob remained unmoving beneath his hand, something Quinn didn't find at all surprising. The police may have done everything they could for now, but the house was still taped off and an active crime scene, or at least that's what she called it thanks to the TV show "Bones," her newest Netflix addiction.

The muscles in Julian's arm bunched and flexed as he leaned on the knob, breaking it away from the door. With his fingers, he shoved the remains of the doorknob away and pushed against the door. It remained locked.

"Deadbolt's locked," he muttered.

Judging by the shine of the deadbolt, Quinn guessed it was a brand new addition, probably added by the police. Julian pulled the palm of his hand back and smashed it into the lock located above the knob. Quinn cringed when the metal gave way and clattered onto the floor of the room beyond.

Her shoulders hunched up as she prepared herself for someone to start shouting at them, or a giant spotlight to beam down on them like the criminals they were. She glanced nervously around, but though she'd thought the sound had been as loud as fireworks, the night around them remained completely still. Julian pressed his shoulder against the door and nudged it open.

The door caught the broken lock that had fallen inside and sent it spiraling away in a dinging clatter across the tiled kitchen floor. Quinn winced at every rattling ting. "We're about as stealthy as a bull," Chris muttered.

Without a word, Julian retrieved the broken knob and lock and placed them on the green marble countertop near the kitchen sink. "Come on," he said with a jerk of his head.

Quinn stepped hesitatingly across the threshold of the home. She felt like the worst form of life for breaking into the dead family's home as she stood inside the doorway. The hush enveloping the house made her feel as if she'd stepped into a tomb. In some ways, she supposed she had. She wrapped her arms around herself and grasped hold of her elbows in an attempt to ward off the chill seeping into her bones.

She couldn't bring herself to look closely at the pictures and drawings stuck to the fridge with magnets. On the wall, beside the phone, was a whiteboard full of colorful doodles, notes, and pins stuck to it. She glimpsed a photo of two young girls hugging each other as they held up blue ribbons before she hastily looked away from the picture.

The warmth that had once filled this house, the love and laughter that had made it a home, was gone. The only thing remaining was this silence and the haunting echo of screams resonating in her head.

"They've already taken the fingerprints from this place too," Julian said. "But just in case they decide to take more, don't touch anything."

"Should we wipe off what you touch?" Melissa asked.

"No one is going to have my fingerprints on file and no bars meant to hold a human will hold me. You two could spend a long time in prison though."

"Don't remind me," Chris murmured as his eyes skipped over the things Quinn refused to focus on.

Julian didn't bother to touch anything else in the kitchen but made his way down the dim hall. Quinn stood, unable to get her feet to move, when he disappeared from view. Finally, she forced herself to put one foot in front of the other as she followed him. No matter how hollow this house made her feel, she couldn't let him face what he might see alone. Unwilling to look at the pictures lining the walls, she kept her eyes focused on her sneakers.

Shadows danced across the wood floor of the living

room when she stepped into it. The scent of blood became more noticeable here; it tickled her nose and caused her fangs to tingle. She *hated* the part of her that reacted to the scent of blood. She loathed the part that made her a little excited, when what she really wanted was to weep for the lives lost here.

Julian had descended the two stairs to a sunken second living room and was making his way toward the dining room. Quinn stopped to watch as he walked across the hardwood floor and through the double doors of the dining room. Beyond the small dining room, she could see the kitchen again.

We'd been eating in the dining room when they knocked, she recalled of the night her family had been torn from her. *Spaghetti with meatballs.*

Her hand fluttered up to the heart-shaped locket around her neck that had belonged to her cousin, Betsy. She wrapped her hand around it, feeling as if the metal burned her flesh while she watched Julian run his fingers over the dining room table. No food was on the table, but papers were scattered across the surface. Perhaps someone had been doing their homework when the attack had occurred.

Quinn's fingers trembled, tears burned her eyes as her own memories threatened to engulf her within their suffocating depths. She struggled to keep herself rooted in the present while the past rose up all around her.

"Did the police clean up all the blood?" Chris whispered.

"If this was a vampire attack, there most likely wouldn't be much blood for them to clean up," Julian murmured.

"Oh, yeah," Chris replied dully.

He looked as pale as she felt right then. Beside him, Melissa's normally olive hue had faded to a pasty color that caused her onyx eyes to stand out.

Quinn spotted specks of blood on the hardwood floor and a few more on the tiles beyond it.

A tremble went through her. "There was a lot of blood when they attacked my family."

Julian's eyes were a vibrant red when he lifted his head to look at her. "They had to be violent and lethal with your family. They knew you were Hunters."

Quinn closed her eyes as she tried not to cry. It had been violent.

Betsy and I were discussing what to pack for college, how to decorate our dorm room. Betsy had wanted pink or purple. I preferred living on the street to either of those color options. I preferred a stereo and no TV. Betsy insisted on both. The bickering had been good-natured, more excited than annoyed or irritated. We both knew, in the end, we were going to have a good time, and neither of us would consider the idea of getting a different roommate.

Barry had risen at the sound of the knock. I barely paid him any attention as he walked behind us toward the door. I couldn't see who was there and barely heard him say, "Come in."

Then, before I could tell Betsy I'd beat her with her old, giant, stuffed elephant if she brought it with her, they were on us. His hand wrapped around my neck, yanking me out of the chair and dragging me into a battle I hadn't been prepared to fight.

"Quinn?" Julian asked worriedly.

She opened her eyes and forced herself to focus on the house before her. Forced herself not to see the home she'd shared with her family until that fateful night. "I'm fine," she muttered. "Do you see anything?"

He continued to stare at her, his eyes narrowing on her face. Melissa rested her hand on Quinn's shoulder, squeezing it reassuringly. Julian shook his head before walking over and running his fingers across the papers on the table. Quinn's legs were wooden; her knees barely bent as she climbed down the two steps to the sunken living room and walked toward him. Julian glanced at her when she stopped beside him to stare at the papers.

"Algebra," she muttered to no one in particular.

"Maybe we should get out of here," Chris suggested.

"Wait." Turning away, Julian walked over and knelt by one of the few splatters of dried blood marring the floor.

Quinn lifted her head, her eyes latching onto a picture sitting on top of a desk in the corner. Her mouth went completely dry as a stab of grief shot through her heart and a startled cry escaped her. At the sound of her despair, Julian's head shot up. His eyes darted around as he searched for some sign of an impending attack.

His eyes came back to hers when her legs began to shake. Before she knew it, he was standing before her. His hands on her shoulders helped to steady her. "What is it?" he demanded.

Quinn pointed at the picture on the desk. "It was him," she whispered. "The vampire who attacked me did this."

Julian turned to look at the photo. Across the center of the glass, a smear of blood partially obscured the clothes of the family in the photo. However, their smiling faces were still evident, all five of them. Two of the children were the young girls she'd seen in the photo in the kitchen, but the girls were older in this one, probably mid-teens. The other was a boy who was only a couple of years younger than the girls were. The mother and father sat in front of their children, their pride in their family evident on their glowing faces. All of them had hair so dark it nearly blended in with the shadows of the room.

"How do you know?" he demanded.

"They look too much like my family for it to be a coincidence. And the blood across the picture, that's what our family photo looked like after the attack."

Julian squeezed her shoulders before turning and striding over to pick up the picture. He held it in his hand as he ran his fingers over the blood smeared across the glass. His head bowed before he placed it back on the desk.

"She's right," he confirmed. Returning to her, he pulled her into his arms. "Let's get out of here."

He didn't release her as he walked with her out the door.

CHAPTER TEN

Julian held Quinn close against his side as he stared at the ceiling in her room. His arm was propped behind his head; the little bit of sun filtering through the blinds and curtains played across the ceiling. His arm tightened around Quinn when she stirred against him, mumbling something before settling down again. It had been a couple of weeks since she last had a nightmare. Tonight, she'd had three.

After each nightmare, she'd bolted upright in bed, her eyes wild in the night as she screamed. Her cries had startled the others and brought Luther to the door the first time, but Julian had sent him away. Turning his face into her, he nuzzled her hair until she settled down again.

He inhaled her fresh scent, which mingled with his own scent in her blood. He was such a big part of her now, his blood mingling with hers, his claim on her evident in the fading marks on her neck. She was his now, and he was *never* going to let her go. She may not know what they were to each other yet, but he had no doubt she was his mate.

Their lives were irrevocably bound together, and he wouldn't have it any other way.

His head turned toward the road when a shout sounded; it was followed by the laughter of people outside. The town had been abnormally subdued since the murders, but it had become louder again today as people fell back into the natural rhythm of their lives.

Julian shuddered as he recalled the impressions he'd received from inside the Kemp's house. In the beginning, all he'd seen was laughter and some tears in the home—along with fights and hugs, shared meals and burnt food. It had been the home of a family who had loved and supported each other. When he'd touched their blood, he'd felt their terror, heard their screams, but it wasn't until he'd touched the photo that he'd seen who had unleashed such ruthless brutality on the unsuspecting family.

The vampire had touched the photo himself, wiping his hand across the picture purposely when he was done killing them. The photo had been meant as a message for Quinn. The vampire had picked the Kemp family because they reminded him of Quinn's. He'd left the blood trail on the photo to remind her of the blood-splattered pictures in her own home. Quinn knew it was the same vampire who'd attacked her; what she didn't know was how badly the vamp wanted her.

Julian did though. He'd sensed the desire in the man's touch, the twisted amusement the vamp took in tormenting her. Julian had no idea who the vamp was yet, but he would, and soon.

Quinn stirred beside him once more. He ran his fingers over the bare skin of her shoulder until she settled again. The vamp hunting her was everything she hated and despised about their kind. Julian had been on the verge of becoming that kind of vampire again the other night. He'd nearly been the one to bring death to this town as he'd teetered on the edge of losing himself to his sinister urges.

Thoughts of Quinn and how badly he'd hurt her if he did such a thing had been the only things that had stopped him. She'd lost too much already in her short life; he couldn't be another of her disappointments and heartaches. He loved her too much for that.

He'd come so close to killing again that he'd stood at someone's back door, his hand on the knob as he'd fought to rein in his baser, more volatile urges. He'd stood there until the sun had sizzled across his back, burning through his clothes down to his skin. Forced away from the door by his burning flesh, no one would welcome a burning man into their home no matter how handsome or charming he was, he'd taken shelter in the pool house. Unable to trust himself around the people as they'd woken and started their day, he'd remained hidden until he could be sure they were gone for the day.

The entire time their coffee brewed and their bacon fried, he'd fought the urge to find a way to coax an invite into their home to gorge on them. Their laughter and inane conversation had grated on his nerves; his nails had dug into his palms so forcefully he'd dug crescent shaped grooves into them until blood dripped from his hands. It wasn't until he heard the slamming of their car doors that he'd dared to emerge from the pool house.

He would have stayed there all day to avoid the sun, but his need to get to Quinn had driven him through the scarce shadows he could find back to her apartment building. Then she'd soothed him, told him she loved him, and given herself to him. She'd completed and calmed him in ways he'd never known possible. What she'd done that day had worked more of a miracle with him than her ability to make his heart beat had. For the first time, he'd *known* he could forever keep the evil part of himself caged in order to be with her and make her happy.

She was his savior; she'd also be his greatest downfall if something ever happened to her.

He wished there was a way to get Devon here without bringing Cassie too, but Cassie would never agree to stay behind if she believed they were in enough danger to warrant calling Devon. Chris and Melissa were her best friends, Luther her Guardian, and he knew she loved him. She'd refuse to stay behind, and with her powers, she couldn't come anywhere near Quinn. Not while a large chunk of the vampire population was hunting her.

"You're very deep in thought." Quinn's fingers brushed over his face, heating his flesh and drawing his mouth instinctively toward hers.

"Thinking about how to catch a vamp."

"Easy," she replied and rose above him. "We use me as bait."

"No."

"Julian, he has no idea what I'm capable of. So far, he seems to be playing this game alone. I can draw him out, we can trap him, and then I can use his own life force to pummel him into pieces."

Despite his intense dislike of her plan, his curiosity pricked at her statement. "Can you do that?"

"I've never tried it before, but I don't see why not. I can give and take, or I can just take. Apparently, I can restart heartbeats too." She smiled at this and pressed her fingers against his chest. That little development still awed him. It had been five hundred and seventy-six years since he'd felt his heartbeat. The sensation had been one of the most amazing of his life, second only to knowing what it was like to possess her body and taste her blood. "I imagine I could also turn that life force against another and bash them with it."

"I'd imagine so too," he murmured.

He threaded his fingers through her hair, drawing her mouth to his. He took her lips with a firm possession. His tongue delving in and out of her hot recesses made him crave more. Wrapping his arm around her waist, he pulled her on top of him.

"Julian, the others," she protested against his mouth.

"Sleeping," he assured her as he reclaimed her mouth.

He'd make her forget all about her harebrained idea to be bait soon enough. Instead, he found himself being the one to forget as his hands skimmed over her flesh. A feeling of contentment and belonging stole through him when she easily slid her body together with his. When her fangs sank into his neck, his entire body arched up. Her ecstasy beat against him so vehemently he could barely separate her pleasure from his. Sinking his own fangs into her shoulder, he gorged on her sweet, powerful blood.

He opened up the pathways between them, allowing her to experience all of the sensations he experienced when he was inside of her, tasting her, allowing her to feel the love he felt for her. She melded against him as her mind opened up to flood his with her love.

His fingers entangled in her hair, he pulled her closer as he fed deeper on her. Her hands dug into his back, and her body moved more rapidly over his as she gave and took of his life in deep pulls. His heart exploded into life, pulsing his blood more vigorously into her.

She moaned against his throat, a delicious sound that nearly pushed him over the edge. Breaking his hold on her shoulder, his head fell back as his heart continued to beat out a riotous tempo within his chest.

He pulled her against him as he lost himself to the pleasure of her body.

~

"IF HE WOULD LISTEN to reason, he would see it's a good plan," Quinn said and actually stomped her foot on the ground.

Julian folded his arms over his chest as he watched her. It was rare that her composure slipped, but the whites of her eyes had turned red, and the red encircling the outer rim of her irises leapt and danced like actual flames.

"Wow!" Melissa breathed and Julian realized it was the first time they'd actually seen the enchantingly strange phenomena of her eyes. Having been born a half-vampire and a Hunter, Quinn had possessed a lot of power before she'd made the transformation into full vampire; it showed in the color of her eyes now.

"Astounding," Luther remarked.

Quinn frowned at Luther before focusing her attention on Julian once more. "It's the best way to accomplish anything," she insisted.

"Putting your life on the line is far from the best way to accomplish anything," he replied.

"It's a good plan, and you know it. If it was anyone else, you would allow it to happen."

"But it's not anyone else," he said. "It's you, and I've sensed how badly this man wants to get his hands on you. I've sensed his thoughts about you, and the depraved things he anticipates doing to you." She paled, but her chin remained thrust out in defiance at his words. "I won't allow it to happen. Do you really think he's going to fall for it, if you go prancing around all alone in the desert?"

"And what would you suggest I do, prance around my job and this apartment while he slaughters more families? I don't know how many families there are with three children in them in this town, but I can guarantee none of them are safe. And that's only if he decided to keep going after families with those numbers. He's made his point; I'd guarantee almost everyone is fair game now."

"She's right," Chris said.

Julian's eyes snapped toward him. "This doesn't concern you, Christopher."

"But it does," he said. "It concerns all of us. Believe me, I know how testy you vamps can be when your mates are threatened. I saw it firsthand with Cassie and Devon. I *really* don't want to see it with you. You're already a little scary at times, but your alternative is to let more people die. Possibly a *lot* more."

"You're making the mistake of thinking I put anyone's life ahead of hers," Julian growled.

Chris's eyes narrowed on him. Quinn stepped forward and waved her hands at him to break his stare with Chris. "Mates?" she inquired when he looked at her.

"I told you about them before, Dewdrop."

"Yes, I remember, but us?"

Julian shot Chris a fulminating look. Chris held his hands up innocently and shook his head. "I assumed you were with how close you two have been. I could be wrong. I don't think I am," he muttered in an aside to Melissa.

"Neither do I," she whispered back.

"Do *you* think we're mates?" Quinn asked Julian.

Julian tried to figure out the best way to answer this. In the end, he went with the truth. "We are."

Quinn's mouth dropped open; she closed it again as the red faded from her eyes. "Oh. I, uh... Oh."

"Just the response every man wants to hear when a woman is informed she'll share her life with him," he said, hoping to coax a smile from her and ease some of the strain from her face.

Finally, a small smile tugged at her mouth, but she still looked as if a freight train had sideswiped her. Walking over, she perched on the edge of the couch. "We can discuss it later," he assured her.

She turned to look at him with her eyebrows drawn together. Chris, Melissa, and Luther grouped closer together. Lou and Zach eyed the door like it was their only hope.

"I saw what that bond did to Seanix when Angie died," Quinn muttered. "And they never even completed it."

"Can you leave us?" Julian asked the others. "We'll meet you at the bar shortly."

"Sure," Lou said and flung the door open. He wouldn't have been more eager to escape from a ticking bomb.

"Good luck," Chris said and slapped him on the shoulder as Julian followed him to the door.

"Thanks," Julian muttered.

Luther stopped before him in the doorway, his gray eyes intent on him. "Hallway," Luther said. Julian glanced back at Quinn before stepping into the hall behind him. "Once you get this straightened out, you really should consider her plan. This vampire has to be stopped before he destroys more innocent lives. I know Quinn is your number one concern, but she will blame herself for every one of those lives, and you know it. She'll also blame you for keeping her from doing this."

Julian's hand curled around the doorknob as he fought the urge to tear it free. "Shit!"

"Shit is right. You can't order her about and expect it to end well. It won't. I don't think being a mate assures you a happily ever after with each other, but working together and listening to her will go a long way toward doing so."

Julian really resented that Luther was always so reasonable and one of the wisest people he knew. Every instinct he had screamed at him to make Quinn bend to his will. She was the most important thing to him. Outside of her and his friends, he really didn't have much concern for anyone else, but she did. She'd been through hell and still somehow had a big enough heart to love and care for others.

"I'll try," he said.

"That's more than I'd expected," Luther replied with a laugh.

Julian smiled at him before stepping back inside and closing the door. He turned to take in an ashen-faced Quinn. Walking over to the couch, he settled beside her and took hold of her hand. "Did you know?" she inquired in a hushed voice.

"I suspected a while ago. I *knew* the first time we were together."

Her eyes were the color of molten gold when she turned toward him. Her chocolate hair tumbled around her shoulders in waves, enhancing her pretty features. Reaching out, he rubbed the scar on her chin. Unlike the first time he'd tried to do this, she didn't pull away, nor did she become angry.

"Why didn't you tell me?" she asked.

"Because I didn't know what to say or how to go about telling you. I love you, Quinn. You love me. Surely, you suspected something more was happening between us when we both allowed the pathways to open between us during the blood exchange. I've never let such a thing happen before."

"My uncle is the only person I'd ever fed from before. At the time, he was dying, and all I felt was a mindless hunger for blood." Tears shimmered in her eyes at the memory, but she blinked them away.

Unable to resist trying to comfort her, he leaned toward her and pressed a kiss against her forehead. He brushed his fingers over her cheeks as he pulled away. "Forgive yourself, love. I'm sure he has."

"He would have, but…" Her voice trailed off.

"It's difficult, I know."

Her head tilted toward him. "Why did you never allow the pathways to open with another before?"

"Because you're the only one I've ever wanted to share the experience with. You made my heart beat again; I'm guessing that's another sign of our bond."

Just as he'd hoped, she grinned at him.

QUINN LEANED against his side as she contemplated his words. She supposed she should be mad he hadn't told her his suspicions earlier, but what would it have changed? She still would have had sex with him. She would *never* take that back. She still would have taken his blood; it had been irresistible to her and still was.

The only way to avoid this happening would have been to have never met him, but that idea only made her heart and mind recoil. She would never wish to go back to the lonely existence she'd been living before Julian and his friends had walked into her life. He'd brought her back to life, had shown her acceptance and love when she'd believed herself undeserving of either of those things.

"Mates," she pondered. "So one of us will die if something were to happen to the other?"

"Or go insane," he confirmed.

The possibility of losing him was enough to make her fangs tingle, but the idea of being bound to someone in such a way was... "Terrifying," she murmured. "I love you so much. I can't imagine losing you."

"You don't ever have to. The Stay Puft Marshmallow Man couldn't squish me."

She couldn't help it; a burst of laughter escaped her as he brushed her hair behind her ear. "And you are okay with this?" she asked. "To being bonded to me for eternity?"

"Dewdrop, I would gladly relive every wretched day of my existence, and believe me, there were plenty, if it meant I would have you in the end."

Her heart may not beat in her chest, but those words caused it to melt completely. She clasped his cheeks in her hands. He was magnificent, and he was *hers*.

"So would I," she whispered and pressed a kiss against his mouth. When heat and passion swirled up within her, she pulled away before she could become lost to him. "But that doesn't mean I'm going to cave on trying to lure out that murderous bastard somehow."

Julian groaned as he dragged her into his lap and rested his chin on her shoulder. "We'll figure something out," he said as he wove his fingers through hers. "Together."

CHAPTER ELEVEN

OVER THE NEXT FEW DAYS, they worked to come up with a plan that would lure out the vampire. Fortunately, no one else was killed in between, but everywhere she went, she felt as if eyes were burning into her back watching her every move. Only in her packed apartment did she feel as if she weren't being watched, which was funny considering her apartment was littered with people.

Luther slept on the couch. Melissa had a cot in the corner by the TV; if she swung her arm out at night, she'd most likely knock the TV over. Zach, Lou, and Chris were sprawled across her living room floor. Trying to get into the kitchen had become a maze of arms, legs, and heads. She had to be a gymnast to maneuver her way through without stepping on something important to someone.

As a child, she'd often played a game with Betsy and Barry called The Floor Is Lava. They would laugh as they jumped from one piece of furniture to the other in an attempt to avoid putting their feet on the "lava" floor.

The adult version was nowhere near as fun, she decided

when Chris rolled over and she barely avoided stomping on his privates. Sometime during the night, Zach had rolled up against her door, blocking it. Finally, leaping like a ballerina over Lou, she managed to get into her kitchen.

There she found Julian already sitting at the table, his long legs stretched out before him and his hands folded on his stomach. "It's like Tetris," he said.

"I was thinking The Floor Is Lava." She walked over to the fridge and pulled out a can of Mountain Dew. Popping the top, she swallowed it eagerly. Caffeine didn't have the same effect on her as it used to—much like alcohol, it would take a lot to have any real impact on her now—but it was still one of the first things she went for after waking in the afternoon. Perhaps it wasn't the best habit, but it wouldn't rot her teeth, so what did it really matter?

"I was considering buying a house to get some time alone with you again."

Quinn almost snorted soda out of her nose as she bit back a laugh. "Could you imagine?"

The hungry gleam in his eyes as they raked over her caused her knees to go weak. "Very much so."

The can crumpled in her hand. She was half-tempted to heave it into the sink and jump on him, but a loud snort from the other room kept her restrained. Rising to his feet, he moved with lethal grace across the room to stand in front of her.

The corners of his mouth quirked into a smile as he rested his hands on the counter beside her and leaned toward her. "I can wake them all and boot them out now if you'd like," he murmured against her lips.

She would like that very much, but she shook her head no instead. "Let them sleep, but as soon as they're up…"

"I'll personally shove them out the door."

Quinn laughed as she grabbed his shirt and rested her head against his chest. The heady, peppery scent of power and the spicy scent of the soap he used enveloped her. Comfort and love stole through her when he wrapped his arms around her and pulled her against his chest.

"Good afternoon." Quinn lifted her head as Melissa stretched her arms over her head in the doorway and released a loud yawn. Her short hair was tussled around her pretty face, a smile pulled at her full mouth as she dropped her arms to her sides. "Aren't you two the cutest?"

Quinn chuckled, but Julian scowled at Melissa. "I'm not *cute*."

"Aw, but you kind of are now," she teased. "You're like a little kitten."

Quinn couldn't hold back her laughter. The look on Julian's face would have made most people cower, but Melissa sauntered forward with a smile as she pulled a glass from the cabinet and removed a bottle of water from the fridge.

"You're lucky I like you," Julian muttered.

Melissa laughed as she uncapped the bottle. She turned toward Julian. "And you're lucky…"

Water shot out, spraying the wall and Julian when her hand compressed around the bottle. Julian jumped back; he opened his mouth to say something, but closed it when Melissa remained unmoving before them, her eyes glazed and her mouth slack.

"Melissa," Quinn whispered and stretched her hand toward the young woman.

Julian snagged hold of her arm and pulled it away. "Don't touch her. She's having a vision."

Quinn's hand fell loosely back to her side. Helplessness filled her as water continued to trickle down the wall and

Julian's face. She wanted so badly to grab hold of Melissa, to shake her, to wake her from whatever held her within its firm grasp.

The bottle tumbled from Melissa's hand. Her arm swung out, catching the glass on the counter. It flew across the room and shattered against the wall as she staggered back. Melissa crashed into the wall, gasps escaping her as tears spilled down her face.

"Melissa," Julian said softly as he carefully approached her. "It's okay, you're safe. Just breathe."

Quinn moved in front of Julian and knelt to rest her hand on Melissa's shoulder. "Easy," she soothed. Melissa took a few more lurching, steadying breaths as the tears dried and she regained her composure.

"Can you tell me what you saw?" Julian asked.

The color had faded from Melissa's face. Her lower lip trembled as her eyes cleared and she focused on Julian. "Death, so much death. We have to stop it."

"Where?" he asked.

Melissa's forehead fell into her hands. "The desert, a bonfire. I'm not sure when. Tonight maybe. It could be tomorrow. It could be…"

Beside Quinn, Julian's body jerked forward and a startled shout escaped him. Quinn stared at him in confusion as his hand shot around to his back. Melissa's gaze latched onto his chest. Still unable to understand why Julian's face was twisted in agony, and Melissa looked as if she were staring into the face of death, Quinn could only gaze in dismay at the blood spreading across the front of his shirt.

Blood!

She jumped up as Julian collapsed into her arms. She cried out in sorrow when his icy-blue eyes briefly met hers before rolling up in his head. "Julian!" she screamed.

Melissa leapt to her feet to take up a battle stance. Quinn couldn't begin to think about fighting as confusion and disbelief swirled through her. Her eyes latched onto the stake jutting out of his back. *What? How? I don't understand. It can't be real! It's another nightmare; it has to be! I can't lose him. Wake up, you idiot!*

Her shaking legs gave out beneath the weight of his body. Falling to her knees beneath him, she cradled him in her arms. *Not real, not real!*

Those words kept tumbling through her mind, but no matter how hard she tried to wake up, she remained sitting on her kitchen floor, trapped in the nightmare. His warm blood, pooling around her, caused her t-shirt and yoga pants to stick to her skin. Her hands frantically ran over his back in a useless attempt to staunch the flow of blood seeping out from the puncture. She knew a mortal wound when she saw it, and this was one.

"No!" she moaned.

Her heart shattered in her chest; jagged pieces of it sliced her open and shredded her soul. Tears poured from her eyes. She lifted her gaze to find Zach standing behind Julian with a glazed look in his eyes as he stared at the body in her arms. *The body,* she shuddered at the realization. *Zach* had made Julian nothing more than a body.

But how? *Why?* He was one of them, their friend. They'd been so focused on Melissa that they'd never heard him approach, and even if they had, they never would have thought anything of it.

Melissa's eyes narrowed on Zach with fury; she stepped toward him but froze when he remained unmoving. He didn't seem to realize what he'd just done. Bewilderment and desperation flitted over Melissa's face. Quinn's fangs began to tingle with the urge to drive them into Zach's throat and tear it out. She didn't care why he'd done this; she only needed him dead. If it wasn't for Julian's body in her lap, she would have leapt on him and tore him to pieces.

"What happened?" Chris demanded from the doorway of the kitchen. His gaze shot back and forth between all of them before comprehension dawned. The color drained from his face, his jaw clenched with fury as he grabbed hold of Zach's arm and jerked him back a step. Lifting his arm, he looked about to drive his fist into Zach's face and beat him to death but his eyebrows knit sharply together when Zach remained unmoving in his grasp.

"What the fuck?" Chris muttered as he released Zach's arm.

Quinn's power began to seep out of her to shake the walls and floor around them. She had no control over it, and she didn't care to try to regain any. There was nothing left to care about as her insides continued to shred apart.

Melissa staggered to the side, her hand falling on the table to steady herself. Luther and Lou pushed their way past Chris and into the kitchen. Lou took an abrupt step back and Luther's jaw fell open when they spotted her and Julian on the floor.

Turning, Luther grabbed Lou's shoulders and pushed him out the door. "Get somewhere safe, now!" he barked at the young man.

Quinn's hands shook as her hair whipped around her and sparks of energy shot from all over her body. The air crackled around her. Chris and Luther gestured frantically for Melissa to come to them. Melissa edged carefully around Quinn and ran toward the door. Chris grabbed hold of her arm and jerked her up against his side.

Julian's blood continued to soak her as his life slipped away. Not slipped, it was gone already. He'd told her once,

"I'm more difficult to kill than a cockroach on steroids and a thousand times faster. You won't lose me."

He was wrong; she had lost him. She'd lost everything. There was nothing left to her anymore except for the fiery burn of fury and the icy chill of a grief so intense she knew she couldn't survive it. Something within her fractured, and the waves of power coursing out of her knocked the others back. Luther pushed them toward the doorway, but Chris and Melissa resisted him as they shook their heads. They were speaking, but she had no idea what they were saying, nor did she care.

From somewhere in the not so broken recesses of her mind, she recalled words Luther had once uttered to her, *"I just witnessed the damage you can do, but you can also breathe life back into things. Humans, animals, plants, you can give them all life again."*

He hadn't said vampires, but then a vampire had already died and been granted an unnatural life. She'd require a vast supply of life, more than her own force to revive a vampire. Lifting her head, she tilted it back to stare at Zach. She didn't know why he had done this, and she didn't care. All that mattered was getting Julian back.

Her hand wrapped around the stake in Julian's back, and then she tore it free. Her belly twisted when it gave way with a sickening sucking sound. Rolling him over, a moan of misery escaped her when she saw his open, unseeing eyes. *So empty.* Not for long, not if she had anything to say about it.

Turning her wrist over, she bit deep into it before pressing it to his open mouth. Her blood flowed into him, but it wouldn't be enough to bring him back. Lurching forward, she grabbed hold of Zach's arm and yanked him toward her. His mouth parted, and his eyes widened briefly. Finally coming back to life, he squirmed in her grasp, but it was too late. The tentacles of her power had already slithered out, grasped hold of his arm, and dug into him.

Zach's eyes flew to hers. Suffering twisted his face as the pulse of his life flowed into her.

"Quinn!" Luther shouted.

She didn't look at him; she didn't tear her gaze away from Zach's. They'd trusted him, and he'd slaughtered the only man she'd ever love in cold blood. Right now, she didn't care what it made her, didn't care if it was wrong, she would do whatever she could to get Julian back. If she had to use his murderer to do so, she would.

Zach's skin became sallow as she funneled his life into her and out to Julian. Keeping her wrist pressed against Julian's mouth, she closed her eyes and tilted her head back as the influx of life within her made her feel as if she'd grabbed a live wire.

Her entire body sizzled with power. The air crackled as her hair whipped about her face and sparks of energy continued to light the air around her. She'd always tried not to drain a person or vampire completely. It had happened before, but the strength and vitality that came with draining someone was like a drug, so addicting and tempting. She could feel that drug trying to drag her under now, trying to twist and turn her into something malevolent and power-hungry.

Perhaps she already was those things.

She hadn't hesitated about using Zach to do this, even though there was a chance it might not work. Luther had said she could breathe life into things, but she never had before. No, she realized. She *had* breathed life into someone before. She'd made Julian's heart beat again. If she could do that without trying, then certainly she could do this when every ounce of her energy was fixated on him.

She kept focused on nourishing Julian, on filling him with the life she stole from the young Hunter. Around her, Julian's blood cooled against her skin and clothes. When she opened her eyes again, Zach's brown eyes had faded in color so they were nearly transparent. His cheeks were hollow, his skin the graying color of an old corpse. His eyes were still on hers, but there was little recognition within them as the last of his life slipped into her and on toward Julian.

Thrusting Zach's body away from her, she quaked as his not yet released life zipped around her body in search of an outlet. She poured all of that life, and more, into repairing Julian's lethal wound. She kept her eyes on the wall, unable to look at either of the bodies before her. Unable to acknowledge she may have become a monster worse than any she'd faced over the years.

Then, beneath her hand, she felt the beautiful beat of a heart stilled years ago. A cry escaped her, and her eyes flew to Julian as his hand wrapped around her wrist. His dazed, beautiful, blue eyes blinked up at her. His heart beat five more times beneath her palm before going still again.

"What did you do, Dewdrop?"

Quinn's eyes rolled up in her head. She passed out before she could answer his question.

CHAPTER TWELVE

JULIAN PACED the room from one side to the other. He felt like a caged animal. His hunger beat incessantly against him, but there was no way he would leave Quinn after the events of this day. He was starving, Zach was nothing but shrunken remains, and Quinn had yet to reawaken. He, on the other hand, felt more alive and powerful than anyone who had just died should.

When he'd died and became a vampire, he'd been out of his mind with thirst and weak with hunger. Now he felt as if he could tear this entire town apart with his bare hands, as if he could take on a thousand vamps at once, but then he'd been flooded with an influx of life to stave off this death.

Dead, he'd been dead again. However, this time he'd died with the belief he wouldn't be coming back. He ran his hand through his hair, tugging at the ends of it as he recalled the feeling of his life slipping away from him. None of the dread that came with the knowledge had been for himself. It had all been for Quinn. He knew his death would tear her apart. He worried about what would become of her after he was gone. What she would do to herself and the others in her grief and rage.

The others all sat silently by. Luther leaned back in the chair he'd brought in from the kitchen; his eyes were focused on Quinn, his arms folded over his chest. Chris and Melissa sat beside each other on the floor; he had her hand wrapped in his as they watched Quinn's unmoving form on the couch. Lou looked tempted to bolt as his eyes kept darting toward the door, but he remained seated beside Quinn's bedroom door.

"If you're scared, then leave!" Julian snapped at him.

Lou jumped. "I don't want to leave."

"Then why do you keep staring at the door?"

Lou glanced nervously at the others before looking at him again. "Because, if he got to Zach and took control of his mind, what if he got to someone else in this room too? What if he's on his way here now, thinking you're dead, that he has an ally in here, and that Quinn will be easy game?"

Julian had already considered the exact same thing, but he couldn't do anything about it, not right now. If that vamp was on his way here, he'd be in for a rude awakening, but Julian had a feeling he would wait to see if Zach's mission had been successful before making his move.

There was no way to know who that vamp may have gotten control of in this room, and the only way to break any kind of control the vampire may have over them was to make sure the vamp was dead, which was something he was going to do as soon as he got a chance.

He would take his sweet-ass time in meting out that death too. He'd savor every second of torture he was going to unleash on the asshole who had almost succeeded in ending his life. Julian cursed himself. He'd let his guard slip.

He'd mistakenly believed they were safe here, amongst friends.

He didn't know when their enemy had gotten to Zach. Ever since his presence in town became known, they'd been in groups of two or three to ensure no one was left vulnerable to his mind control. Which meant there were two possible situations playing out now. There could be someone else in this room under his spell, maybe *two* somebodies, or the vamp had been stalking Quinn before he'd stepped into the bar. It was possible that he'd gotten to Zach long before that night at Clint's.

He didn't like thinking about any of those scenarios, but he also didn't want to consider his most trusted friends possible threats either.

"Anybody who thinks she's easy game is going to get the rudest awakening of their life," Chris muttered.

"That they will," Lou agreed.

Melissa shuddered as she focused on the blood on his shirt. "I've seen Cassie turn into a ball of fire, but that… Well, that was impressive and terrifying."

Julian recalled opening his eyes to find Quinn kneeling over him, her hair whipping around her as sparks of life shot from her fingertips and around her body. Her eyes had been their fiery red combination that never failed to amaze him with their unique beauty. They'd also been unseeing, as she'd stared at the wall. She'd been awesome and frightening, breathtaking in her wildness, and enticing in her power and ruthlessness.

She'd never killed for pleasure or spite, but she'd *never* hesitate to strike someone down in order to save the lives of the ones she loved.

And this time, it had been *his* life.

He didn't know how she would feel about what she'd

done when she woke, but he would deal with it then. Now, he just wanted her to wake so he could feel her arms wrap around him again and pull him close.

Shock was nowhere near big enough a word to describe what had gone through him when he'd felt that stake pierce his heart. His disbelief had swiftly been replaced with grief over the loss of her, the loss of all the things he desired for them, for the eternity he'd dreamed of with her. He'd grieved over leaving her behind to deal with his loss, for effectively ending her life too.

That had been the worst, most hideous realization of his life. Far worse than when he'd realized he'd lost Devon as his friend and kill mate, far worse than when he'd realized Cassie could never be his. Both of those life-changing events had been nothing compared to what would become of her in the wake of his death. He'd let her down. He'd left her behind to deal with something *no* vampire should ever have to face, especially not his Quinn.

He rushed back to her side when she stirred on the couch, but she settled down again. She looked so fragile and small, so drained. Looking at her, he realized she'd used some of her own life to bring him back too. Spinning on his heel, he ran a hand through his hair as he paced over to the kitchen doorway. Zach's wasted body remained sprawled on the floor there.

He spun when he heard the sound of footsteps behind him. He'd heard Zach approach earlier too, but hadn't paid him any attention, as he'd been more concerned with Melissa at the time and mistakenly believed they were safe. It could have been Quinn, instead of him, who'd died, and he wouldn't have been able to bring her back.

"You know you can trust us, under ordinary circum-stances," Luther said to him when Julian eyed him.

"I do, but these circumstances aren't normal."

"No, they're not." Luther's gaze lingered on the crumpled, shrunken form of the Hunter.

Julian still couldn't believe she'd done this for him. He could only hope it didn't change her too much, that she didn't hate herself for it. When she woke, her anger and sorrow over his death would be gone, and she would realize why Zach had staked him. Julian could try to keep it hidden from her, but it would put her in danger if he did, and she would never forgive him if she ever discovered the truth.

"We should probably get him out of here," Luther suggested. "Before she wakes up."

"I'd like to," Julian said. "But I think it's better if *none* of us separate right now."

Luther lifted his glasses and rubbed at the bridge of his nose before settling them into place again. "Then let's at least cover his body. She shouldn't see this when she wakes."

"No, she shouldn't," Julian agreed. "There's some extra sheets and maybe some blankets in her closet."

"I'll get them," Lou offered and rose to his feet.

Lou glanced at Quinn before shuffling into her bedroom. He emerged a minute later with a gray sheet and a tattered blue blanket. Julian took the sheet from him and walked over to drape it over Zach's form.

Zach looked as if he'd been decaying for a hundred years, not merely dead for an hour. *At least he doesn't stink yet*, he thought to himself. Then again, he probably wouldn't stink too badly as there was very little left to Zach's once strong body. Julian settled the sheet into place and turned back to Quinn.

"Are you sure he was under mind control?" Julian

inquired. "I wasn't exactly his favorite vampire in the world."

"No, you weren't," Luther agreed, "but I'm sure. He never tried to move away from her. He stood there, staring at her as she unraveled. No one would have willingly stayed so close, never mind that he barely registered what was going on until she started to drain him."

"His eyes were completely blank," Melissa added. "There was absolutely nothing within them. He had no idea what he'd done."

Julian actually felt a tug of remorse over the young man's death. Zach had stabbed him through the back, but it was what his mind had been manipulated into doing. "Do you think he was told he had to kill you today?" Lou asked.

"We'll never know." Julian walked back toward the doorway to look out at them. "I know a fair amount about the ability from watching Devon wield it over the years, but only the vampire or Hunter who is controlling the mind ever knows the full extent of that control or the commands they issue to the one under their control. Zach could have been told to do it today, or the command could have been to kill me the first chance he got. My guard was down earlier, and he seized the moment."

Melissa bit her bottom lip as she glanced away from him. "I didn't mean to distract you…" Her voice trailed off, but what could she say? She had no control over when her visions hit her, and she certainly hadn't been responsible for what had happened.

"It's not your fault," Chris said.

"It's not," Julian assured her. It was one *ugly* vampire's fault, and Julian was going to make him uglier by the time he was done with him.

Melissa thrust her shoulders back when she met his gaze

again. "Wouldn't we have seen a difference in Zach? I mean, something, *any*thing."

"No," Julian replied. "He would have acted completely normal until he'd fulfilled his duty. Even then, I've seen Devon command people and vamps to do something and continue about their lives as if nothing happened afterward. They never remembered they'd killed their wife, mother, brother, sister, or someone else."

Melissa shivered and Chris squeezed her hand. "Why wouldn't he tell Zach to do the same thing after?" Lou asked.

Julian stared at the body and his blood staining the floor before pacing away. "I believe this vamp has been watching Quinn for a while." The minute the words were out of his mouth, he realized how much he believed them. "He probably doesn't know how deep the bond is between the two of us. Few vamps who murder and kill actually believe in mates, and some have never even heard of such a thing. However, he knows there is something between the two of us, and I think he wanted Quinn to be the one to kill Zach after he'd fulfilled his command."

"Why?"

The croaked question caused him to spin around. Quinn sat up on the couch, her hair a tangled mess around her shoulders, her eyes bloodshot and swollen. The paleness and translucence of her skin would have made a ghost look solid. He could see all of the thin blue veins running through her cheeks and around her eyes and forehead. Her sunken cheeks had caused her cheekbones to stand out starkly under her skin, but she was still enchantingly beautiful to him.

He moved so fast, he was around the couch and at her side in less than a second. Falling before her, he clasped hold of her hands. Looking at her, he realized that funneling Zach's and her life into him had caused her to lose a good fifteen pounds. Already slender with an athletic build, the weight loss had affected her greatly. He could feel the delicate bones of the backs of her hands in his grasp.

Earlier, before placing her on the couch to sleep off the aftereffects, he'd taken her into the bathroom, scrubbed his blood from her skin, and changed her into a t-shirt and shorts. She hadn't been this thin then, he would have noticed. The impact of forcing her life into him had taken its time showing up on her.

The sleeve of her baggy tee slid off her shoulder to reveal the sharp edges of her collarbone. His fingers trembled as he stroked gently over the bone and the blue veins running beneath her skin. "Look at what you did to yourself."

A single tear rolled down her cheek and fell on his hand, drawing his attention to her face once more. "You mean what I did to Zach."

"No, I mean what you did to *you*. Zach doesn't matter."

"Of course he does," she whispered.

"Not anymore." He glanced at the others, wishing he could tell them to leave, but with night upon them, he didn't dare send them out alone.

"Because of me." Another tear slid free, she grasped his hands more firmly as her eyes closed. He didn't know how to make it better, didn't know how to ease this for her. Leaning closer to him, her eyes fluttered open to reveal their honey color. "I'd do it again, for you."

His hand wrapped around the back of her head as he pulled her down for a tender kiss. He didn't want to harm her by hauling her against him and kissing her senseless like he longed to do; she was too frail for that right now. He forced himself to pull away from her and sit back.

"You'll never have to worry about something happening to me again," he promised.

"You'd said that before this too."

"I got overconfident. I won't again," he vowed. "Now, we have to get you some nourishment."

Her hands were surprisingly strong when they took hold of his. "It can wait. Why do you think that monster wanted me to kill Zach?"

Julian ran his thumbs over her lip before taking hold of her hands and resting them in her lap. "To push you over the edge. To have you go after him so he could catch you."

The words caused his fangs to lengthen; he tried to keep it hidden from her, but her gaze fell to his lips. She'd had enough happen today without having to deal with the wrath mounting steadily within him. That vampire wanted her, and not only for the prophecy, which he had to know about now, if he hadn't before. If he'd had the chance to get to Zach and bend him to his will, he would have taken some time to question Zach about Quinn and the others too. The sick prick planned to keep Quinn as his own.

It would never happen.

"And you believe he got to Zach before he ever walked into the bar," she murmured.

His brow furrowed as he studied her. "How long were you awake?"

"Not really awake. Trying to wake. I was caught in a strange in-between I couldn't quite escape from. I could hear you all speaking, but couldn't respond to you." Her eyes were haunted when she lifted her head to him. "It was horrible, but I deserved to know the fear and uncertainty of possibly being trapped like that forever after what I did."

"Oh, love," he murmured before pulling her into his arms and off the couch. "You deserved no such thing."

He rocked her as he pressed her close and kissed her forehead. Her slender arms slid around his neck, and her mouth rested against his throat. He felt the press of her fangs before she turned her head away. She tried to hide it, but her hunger beat against him. It didn't matter how hungry he was, or that they had things to discuss, her needs came first.

Rising, he didn't glance at the others as he carried her into her bedroom. "Don't leave," he commanded before kicking the door shut with his heel. Carrying her over to the bed, he placed her on the edge of it before settling beside her. "You have to feed from me."

"Julian..."

"Quinn, not only did you force Zach's life into me, but also some of your own. You need blood and life, and I am the most powerful being here." Red bled into the whites of her eyes before she closed them. "Don't punish yourself for what happened today. You were pushed into it."

"I chose your life over Zach's."

"I would have done the same. I would choose your life over my *own*. When Zach killed me, he also signed your death certificate. Recall what you were feeling before you grabbed hold of Zach. That feeling *never* would have gone away. You would have had to be destroyed if you didn't walk into the sun yourself. You very likely would have gone after the others too in your insanity. You killed *one* today. You could have killed countless others before you were stopped. One life is small in comparison."

"One life is never small in comparison to anything else. Sacrifices may be made for the greater good in some cases, but a life is *never* small. I know all of those things you said are true," she whispered. "I realize what I could have done. I felt the need to destroy and kill shaking my entire being, and I wouldn't have been satisfied with just Zach if you hadn't returned to me." Her gaze slid away as she nervously licked her lips before focusing on him again. "I regret what I did to Zach, but I would do it again. What does that say about me?"

"That you're a survivor, and all survivors do what is necessary to live. Now, drink from me and take from me the life force you need to grow stronger."

"The others, they didn't sound like they hated me..."

"They don't."

"But they're afraid of me, what I was, what I *became*."

"I saw you, in the end; it was a sight to behold for sure. They are afraid of what is to come, of what this vampire is willing to do, and of you." There was no reason to deny it. She'd scared them today, and she knew it. "But they know you wouldn't injure them under normal circumstances."

"If it had been one of them who staked you, I would have done the same thing."

"I know and so do they, but I can guarantee none of them would want to live under his control. Just as you wouldn't."

"No, kill me yourself if that ever happens."

Wrapping his hand around her neck, he pulled her closer to him as he lifted her up and settled her on his lap. "We'll kill him in order to ensure it doesn't ever happen, and to break whatever control he may have over someone else. Now, stop talking and drink," he commanded brusquely.

She fought him for a second more before easing in his grasp. Her lips pressed against his neck, heating his flesh. His hand clasped her thigh as he willed her to take the nourishment she required. Finally, after what felt like endless seconds, her lips pulled back and he felt the press of her fangs against his throat.

A groan escaped him when her teeth pierced his skin and she drank from him in greedy pulls. Her joy over being able to touch and hold him again filled him. He felt her terror and anguish over losing him, felt the shattering of her soul that had preceded the moment she'd lost control and grabbed hold of Zach.

All of her feelings washed over him as her tears wet the collar of his shirt. He held her closer against his chest while he felt the subtle pull of her power taking back from him some of the life force she'd given.

"I understand and I love you," he murmured. "Nothing will turn me away from you."

CHAPTER THIRTEEN

Quinn lifted her head from his shoulder and stared around her bedroom before looking at him.

"Did you see anything?" she inquired. "You know, when you died? Was there a light or anything?"

He frowned as he pondered her question. "No, I saw nothing. There was only blackness, like the last time I died."

"I only saw blackness too before the change into vampire started to take hold," she murmured.

He brushed back a lock of her hair, drawing her attention back to him. "Why do you ask?"

"I may be immortal, but death isn't out of the question. I'd like to know there is something after."

"I think we all would. I wasn't dead for long, either time, so perhaps there is something after and I haven't found it yet."

"Maybe," she agreed.

"If it does find me, I have a feeling there will be a lot of fire involved."

"You don't know that. You're doing a lot of good now."

"I have *centuries* behind me of being about as far from good as one can get."

She rested her hand against his cheek. She'd almost lost him. The sorrow of that reminder was like a stake to her heart. "Then we'll have to make sure you get a *millennia* of being who you are now," she told him.

He smiled as he pressed a kiss against her forehead. "I like the way you think."

"Besides, I may be joining you in the fire."

"No, never you."

She hadn't been so sure before today, and she was less sure now, but she wasn't going to argue with him. "We should rejoin the others." His hands tightened on her, the corded muscles of his neck and arms stood out. "Julian—"

"Yes," he agreed.

He didn't release her, but kept her pressed against him as he rose to his feet. Ever so slowly, he allowed her to slide down the front of his body. A delicious shiver went through her at the friction the motion caused. She bit her bottom lip as she tried to suppress the arousal the movement awoke in her. She knew she'd failed when his mouth quirked in that cocky half grin of his.

"I have to wash my face first." She pulled away from him and walked into the bathroom.

Flicking on the light, she blinked at the vision of the woman staring back at her within the mirror. Her cheeks were sunken, the blue veins in her flesh clearly visible. The shadows under her eyes made them shine nearly as bright as the sun. Her fingers pressed against her cheeks, and she gawked at her bony hands. She'd never considered herself beautiful, but now she looked like a walking corpse.

She shuddered at the reminder of a corpse. There was one in her kitchen right now after all, and *she* had put it there. *And I'd do it again to save Julian.* She didn't bother to deny it, and Zach hadn't been innocent.

But wasn't he? He'd had no control over what he'd done. If he was still alive, Julian would be dead, you'd be a monster, and Zach would be useless to us. Untrustworthy and corrupted. He would have had to be locked away or destroyed anyway, and so would you, eventually.

No matter what, if Julian had died, she knew she would have been able to keep herself together until she'd managed to destroy the monster stalking her town, turning who knew how many countless others against them. She would have taken her revenge on him before destroying herself.

Now, there could be other friends turned enemies out there, waiting for their chance to attack. And there was no way to know who they were, until they made their move. Julian was the only one she could trust completely. If he'd been under the control of the vampire who wanted her, she would no longer be standing here. She was strong, but she'd never be able to fight Julian off if he was ever compelled to hand her over to their enemy.

"You look better." She glanced at Julian as he appeared in the doorway of the bathroom.

"I looked worse than this?" she croaked with a wave of her hand at the mirror. "I look like the corpse bride."

He smiled as he came forward to stand behind her. Their eyes met in the mirror. Resting his hands on her waist, he leaned over her until his chin rested on her shoulder and his lips were against her ear. "But you're my corpse bride," he whispered, "and I still think you're stunning."

"If you weren't a vampire, I'd swear you needed glasses."

Her hands trembled when she turned on the water. Dipping her hands into it, she bent to splash it over her face. What she wouldn't give for the longest, hottest bath of her life, but with a corpse in her kitchen, there were more pressing issues than her achy, bony body.

Julian handed her a face towel, and she quickly dried herself. Her eyes met his in the mirror again before she turned to face him. "Some more blood will help," he said and brushed her hair over her shoulder. "We'll get you some now."

"I think there are more important things to deal with first. And what about Melissa's vision? It's Tuesday, I don't think there are any bonfires tonight, but what if the fire in her vision isn't the same bonfire we went to before? It's not like people don't have fires in their backyards all the time around here."

Julian tugged the towel from her hands and draped it on the sink. "We'll deal with that later."

"I couldn't stand it if more innocent people die because of this d-bag," she muttered.

"I know, but you're not exactly up for a fight right now."

She tilted her chin and thrust back her shoulders. "I can still drain him dry if necessary."

"That's my girl." He kissed her so tenderly, her heart melted before he pulled away from her. "Come on."

He slid his hand into hers and led her from the bathroom. She followed him into her crowded living room, though it was less crowded now than it had been before, she realized guiltily.

"I'm sorry about what happened." She couldn't bring herself to apologize for saving Julian's life by taking Zach's, but she *was* sorry it happened, and she needed them to know that. Julian's hand squeezed hers as he surveyed the people gathered within. "I wish you all hadn't seen it." That was very true; she could only imagine how appalling and frightening it had been for them to witness what had unfolded here earlier.

Melissa released Chris's hand and rose from the couch. Quinn braced herself for whatever the young woman had to say. They may not have dated seriously, but there had been something between Melissa and Zach at one time. She'd come to consider Melissa a friend and believed Melissa saw her the same way, or at least she *had* before Quinn had killed Zach. Now, she deserved Melissa's condemnation and resentment, and she would take them both without complaint.

"We understand why you did it," Melissa said.

Quinn opened her mouth to sputter some kind of response, but she had none. Chris rose to his feet and walked around the milk crate coffee table toward her. Quinn took a step away from him, but he rested his hand against her arm.

"You shouldn't touch me," she protested as her power hungrily slid toward him.

She was drained and her ability was seeking out a source to replace the life it had lost. Clamping down on it, she kept it from latching onto Chris. She could keep herself from hurting him, but she didn't believe she deserved their sympathy and understanding right now. She'd killed a man; she'd killed a *Hunter.* One of their own, one of her own too.

She tried to move further away from Chris, but Julian's hand on hers would only allow her to go so far. Attempting to tug her hand free of Julian, she gave up when he refused to release her. She didn't have it in her right now to give him the zap he deserved for keeping her restrained.

Chris kept his hand wrapped around her arm. She'd lost

so much weight that his fingers met on the underside of her arm. Her shoulders heaved with the helplessness filling her. "It wasn't Zach's fault, and it wasn't yours either," Chris said. "He did what he'd been compelled to do. You reacted on instinct and your need to keep your mate alive. We trust you."

"Why? You shouldn't."

"Because you are also one of us, a Hunter."

"I was also part vampire before I became a full vamp."

"In truth, all Hunters are also part vamp. You were just a little bit more than the rest of us. If you were truly a danger to us, you would be taking some of my life from me right now. Judging by the look of you, no offense, you could *definitely* use it, but you're not taking anything from me."

Quinn released a small snort of laughter. "No offense taken; I have a mirror." He smiled at her, squeezed her arm again, and released her. "Why are you so understanding?" she blurted when he turned to walk back toward the couch.

"Because I can feel evil. I can sense when something is wrong in someone and they're a threat, unless they're under the influence of mind control, apparently. You're none of those things. Not unless someone's life is on the line. Every single one of us can become someone you don't want to mess with when our loved ones are threatened."

"What if it had been Melissa or Luther, instead of Zach I had done this to?"

Chris winced, bowing his head and hunching his shoulders forward. Finally, he lifted his head to meet her gaze again. "But it wasn't, and for that I am eternally grateful. What does it say about me that I would have traded Zach's life for Julian's, or anyone else's in this room?"

Quinn didn't know how to answer him. There was no

answer to it. Judging by the expressions on the faces surrounding her, they all felt the same way. But then, she believed they'd trade her life for the others too. They liked her, but they had all been together for years, especially Chris, Melissa, and Luther. She had no doubt they would do anything to protect each other's lives.

And she understood that.

Finally, tugging her hand free from Julian's, she wrapped it around his arm and stepped closer to him. "The bonfire you saw in your vision, was it the same one we went to before?" she asked Melissa.

Melissa tilted her head to the side as she mulled it over. "With everything else that's happened, I'd almost forgotten about the vision," she said with a small snort. "You know, I'm not sure. It was in the desert, but everything around here is. The flames weren't overly large, so it could have been starting or ending."

"If there's going to be a big bonfire, it won't be until Friday, but anyone could have a fire in their yard over the coming nights," Quinn replied.

"There were at least ten bodies there," Melissa said. Chris rested his hand on her shoulder when she began to pull anxiously at the sleeves of her shirt. Her fingers stilled.

"The best place to start will be the big bonfire," Julian said. "And we'll stay alert for any other fires in the area. We have to destroy this vamp as soon as possible. Until he's dead, anyone could be an enemy."

Quinn's gaze slid over the others. She didn't like to believe any one of them could be a danger, but there was no denying they could.

"We have to get the body out of here," Chris said.

"We'll do that now," Julian said. "I'm going to need all of you in the hallways and outside to keep an eye out. I can get him out of here and into the desert before anyone sees me, but I can't take the chance of walking into a human."

"Dusty probably wouldn't flash you another peace sign after he saw you with a dead body," Quinn said.

"That might be worth it," he replied before turning to the others again. "You're all to stay near this building until I get back from disposing of his body."

"No," Quinn said. "We're going with you, and he's going to be buried. Maybe no one else will ever know he's there, but we will, and he deserves more than being dumped out for the animals to find him."

Julian opened his mouth to argue with her, but Melissa spoke before he could. "She's right. We will give him a proper burial."

He glanced at Quinn before looking over at Melissa. "Fine," he relented. "We'll need shovels."

"The hardware store is probably closed by now," Quinn said.

"He's not staying in here until tomorrow," Lou said.

"No, he's not," Quinn hastily replied. Turning to Julian, she smiled at him. "But you can get them."

"You expect me to break into the hardware store?" he asked.

"Aren't you the one who's always telling me to embrace my vampire nature and that we never have to want for anything?"

"This is not what I meant."

"Of course it is. We need, and we don't have to."

He scowled at her, but didn't protest as he turned away. "You're coming with me," he said to Chris who nodded his head in agreement.

~

"Freaking women have us breaking into a hardware store in the middle of night to steal shovels for the man who stabbed me in the back," Julian muttered as he slunk through the shadows of the store toward the shovels hanging on the back wall.

Chris's eyes darted around constantly; he jumped at every shadow he saw. "Still can't believe that happened. Shock is the understatement of the century for that whole traumatic event," Chris said.

"You didn't get the stake through the heart, that was trauma," Julian retorted.

"No, but you didn't have to witness one of your best friends dying, again. I'd hoped to never see that again after Cassie."

Julian glanced back at him. Chris was crouched low as he walked, looking like every ridiculous burglar in a bad comedy movie. *Best friend?* They'd grown closer over the past couple of years, but he'd always believed a part of Chris would never forgive him for what he'd done to them when they'd first met. Chris had never acted that way, but Julian certainly wouldn't have been so understanding if the roles had been reversed. Apparently, Chris had a bigger capability for forgiveness than he ever would, but then, he already knew that.

Watching him, Julian had to admit he didn't know what he'd do without the kid. Chris could be a pain in his ass, but he also kept him in line and called him on his crap. Chris stopped walking when he realized Julian had halted before him. His sapphire eyes glinted in the dim light as he searched for a threat.

"What is it?" he demanded.

"Nothing," Julian said with a shake of his head and turned away from him.

"By the way," Chris continued, "I'm getting really sick and tired of seeing my friends die, so could we stop that now?"

Julian snorted with laughter. "It wasn't in my plans for the day; I can assure you of that."

"I think you're getting soft in your old age."

Julian shot him a ferocious scowl. "I was, but it most certainly won't happen again. Quinn depends on me now, and I messed up, big time."

"*No* one saw that coming, ever. This vamp after her, he's a conniving prick."

"He's going to die the most agonizing of deaths, if I have anything to say about it."

Chris jumped when a car went by on the street and the spill of its headlights briefly illuminated the store. "I can't go to jail."

"You're not going to jail," Julian replied impatiently. Arriving at the back wall, he tugged down two shovels and handed one to Chris before making his way toward the front of the store. He pulled some money out of his pocket as he walked.

"What are you doing?" Chris hissed.

He may have let Chris behind him, but Julian kept his senses and his ears acutely attuned to every sound and move he made. Under normal conditions, he'd never hesitate to trust Chris with his life. These weren't normal conditions. He'd have him by the throat, on the ground, and hog-tied with the nearest piece of rope if Chris made one wrong step toward him.

"Quinn told me to leave money behind for the tools. She said the couple who own this place work hard to keep their store going," he answered.

Chris released a snort of laughter. "She has you wrapped around her little finger."

"She does." He wasn't at all ashamed to admit it either.

"But then, I think she's pretty far gone for you too." Chris stopped at the counter beside Julian. He reached out to flip through the brochures and coupons stacked near the register before snatching his hand back. "No jail," he scolded himself.

"I think she is too," Julian replied. Tossing a couple of twenties on the counter, he lifted his head to stare around the shadowed interior of the store. He couldn't shake the feeling he was being watched.

"It's a good thing too. If she wasn't, you'd be ash in the morning."

Julian shot him a look over his shoulder, but Chris assumed a completely innocent expression that set his teeth on edge. Had he really just been thinking that he didn't know what he'd do without him?

Turning away from Chris, he scanned the store again. Chris released a loud grunt of displeasure when Julian moved toward the plate glass windows making up the front of the building.

His eyes scanned the horizon, but he saw nothing moving amongst the shadows. Turning, he focused on Quinn's apartment. He spotted her sitting in her garden window with her back to the street. He believed it highly unlikely the vamp had managed to get to Luther, Melissa, and Lou too, but relief still filled him at the sight of her sitting where he'd asked her to. If he'd thought she was up for it, he would have brought her with him, but until she got some more nourishment, he didn't want her to exert herself.

"Look, human bars may not hold you, but I don't look good in orange, and I am *way* too good looking to go unnoticed in prison," Chris said from beside him. "Can we please get out of here?"

"Yeah," Julian murmured as he turned away from the window. "Let's go."

Chris eagerly led the way back through the aisles crowded with an assortment of hardware supplies.

CHAPTER FOURTEEN

JULIAN TOSSED the last shovelful of sand onto the grave and patted it down with the back of the shovel. Quinn's head bowed as she silently said a few words of prayer, even though it was something she'd rarely done before. Right then, she really hoped Zach had somewhere to go beyond this plane, and he had a chance to experience something other than the brief and brutal life he'd lived here.

Beside her, Julian's nostrils flared as he relentlessly searched the night. Quinn lifted her head to look at the shifting sand of the dunes around them. She was convinced something menacing lurked behind every cactus or rock outcropping on the horizon, maybe multiple somethings, but nothing came at them.

"We have to feed and get back," Julian said.

Melissa lifted her head from where she was drawing a small cross into the sand at the head of the grave. "We'll leave you."

"No," Julian replied. "I'll find something and bring it

back. Splitting up while we're in the middle of nowhere is *not* a good idea."

He handed his shovel to Chris before rushing into the night so fast Quinn only saw a blur in the sand he kicked up in his wake. The protest she'd been about to issue died on her lips. "I don't know why he thinks it's okay for him to take off on his own then," she muttered.

"Because he's stubborn," Chris replied and shoved the heads of the shovels into the ground.

"Too stubborn," Quinn agreed.

The moon had barely shifted in the sky before Julian reappeared with a coyote in his grasp. The animal squirmed against him, but Julian didn't release it. Quinn followed Julian over to a set of rocks and knelt to feed. The rush of warm blood filling her made her groan in ecstasy. His blood and life force earlier had helped to replenish her a lot, but she hadn't realized how hungry she was until her fangs sank into the animal's throat.

"Are you still hungry?" Julian inquired when she released the coyote to stagger away into the night.

She wiped the blood away from her lips. "Yes, but…"

She never got a chance to finish before he turned away and vanished once more. Red stained his lips from having fed too when he brought her back two coyotes the next time. "Still hungry?" his eyes ran anxiously over her after she'd fed from them.

"I'm full," she said. "And you really need to stop disappearing. I already lost you once today."

His jaw jutted out, but his shoulders sagged. Taking hold of her hand, he helped her rise from behind the rocks. The others were all sitting at the front of the rocks, their knees drawn up to their chests as they hugged themselves against the increasing chill of the night.

"You look a lot better," Melissa said to her.

"I feel a lot better," Quinn replied. "I still wouldn't mind standing in the shower for hours and sleeping until next week though."

"We can arrange that," Julian said as he took hold of her hand and led her across the sand.

"I have to work tomorrow night," she reminded him.

"I'm sure Clint will understand."

"No. I'm not going to let that bastard continue to interfere with my life. He's done far too much damage already."

She could feel Julian's displeasure, but he didn't comment as they covered the two miles back to town. Entering her building, she walked tiredly up the stairs and unlocked her door. She hurried into her bedroom and grabbed a fresh set of towels before heading into the bathroom.

Turning the shower on as hot as she could stand it, she sighed with pleasure when she stepped beneath the stinging water. She was in the process of scrubbing her hair when the bathroom door opened. Grabbing the curtain, she peeked around the edge. She blinked against the shampoo sliding toward her eyes when she spotted Julian tugging his clothes off.

"What are you doing?" she whispered.

He glanced at her before pulling his shirt off and tossing it on the floor. "Joining you." Her eyes hungrily drank in his chiseled physique as mist from the water swirled around him, dampening his pale skin. When he was naked, he tugged the curtain away from her clenched hand. He'd already seen all there was of her, but this was so strangely intimate and new to her. She tried not to gawk at him when he climbed in and pulled the curtain closed. "Now, let's get that stuff out of your hair before it blinds you."

With gentle hands, he maneuvered her beneath the spray of water and tilted her head back. She closed her eyes as his fingers ran through her hair, massaging her scalp as he washed the shampoo from her. His hands slid over her, rubbing and kneading her aching muscles as he progressed lower over her body. Her legs quivered as his touch eased the discomfort in muscles denied life. She hadn't realized how badly they'd been cramped until he worked his magic over them.

She could feel his growing arousal against her, but there was nothing sexual in his touch, as he remained focused upon easing her soreness. Kneeling before her, his hands worked over her calves. A moan escaped her when the knotted muscles in the backs of her legs gave way.

Rising back over her, his hands slid through her hair as he brushed it over her shoulders. "Feel better?"

"Much." She rested her hands and head against his chest. Love swelled within her as she relished the feel of the hot water sliding over them both. His muscles tightened when she licked away a bead of water trickling down his pale flesh. His hands settled into the hollow of her back as he pressed her against him. "I'd like to go to bed now."

"I can oblige that." He turned the water off and wrapped her within a towel before carrying her out to her room.

STANDING OUTSIDE, Julian stared in the front window of the bar. He watched Quinn as he impatiently waited for his phone call to be answered. Finally, when he thought it was going to voicemail, Devon picked up. "Hey."

"Hey to you too," Julian said. His hands clenched around

the phone when Quinn moved out of view and into the pool-room. *Don't break it.*

"What happened?" Just like Devon to cut straight to the chase.

"Well, I died and came back to life."

There was a moment of silence before Devon replied, "Again?"

Julian started to pace when Quinn reemerged from the poolroom. "Yeah, and believe it or not, it was less fun this time. More of a permanent thing."

"Obviously not too permanent. Care to tell me how this non-death came about?"

Julian filled him in on what had occurred yesterday. As he spoke, he could hear Devon moving about and closing doors. By the time he got to the end of his story, he was fairly certain Devon was in a closet in an entirely different house than the one he'd started in.

"What kind of trouble are you into down there?" he asked when Julian stopped speaking.

"Nothing I can't handle."

"Julian—"

"You wouldn't have seen one of *our* Hunter's staking you through the back either," he said.

"No, I wouldn't have. But a vamp with that strong of mind control is going to be an issue."

"He already is."

"Do you need help?" Devon asked.

"No, neither of us can risk Cassie here."

"It would be only me."

"Like she'd ever allow that to happen." Another door opened and closed on the other end of the line. "What are you doing, going through *all* of the houses?"

Devon chuckled, and Julian could hear wind blowing

around him now. "There are big and little ears all over this place. Trying to find somewhere to hide out is damn near impossible. What if I send Dani to you?"

Julian's hand squeezed the phone. He'd never gotten over his dislike or distrust of that girl. *Chris has forgiven you, and you would have gladly ripped out his throat at one time.* Still, it was Dani. "You want to send me the Hunter who betrayed Cassie and planned to leave my ass in that hellhole the Commission created, thanks but no."

"You know why she did that. She's one of us now. She's proved it multiple times. Plus, she's strong and getting stronger. She'd be able to zap him before he ever got close enough to control her mind, or anyone else's."

Julian's stomach twisted with turmoil as he pondered Devon's words. Dani would be a powerful ally, but she'd been a big part of the reason he and Cassie had been imprisoned together beneath that school. Imprisoned and tortured. The idea of her anywhere near Quinn made him see red, but Dani would be able to knock that vamp on his ass with her ability to wield electrical currents. She'd knocked *him* on his ass before.

And she has done nothing but prove herself these past two years, like you.

"Julian?" Devon asked.

"I'm thinking."

"Don't hurt yourself."

"You're funny. Hold on." Walking over to the glass, he tapped on the window to get the attention of Chris, Melissa, and Lou sitting on the other side. He pointed to Luther at the bar before gesturing for them to meet him outside. "How is everyone doing there?" he asked as he waited for them.

"Far better than you. I may be able to convince Cassie to

stay behind and let me come on my own. That vamp won't know what mind control is if I get a hold of him."

"I don't think we're there yet, but I'll call you if it becomes necessary."

"You want him for yourself," Devon deduced.

"Yes. You have no idea what I'm going to do to him when I get my hands on him."

"Oh, I have a very good idea. We did run together for centuries after all."

"This will be worse," Julian vowed. "They're coming." Luther, Lou, Melissa, and Chris stopped before him. He moved the phone away from his mouth as he spoke with them. "Devon has suggested sending Dani here to help. Since we all know my feelings on her, I'd like to hear your opinions on it."

They all exchanged a look before Luther spoke. "I think it's a good idea."

"Cassie will know something is up if he sends Dani," Melissa said.

"She's going to know anyway," Devon said through the phone. "I can't keep this from her. I can keep her from there, but she has to know. She'll never forgive me if something happens and I knew about it but didn't tell her."

"Devon is going to tell her anyway," Julian said to them.

Melissa folded her arms over her chest. "I agree with Luther. If more innocent people die, and Dani could have helped us do something to stop it, but we refused her help, then we'll be at fault too."

Julian couldn't keep the scowl from his face; he glanced through the window at Quinn again. "I know you don't like Dani," Chris said. "I understand why, but she has changed, and she is trustworthy. I *know* she is."

Everything in him screamed against it, but he knew it

would be foolish to let past grudges stand in the way right now. "Fine, send her," he muttered into the phone. "I'm going to have to buy a house to have any alone time with Quinn again."

"I'm sure with that attitude, Dani will feel very welcome and at home," Devon said with a laugh. "And just keep building houses, like I do."

"Look at how well that's working out for you. You're standing outside in February in Canada. If Dani makes one wrong move toward Quinn, I'll tear her head off," he promised.

"That will help her feel more welcome."

Julian turned away from the others and stalked over to a pickup truck. He watched as they made their way back inside the bar. "Are you sure you're going to be able to keep Cassie away from here?" he asked.

"It's going to kill her, but yes. She has numerous lives depending on her here right now."

"Good."

"Your mate, Quinn?"

"What about her?"

"They can't get their hands on her, Julian, not if she can do something like bringing a vampire back to life. Her power will only grow every year. What she could do in a hundred years, or fifty years, could be devastating in the wrong hands."

"I know."

"I know you do."

"Are you flying Dani or having her drive here?" Julian asked.

"The soonest day flight I can find, hopefully tomorrow, she'll be on it. If it's still daytime when she arrives, she'll be safe getting to you. You do realize she's the only one, besides Quinn, you'll be able to trust not to possibly be corrupted by this vampire."

"The thought has occurred to me."

Devon's laughter made him wish his friend were standing before him so he could throttle him. "That makes you so happy, I can tell."

"Thanks for the sympathy."

"Only the same amount you gave me when Cassie and I were first struggling through everything. In fact, you tried to kill her, multiple times. We've gotten past it; you should do the same with Dani."

"Dick."

"Yep."

"Dani may not want to come," Julian said.

"She will. She's a fighter."

"I'll text you the address here."

"Okay. Oh, and, Julian?"

"Yeah."

"Tell Quinn I said thank you."

Devon hung up before he could respond. Julian texted Quinn's address to Devon and slid the phone in his pocket. Devon was right, but he still couldn't help his resentment at the idea of seeing Dani again. Climbing the stairs, he stepped into the bar and surveyed the meager crowd.

Most men were gathered around the bar, where Quinn was pouring drinks. She smiled and laughed as she talked with them and slid the mugs across the bar. She still looked about five pounds lighter than she had before she'd brought him back to life, but the blue veins were no longer visible in her skin and the shadows were gone from under her eyes. Her cheekbones were still more pronounced, her collarbone more visible, but there was a healthy glow about her once more.

He was going to have to chase off some overeager patrons who mistakenly believed they had any chance with her. Stalking toward the bar, a scowl twisted his face when Clint's short, stout form stepped in front of him.

"She's going to have to wait, Children of the Corn." Julian's scowl deepened at the new freaking name. His fingers curled into fists as he fought the urge to break Clint's neck. The worst part was Julian grudgingly admired that Clint kept coming up with ways to needle him and the man had no fear of him. Clint didn't know what he was, but most men still stayed far away from him and cowered from the very look Julian gave Clint now. "I need your help with something."

"Are you out of your mind?" Julian demanded before he could stop himself. "Why do you think I'd help you with anything?"

"Because Quinn would want you to. This way." Clint spun on his heel, leaving Julian staring after him as he made his way through the tables toward the kitchen without so much as a backward glance to make sure Julian followed him.

Quinn was turning away from the taps when Julian made his way around the bar, grabbed hold of her waist, and dragged her up against him to kiss her. A small squeak escaped her. Her hands flattened on his chest as she tried to push him away, but as his tongue slid over her lips, her body melded against his.

She swayed on her feet and blinked at him when he released her. He forced himself to step away before he forgot all about the people surrounding them, lifted her onto the bar, and stripped her clothes from her sweet body. That was an idea for later, he decided as he gazed at her dazed eyes and swollen lips.

"I have to help Clint with something," he told her. "I'll be right back."

"Really?" she blurted.

"He told me he needs my help."

"Oh, uh… okay," she stammered.

He sent a scathing look over at the men gathered too close for his liking before hurrying over to join Clint by the kitchen doors. "Why don't you just brand her?" Clint demanded.

Julian merely smiled in response. Clint shook his head and shoved the door open. The clattering of pots and pans greeted him as they stepped into the kitchen. Grease sizzled on the stove as water sprayed into the sink. The two men in the back barely glanced at them before continuing on with their work in the sweltering kitchen. He wiped the sweat from his brow as he followed Clint past the stainless steel appliances toward the back door.

"Where are we going?" he demanded as Clint opened the door and held it for him to walk out.

"She'll survive without you for ten minutes," Clint grumbled when Julian hesitated, his gaze going back to the swinging doors leading into the bar. Clint couldn't know, but ten minutes was nine and a half minutes more than someone would need to take her from him. "No one is going to attack her in such a crowd."

Julian frowned as he turned toward Clint. What an odd choice of words for him to use. Why would he even think about someone attacking Quinn?

"You have to see this," Clint insisted.

Julian kept one eye on Clint when he stepped out the door. Had the vampire they were hunting gotten to Clint too and was now using him as bait? The smell of blood filled his nostrils; he kept his instincts honed on Clint while they walked down the back alley. Clint remained focused on him, his brown eyes intense. He didn't ask the man where the scent of blood was coming from, most humans wouldn't be able to detect the odor.

"What am I supposed to be seeing?" he asked.

Clint snorted and jerked his head toward where his garage was. Julian walked stiffly beside him, his gaze moving over the alley as they made their way to the back. Once there, Clint pulled a flashlight from his pocket and clicked it on.

The scent of blood was stronger here, more intense as the copper tang of it seared into his senses. Julian didn't need the light to reveal the streaks of red all over the back of the bar. His muscles tensed as he fully took in the image painted there.

The twisted asshole had used human blood to paint Quinn on the back of the building. Her hair fell over her shoulder, her head bent and turned to the side in the way it often did when she was being playful with him. Few saw that look from her.

The blood mural became shaded in a thick red haze. His muscles shook, his nails dug into the palms of his hands as a low hiss slid out from between his gritted teeth. Beneath the mural, a single word was scrawled: *mine.*

That was nearly his undoing. Stepping closer to the bar, he reached out to tear the shingles off. To rend the back wall to pieces in order to remove the hideous image from the building. "Don't tear my bar apart," Clint said.

Julian almost lunged at him with the intent of ripping his throat out in order to ease some of what was burning so hotly within him, but he managed to keep himself restrained at the last second. *Control it. Control it.*

But it was so difficult when he couldn't tear his gaze

away from the scene before him, and his body shook with the bloodlust consuming him. Quinn was *his*. Everyone, especially vampires should recognize this, but this vamp wanted to take her from him.

"Come with me," Clint instructed.

"No."

"She'll be fine. Come with me."

Julian finally turned toward the short man. "You have no idea what is going on here."

Clint pointed toward his garage. "Come. I plan to wash this off after."

Julian glowered after Clint; he turned to head back to the bar and Quinn, but his foot froze in mid-air. His gaze returned to Clint as he pulled open the door of his garage and stepped inside. He didn't bother to look back at Julian but continued out of sight.

Julian glanced at the bar. Quinn was safe inside, if the vamp did enter, she wouldn't chase him into the night again. He hoped she wouldn't anyway, but she might, and if the vamp knew Julian was outside, he might be bold enough to try to lure her away again. The others would stop her, or they would at least try to.

He should go back, but he found his curiosity drawn to the strange little man as the light inside the garage flickered on. Clint was far too calm for someone who had recently found a bloody mural painted on his wall. Perhaps he assumed it was only red paint, but Julian didn't believe so.

Walking over, he found Clint waiting patiently inside the door for him. Clint closed the door behind him before walking around his souped-up Jeep toward the back wall. He knelt to pull up a panel discreetly tucked within the floor. The opening in the floor revealed a set of stairs already illuminated by a light below. The man vanished down the stairs with far more speed and agility than Julian would have suspected from someone with his build.

"Don't be a chicken!" Clint called up to him.

If you snap his neck, you could make it look like he fell down the stairs. But he knew it would upset Quinn if Clint died, and he couldn't bring her anymore distress.

He descended the stairs, prepared to attack Clint if he tried to stake him or attack him. Stepping off the bottom step, surprise slammed into him, but he managed to keep his face impassive as he realized how likely an attempted staking could be. He may get his chance to kill Clint after all, he realized as his gaze ran over the room.

CHAPTER FIFTEEN

QUINN CLOSED the dishwasher and hit the button to turn it on. Because it was a typically slow weeknight, she was the only waitress on. Clint would jump behind the bar to help if she needed him, but it was rare she ever did, and he'd disappeared out back with Julian. *Please don't kill him,* she inwardly pleaded.

She knew how Clint could push Julian's buttons, but she hoped Julian had enough restraint not to hurt the man who had become the closest thing she'd had to a father since her uncle. Her gaze slid to the kitchen doors. All the customers were set with drinks in the bar right now; she could slip out back and see what the two of them were up to and make sure Clint was safe. It wouldn't take long.

"Would you like me to check on them?" Melissa asked as she leaned over the bar.

Quinn shook her head. "I'm sure they're fine."

"You don't look so sure."

"That's because I'm not."

"I really don't think Julian will kill him."

"That's reassuring," Quinn replied with a laugh.

Before Melissa could respond, the door opened and five more men entered. They walked up to the bar and settled onto some stools. She recognized Jeb, Ernie, and Ross, but she'd never seen the other two. That wasn't unusual, sometimes new hands rotated through to work the ranches, depending on the needs of the ranch at the time.

Still, her instincts went on high alert as she smiled and approached the group. "Good to see you, Quinn," Jeb greeted. She'd always really liked Jeb; he was easygoing with a charming smile. He'd had a bit of a romantic interest in her over the years, but she'd made it clear it wouldn't happen even before Julian walked into her life.

"You too, Jeb. Where you been hiding?"

"Been having a lot of problems out at the ranch. Someone's been slaughtering the livestock."

"Who would do such a thing?" Melissa gasped.

"Don't know," Jeb replied. He pulled his cowboy hat off to run a hand through his curly blond hair. "We put up cameras and still can't catch whoever it is. It's a mess. Losing a lot of money. We had to move what remained of the animals to the boss's main ranch up north. Can we get a round of shots?"

"Sure." Quinn walked down the bar and pulled a bottle of Jack she knew was Jeb's preferred choice from the shelf.

Luther and Chris had moved closer throughout the conversation. Lou sat on the other side of them with his head tilted toward the men. "How come you haven't caught them on the cameras?" Luther inquired.

Quinn placed five shot glasses on the bar and filled them all.

"You wouldn't believe me if I told you," Jeb muttered before lifting his glass and downing the liquid.

He put the glass on the counter and gestured for Quinn to refill it; she lifted an eyebrow, but poured the drink. Jeb was more of a beer man. When he did do a shot, it was usually one a night and he was done. In her three years here, she'd *never* seen him do two in one night. The other men all drank their shots and made the same gesture to refill as Jeb had.

"You'd be amazed at the things I'll believe," Luther said. "I've seen shit no one would believe."

Jeb downed his second shot. He turned toward Luther, his elbow resting on the bar as his hand gripped the glass. "Ever see something move so fast it can't be caught on camera?"

The hair on Quinn's nape stood up. She was half-tempted to take a shot for herself as she studied Jeb's profile. His normally tanned skin had paled considerably; his fingers on the shot glass trembled, and she knew it had nothing to do with the whiskey he'd consumed. Behind him, the other four cowboys had their heads bent and their eyes focused on the bar. One of them crossed themselves before kissing the cross hanging around his neck.

"Because that's what we saw," Jeb continued. "Just this blur and then a dead sheep. Another blur and a dead steer, another and my favorite horse was killed. There were so many of them…" He broke off with a shudder and lifted the shot glass toward Quinn. "Another?"

"You know Clint's rule," she said, but she still took the glass from him and refilled it. Under these circumstances, she was pretty sure Clint would understand the breaking of his 'two and done' shot rule.

"We're staying at the motel tonight, before heading back north. Ross wants to spend some time with his wife before we go back, so no driving for us."

"You're not going to the ranch?" she asked.

"No." His eyes were haunted when he lifted his head to look at her. "We're going to be working up north for a bit. Probably come back in the spring, maybe."

She refilled the other glasses and slid them toward the rest of the men. Luther's eyes were troubled when they met hers; he pulled his glasses up and rubbed at the bridge of his nose.

"It sounds crazy," Jeb murmured as he stared at the amber liquid in his glass. "But we saw them, and when we showed the video to the boss, not only did he not fire our asses, but he ordered the remaining stock be taken somewhere safer. We weren't imagining it."

"I didn't think you were," Quinn said quietly.

Jeb's normally jovial face was grave and remote when he looked at her. "I did," he admitted. "Even when these guys saw it too, I still believed we were all imagining it. That it was some sort of strange, group hallucination. I mean it's *insane*."

Quinn rested her hand on his and gave it a pat. "Sometimes there are things in this world none of us can explain."

Jeb snorted before consuming his shot. "You're telling me. Beer, please."

"You got it."

She looked to the others who all gave her their orders before she walked away to pour their drinks and pop the tops off their beer bottles. Her mind spun as she contemplated Jeb's words. *Why would vampires be slaughtering livestock?* Unless they abstained from human blood like her, Julian, and his vampire friends, but they didn't kill the animals. However, not every vampire who didn't kill humans wouldn't kill animals. As much as she didn't like it, better an animal than a human, she supposed.

But for some reason, she didn't think these were

vampires like her. There was something awful and *off* about what they were doing. Why would they keep going back to the same place? Why weren't they hunting the animals? She didn't like that it happened, but she couldn't deny a part of her thrilled at the hunt. The excitement of the chase may be the best part of feeding.

Yet these vamps were denying themselves that thrill. And how many vamps were there that they were decimating live-stock numbers to the point where they had to be moved?

Her hand trembled so much she clinked two of the beer bottles together when placing them on the tray.

"Do you have any idea how many are doing this?" Luther asked as she set the tray on the bar before Jeb and the others.

"At least ten blurs," Jeb replied and bowed his head in thanks when she pushed his beer toward him.

A sick feeling twisted through her stomach as she handed out the rest of the drinks. What was going on? She glanced back at the doors, but Julian and Clint had yet to return. She highly doubted Julian had ever heard of anything like this before either.

Grabbing a shot glass, Quinn broke another of Clint's rules when she poured herself one and downed it. Her face twisted as she stuck her tongue out at the potent taste of the whiskey. It wasn't as good as her rum, but she enjoyed the burn.

∼

"RED," Julian greeted when he spotted Hawtie sitting in a chair across the way. She bowed her head in greeting, but didn't say anything. Her thick red lips were pursed and though she rarely looked her fifty plus years, there were lines etched around the corners of her mouth and eyes. His gaze slid back over the cache of weapons stored within the room. "Are we preparing for the zombie apocalypse?"

"Let's not play games," Clint replied as he settled himself onto a crate.

"Oh, yes, let's not," Julian drawled as he looked pointedly at the hundreds of crossbows, stakes, axes, swords, and guns big enough to take down an elephant, hanging on the wall. There were more weapons leaning against the wall, or stored inside glass cases. It made the stash in the RV look like a joke, and Julian had believed them over-prepared. "What is your point here, Clint?"

"My point here, Julian, is I know what you are. I have a good idea what your friends are, and I know what Quinn is." Julian's jaw locked. He shifted his stance so he could be across the room and have Clint's neck snapped before either he or Hawtie blinked. "There's something nasty out there after her, hunting in our town, and it has to be stopped."

Julian's gaze ran over the stout man as he tried to figure out exactly what he was. Not a Hunter, he would have sensed the power in him. Certainly not a vamp as both he and Hawtie had steady heartbeats. Guardians? But wouldn't Luther have known if they were?

He tried to recall the times he'd touched either of them. He wasn't sure he'd ever touched Clint. He was almost certain he hadn't, but he'd certainly touched things Clint had. Hawtie, he'd touched a few times, and he'd touched things she had. But he'd almost always had his ability shut off around them and in their places of business, and he'd never been focused on them when using it. Even if he'd had it on, he couldn't have guaranteed he'd see something from them, not with the rotating amount of people they had coming in and out of their businesses every night.

Clint and Hawtie were humans, and he'd wrongly assumed both of them would have little useful information for him. He kept his ability turned off most of the time, unless he believed he needed it. Years of seeing things he didn't want to had made it so he preferred not seeing them now. Not to mention, most people were beyond boring. He'd rather beat his head against the wall than see into the life of one more soccer mom in a mini-van.

"And how did you come by this information?" Julian inquired of Clint.

"Someone painted a bloody picture of her on my wall."

"Let's not play games," Julian said. "That alone wouldn't lead you to believe Quinn and I were somehow different, or my friends."

Clint folded his arms over his chest and tilted his head to the side. "I pay attention."

"And what exactly do you think you've learned by paying attention to us?"

"That you're not human."

Julian held Clint's steady gaze as a patronizing smirk curved his lips. "So I see someone hopped on the crazy train. Enjoy the ride."

"Enough boys," Hawtie interjected. "Jesus, the two of you are like dogs circling a bone." She turned toward Clint. "He's good for Quinn. You've seen the change in her, how much happier she is now. And you," her warm brown eyes seared into Julian, "we protected Quinn this whole time. We've looked out for her and tried to keep her safe for three years. Even while knowing she was a vampire—"

"Chelsea," Clint groaned, and despite what Julian had already suspected them of knowing, a jolt of disbelief went through him at hearing her confirm it.

"We welcomed her here," Hawtie continued as if Clint hadn't spoken.

"Why would you do that?" Julian inquired.

"Because when she first came here, she was a broken soul. More broken than anyone I'd ever seen before, and in my business, I've seen my fair share of haunted and hurting people. All I wanted was to hug her, but she wouldn't let anyone near her. Gradually, she came out of her shell, but it took a while," Hawtie replied. She dabbed at the corners of her eyes as she spoke. "We never had children—"

"Maybe if we'd gotten married," Clint interrupted.

"Pfft," Hawtie said with a wave of her hand at him. "Marriage wouldn't have made you want children."

"And you know why I didn't," Clint muttered.

Hawtie patted his hand reassuringly before turning to focus on Julian again. "There was something so forlorn about Quinn that I couldn't help but care for her, even if she was supposed to be a monster."

"But she's not," Clint said.

"Of course she's not," Julian growled.

Clint's eyes narrowed on him. "You are though. You *may* be better than most vampires, but there's a viciousness in you."

"There is." There was no point in denying it. They were all laying everything out on the table, subtlety and denial had no place in this conversation. "But I don't kill humans. I don't feed from them, unless it's necessary, and then I will do what has to be done. Quinn will do the same."

Clint nodded, but Hawtie shook her head. "No, she's—"

"A survivor," Julian interrupted. "One of the strongest survivors I've ever encountered. You're right; she's vulnerable and kind. She's been broken, and she's done things she regrets, but in order to be a survivor, you must be willing to do whatever it takes to keep going. But she also loves with all she has, and she loves you both very much," Julian told them, sensing Hawtie needed to hear this bit of truth. "You're the whole reason she won't leave this town, even if it would probably be safer for her to do so."

Hawtie dabbed at her eyes again. Clint rested his hand on her thigh and gave it a squeeze. "It wouldn't be safer for the town if you left," Clint said.

"And she knows this."

"As do you."

"Yes, but I'd have her out of here faster than either of you could blink if it meant ensuring her safety."

There was actually a grudging flicker of admiration in Clint's eyes as a smile curved his mouth. "I don't like you, but I do like that she has you looking out for her now too. What is this thing in our town?"

"It's the vampire who ended her mortal life," Julian said.

"And turned her?" Hawtie asked.

"Not in the way you're thinking."

"What do you mean?"

Julian ran a hand through his hair before glancing at the stairs. "I think that's something for Quinn to tell you, if she chooses to."

Hawtie and Clint exchanged a look before they focused on him again. "Fair enough," Clint replied.

"What do you suspect my friends are?" Julian inquired.

"Hunters, Guardians, maybe both."

"What gave you that impression?"

Clint shrugged. "I know what to look for."

"And how do you know what to look for?"

Clint's mouth clamped shut. Hawtie leaned against his side, nudging him with her elbow. "Tell him."

Clint heaved a large sigh before rising to his feet. "My grandparents were Guardians," he finally answered.

"I see. And so are you?"

"I suppose, but I wasn't raised in the same way most Guardians are. My grandparents fled the Commission with my mother and came to the U.S. during World War II."

"Why did they flee?" Julian inquired as he leaned back on his heels to peer up the stairs. He really should return to the bar, but he had to learn as much as he could about these two before he let them anywhere near Quinn again.

"Because they disagreed with the Commission's policies. In England, during the war, the Commission did a lot of testing and experimenting on Hunters and vampires."

"I am well aware of the Commission's *experiments*," Julian spat.

Clint lifted an eyebrow at that but refrained from commenting. "My grandparents were aware there were vampires out there who didn't kill and lived in peace. They'd encountered a few of them and allowed them to live. A couple years later, they recognized one of the vampires they'd let go as a vampire the Commission had captured to experiment on. They tried to make the Commission understand what they did about vampires, but they wouldn't hear of it. My grandparents feared their protests would turn the Commission against them."

"Rightly so," Julian muttered.

"So my grandparents fled. They spent the rest of their lives in hiding, as did my mother. My father also went into hiding to be with her. I've spent my whole life hiding in this town." He squeezed Hawtie's hand and lifted it to his mouth to press a kiss against the back of it. "Though it was a fun hiding place." She grinned at him as she briefly rested her head on his shoulder. "Hawtie is the only one who ever knew the truth about me, until now."

"And believe me, I considered him insane at first." Hawtie chuckled.

"You still do," Clint teased.

"I do."

"My parents taught me what I was and trained me to be prepared in case someone came after me," Clint continued. "They taught me how to recognize vamps by their movements and actions. The same with Hunters. Guardians are more difficult to pick out, but they're less of a menace to me, in small numbers. They most likely don't know about my existence but I'm not willing to take the chance they do."

"So that's why you didn't go after Quinn when she came into town," Julian surmised. "Because you thought she might be one of the vamps who didn't kill."

"Yes. I've encountered a few vampires who came through here over the years. Some I've allowed to pass freely when they made no move to attack anyone. Some of the others I put down. I was waiting to see which category Quinn would fall into. I was relieved to learn she was simply looking for a place of her own to hide, and I know this town is a good one."

"So what exactly do you plan to do to help us?" Julian inquired.

Clint gestured at the weapons surrounding him. "You might not think it, but I'm tougher than I look. I want this vampire out of my town and as far from Quinn as possible."

"You and I finally agree on something," Julian said.

CHAPTER SIXTEEN

"Aren't you going home?" Quinn asked Clint as she gathered the remaining glasses from the tables.

"In a little bit," Clint replied. "We have some things to discuss first."

Quinn froze, her head lifted to stare at him and Hawtie sitting at the bar. She glanced at Julian when he walked over to lock the front door with Melissa, Luther, Lou, and Chris still inside. Clint didn't protest the action.

"Is everything okay?" Quinn demanded as she placed the glasses on the table.

She turned accusing eyes on Julian. Had he somehow managed to persuade Clint to fire her so she would reconsider leaving? "It's fine," Julian assured her and rested his hands on her shoulders.

Quinn turned toward her boss. "What is it?"

"You should sit," Julian suggested and pulled out a chair for her at the bar. "And the rest of you will want to hear this too."

Quinn glanced uneasily at him before settling into the

chair. She turned to face Clint and Hawtie, prepared to fight for her job, no matter what Julian had told them. She was also prepared to sock Julian in the jaw for trying to take control of her life, *again*.

"What is it?" Quinn demanded.

"I'm a Guardian," Clint said flatly.

Out of everything running through her mind, that declaration had been so unexpected that she couldn't process it at first. Chris sprayed his beer over the bar, and Melissa started to laugh before abruptly silencing it when she realized Clint wasn't kidding; he'd dropped a word most humans wouldn't use to describe themselves. Luther and Lou both had their eyebrows so high into their hairlines that Quinn didn't think they'd ever come down again.

"I don't understand," she finally managed to get out.

Leaning forward, Clint took hold of her hands while he told her about his family and their history. "I was born in this town, I've never left, but I know of your world."

Quinn couldn't help but squeeze his hands as she fought the shock washing through her. "Why didn't you tell me sooner?"

"I was hoping the three of us could live here peacefully and find the shelter, refuge, and friendship we were seeking with each other. Hawtie and I wanted to protect you and keep you safe. We were afraid you might bolt if you knew the truth about me.

"When these guys came into town," he waved a hand at the others, "I knew our peace was going to come to an end, but when they didn't hurt you, I decided to let it play out and see what happened. I didn't realize there were still Hunters and Guardians who realized all vampires weren't evil. When this group walked in with a vampire, I have to admit my curiosity was piqued."

"It took some time for many of us to learn that not all vampires are killers. We didn't believe it until only a couple of years ago," Luther said. "I know of no other Hunters or Guardians before then who believed some vampires deserved to live."

"My grandparents said there were others," Clint replied.

"The Commission either killed them, they fled, or they remained silent in order to ensure their safety," Julian replied. "I'd lean toward the Commission killed as many of the dissenters as they could find."

"I would too," Lou murmured.

"Bunch of bastards," Clint muttered.

"They're gone now," Quinn said. "They were destroyed."

Clint spun toward her, his jaw slack, and his eyes bugging out of his head. Beside him, Hawtie sat up straighter in her chair. "What?" Clint demanded.

"We destroyed them," Julian replied. "There may be some out there still, but they're more scattered than the Hunters and Guardians were after The Slaughter. They're also an open target for *every*one who stumbles across them as far as I'm concerned. There are no innocents in that bunch."

"Julian." Quinn rested her palm on the rigid hand grasping her shoulder. He eased his grip a little before beginning to massage her shoulders.

"That means…" Hawtie whispered before shaking her head. "It doesn't matter; I'm a little too old to have children now."

Clint took hold of her hand and squeezed it within his. "I'm sorry."

"It's not your fault. I knew you didn't want children when I chose my path years ago. I'm happy with it, until you piss me off."

"Most likely tomorrow," Clint said.

Hawtie laughed. "Most likely."

"The Commission is the reason you never had children," Quinn guessed.

"I couldn't have my children living with the worry they could be discovered at any time," Clint replied.

"And I refused to marry him if he refused to have children in the beginning. Now, it's become our thing," Hawtie said.

"One of these days, I'll convince you to marry me."

"Don't count on it."

Quinn couldn't hide her smile over their banter. "So why did you reveal this to Julian?" Luther inquired.

"We want to help," Clint replied. "I have a large stash of weapons—"

"He has enough to bring down a vampire horde," Julian said, not looking at all pleased by the notion.

"Good, because I think we're going to need it," Luther said.

"What do you mean?" Julian demanded.

Quinn rose and paced over to look out the window as she spoke. "Jeb came in earlier."

"I was wondering where that boy has been," Clint said as he rubbed at his chin.

"Busy," Quinn said and then filled them in on what Jeb and the others had revealed. The white band encircling Julian's pupils burned a fiery red. She'd come to recognize the reddened band signified he was angry, but still mostly in control of himself.

"How many did he think were there?" he demanded.

"At least ten," Quinn replied.

"What I don't understand is why they're killing animals and not people," Chris said.

"They're trying to go undetected," Luther replied. "They've brought attention to themselves with the slaughter of the livestock, but they believe humans will pass it off as a bizarre animal attack. I don't think they realize they're on camera."

"Why wouldn't they think they were on camera?" Melissa asked.

"Not all vamps have caught up with technology," Julian replied. "And those who have are often too arrogant to think they'd ever slip up in some way. Besides, no one would be able to tell what those blurs were. Slowing the video would do nothing as the vamps themselves are moving at a speed undiscernible to the human eye."

"So we have a growing number of vamps on the outskirts of town, trying to go unnoticed. Why?" Clint asked.

"Because of the prophecy," Julian replied. When he lifted his head to look at Quinn, his eyes were a fiery red now. "They know it's you and they've come for you."

"What are you talking about?" Clint demanded.

Quinn filled him in on the stupid prophecy and the truth surrounding Angie's death. She knew there was a chance Clint and Hawtie were also under that ass's mind control, but most vamps probably already knew about the prophecy. Besides, Zach had most likely spilled all the beans about her anyway.

"Jesus, Quinn," Hawtie whispered. "Why didn't you run from here?"

"Because I had to make sure you were safe. It doesn't matter where I go; there are vampires everywhere, and they'll hunt me until the day I die. I didn't expect the vamp responsible for my turning to walk in here after all these years or for him to amass a small army. If we left now, I think he'd be enraged enough to slaughter everyone in town before trying to follow me, and I can't allow that."

"No vamps in Antarctica," Julian muttered.

"Like you would live there," Chris said. "You're more cold-blooded than a snake."

"I would if it meant no one would bother us."

"I'm not running!" Quinn snapped. "And I'm not living in the land of snow and ice."

"They have penguins," Julian said with a coaxing smile.

"I do like penguins. We can *visit* someday."

"This vampire is obsessed with you, Quinn," Hawtie said.

"And the only way to end that is to kill him," she said firmly, "before he brings more of the undead here."

"Why is he so obsessed with you?" Clint inquired.

"I think because he doesn't understand how I'm still alive. He certainly didn't expect me to survive the night he attacked me."

"How did you change?" Clint inquired.

Quinn turned to look at the window again as she revealed her Hunter and vampire heritage to them. "Between being born a Hunter and part vampire, I had enough vampire blood in me to keep me from dying that night," she said.

"Aw, honey." Hawtie walked over to pull Quinn's hair forward and tug at the ends of it. Quinn couldn't help but smile over the familiar, comforting gesture. "I'm so sorry for what you've gone through."

"Others have been through worse," she said as she squeezed Hawtie's hands.

Hawtie dragged her up against her ample chest, hugging her so close that Quinn never would have been able to breathe if she were still human. She smiled as she wrapped her arms around Hawtie's back.

"Not many have," Hawtie said as she stepped away from her.

"He probably knows how I was able to survive the change now, because of Zach," Quinn said.

Clint looked around the bar at the others with a look of confusion. "Wait a minute, what do you mean because of Zach he probably knows, and where is Zach?"

Guilt slithered through Quinn. She turned her eyes away from the man who thought better of her than he should. She moved further away from Hawtie. Julian stepped closer to her and wrapped his arms around her waist. He pulled her against his chest and rested his chin on her head.

"He's dead," Julian said flatly.

Clint's eyes widened. Hawtie's hand flew to her mouth. "What happened?" Clint demanded.

Julian looked questioningly at her, but she shook her head. She didn't much feel like retelling that tale. He focused on the two of them again. "The vampire hunting Quinn has the ability to control minds. He got hold of Zach at some point, probably before he ever let his presence in this town be known to us. Zach staked me, killed me, and Quinn brought me back."

No one spoke for a minute. "How were you able to do that?" Hawtie finally blurted.

"I drained the life from Zach and gave it to Julian," Quinn said flatly.

Clint pulled a piece of gum from his pocket. He unwrapped it and folded it into his mouth as his gaze slid from her to Julian and back again.

"You can *do* that?" Hawtie asked with a hitch in her voice.

"I never had before, but yes, I can and *did* do that," Quinn replied.

"By taking my life, Zach was also taking Quinn's, but I'm not sure he knew that. I'm not sure if this vampire knows we're mates or not, but—"

"Wait, wait, wait," Clint said and held a hand up to halt him. "The mate thing is real?"

"It is," Julian confirmed.

"And you two are mates?"

"Yes." Julian's arms tightened possessively on her waist as he growled the word.

Quinn rested her hand reassuringly on top of his. "I didn't mean to kill him," she said. "Well, I did, but I never would have under normal circumstances. I just lost it. I only knew I had to get Julian back."

Clint's eyes looked about to pop out of his head as he chomped on his gum and stared between the two of them. "But like I was saying," Julian continued, "if this vamp does know we're mated, I think he intended to test the strength of the bond by killing me and see what Quinn could do if pushed beyond reason. If he didn't know, then he was simply looking to get me out of the way so he could get to her."

"And if what Jeb said about the ranch is true, he's either creating vampires or he's gathering them here," Clint said.

"Or both," Julian replied.

"Shit."

"That about sums it up," Chris said.

"What's your plan?" Clint inquired.

"We haven't formulated one for this yet," Luther answered. "I'm not sure there is one, other than sticking together, staying on our best defense, and preparing ourselves for what could be one hell of a battle."

"I can help with the preparing," Clint said with a grin.

~

THE KNOCK on the door roused Julian from bed. Devon had called earlier to say Dani was on her way and should arrive early in the afternoon. Opening the bedroom door, he peered out at the people strewn about the room. Melissa sat up on her cot and rubbed at her eyes. Luther's head emerged around the kitchen doorway, but Chris and Lou remained sleeping on the floor.

Shaking his head, he stepped over their bodies to get to the door. He pulled it open to reveal Dani on the other side. The sight of her caused a jolt of anger to go through him, but he shoved it aside. *Here to help, and right now, she's the only one you can trust other than Quinn. If that vamp had control of Quinn, she wouldn't be with me right now.*

The small, slender girl had her normally dark hair bleached blond now; rainbow streaks of color framed her face as it fell around her shoulders. Since he'd seen her last, she'd pierced her eyebrow and lip with silver hoops.

"I bet you're throwing me a party to celebrate my arrival," she said with a smile.

Julian scowled at her, but he stepped aside and gestured for her to enter. "Wow, I'm having flashbacks of fifth grade sleepovers," she muttered as she surveyed the people sprawled across the floor. "Except these guys smell *much* worse."

Chris didn't bother to open his eyes as he lifted his hand to give her the finger.

"Forced to buddy up because of a crazed vampire and all that," Melissa said.

"So, the usual," Dani replied.

"Yeah."

"What's with the face metal?" Chris asked as he pushed himself up onto his elbows.

Dani grinned at him as she set her bag on the floor near the door. "Eighteenth birthday present to myself. Like?"

"It's you," Chris replied.

Dani turned toward him, but before she could speak, Quinn emerged from the bedroom. Julian took hold of her hand and pulled her against his side. "Quinn, this is Dani."

He'd told Quinn enough about Dani that she hesitated before extending her hand. "Thank you for coming," she said.

Dani thrust a thumb at him. "I kind of owe this guy."

Quinn glanced at him as Dani took hold of her hand and gave it a shake. He remained unmoving, his gaze on the young girl. *And she is young*, he reminded himself. *She was even younger when she betrayed Cassie.*

He kept his eyes on Quinn's hand as Dani wrapped both of hers around it. "It's nice to meet you," Dani said.

"You also," Quinn replied and glanced at him again. She rested her hand on his chest, causing his muscles to relax a little as some of his tension eased.

"So, why don't you guys fill me in on what's going on," Dani said as she weaved her way through the sleeping bags to settle on the couch. Luther grabbed a chair from the kitchen and brought it out as they all gathered around to fill her in on the details.

CHAPTER SEVENTEEN

D<small>ANI LEANED</small> against the hood of the pickup she'd rented from the airport with her fake ID and stared out at the desert. Quinn sat in the driver's seat, watching as Julian and the others moved around the truck, tossing the last of the supplies into the back. There was a never-ending supply of death wielding power beneath Clint's garage. She never would have suspected that room was beneath the building, or that Clint was actually a Guardian. He'd shown no indication he'd known what she was over the last three years.

But then, how well could anyone ever really know someone else? The surface of a person painted one picture, but beneath it were thousands of hidden secrets. Quinn's gaze drifted back to Dani. It had been the same with her, but the others seemed to have forgiven her and moved on. Julian had only forgiven her grudgingly, but he was trying.

Quinn didn't know if they could trust her, but she'd come to like the young girl over the past couple of days. She was her own person, confident and outgoing with an easy smile that was tough to resist. Quinn wouldn't mind punching her for what she'd done to Julian, but she liked Dani far more than she'd believed she would when Julian had told her she was coming.

Julian walked over beside her. He leaned his arm against the driver's side mirror as Chris tossed two shovels onto the pile in the back and pulled the canvas covers over the load. Quinn didn't want to think about the fact the shovels had been added in case graves needed to be dug. She was holding onto the hope they would be saving lives tonight.

"That's it," Julian said.

Quinn turned the truck on. He didn't move away from the vehicle. "We'll be fine," she assured him and patted his hand.

"I don't like this."

"I know, but look at the weapons we have. Besides, between Dani and me, we can fry anyone who tries something funny. Plus, all of you will be right behind us. If something is going to go down at the bonfire tonight, it will be better if we have the element of surprise on our side."

"I still don't like it," he grated through his teeth.

She squeezed his hand as Dani opened the passenger side door and jumped in. "We can't keep letting him come at us; we have to take the fight to him." She'd seen what he'd painted on the wall of Clint's bar. The memory of it caused her to tremble, but thankfully, Clint had hosed the blood away that night. "He's only going to destroy more lives until he's stopped."

Julian's gaze slid to Dani.

"Besides," Quinn continued. "I've got the only person we know isn't under mind control with me. I should be more worried about you."

"Don't worry about me, keep yourself safe."

"I love you."

His hand wrapped around the back of her head and he pulled her close. His lips pressed against her ear as he held her. "I love you too," he murmured before giving her a kiss that had her blinking dazedly after he'd stepped away from her. The arrogant grin he shot her caused her to scowl at him before she shifted into drive and hit the gas.

The vehicle lurched forward, kicking up sand as the wheels spun. Dani grabbed hold of the handle over her head and pressed her feet into the floorboard as the back wheels continued to spin. Finally, the truck found traction and lurched forward. Quinn laughed loudly when Dani pressed her back flat against the seat.

"Hold on!" Quinn yelled over the whipping wind as the truck sped across the packed sand of the desert trail.

"Good thing I rented this with my fake ID," Dani muttered as the vehicle went airborne over a dune and landed with a loud groan of springs and struts.

Quinn laughed again and hit the gas harder.

～

"Is that the way she drives my Jeep?" Clint asked as he popped a piece of gum into his mouth.

"Oh no, she treats it like it's a delicate flower," Julian replied with a straight face, earning him a sizzling glare from Clint.

"The look on Dani's face!" Chris laughed as he hugged his belly. "Oh, I don't envy her. That vampire is one nutso driver!"

Julian watched as the truck flew into the air over a dune before crashing back to the ground. Shaking his head, he turned away and tossed the last of the bags into the back of Clint's Jeep. He climbed into the driver's seat and started the engine as Clint walked over to join Hawtie in her black Bronco.

Hawtie had asked some of her employees to help at Clint's tonight while her strip club was still closed, saying both Clint and Quinn had fallen ill. It would make many of the patrons at Clint's happy, Julian was sure, and it allowed Quinn and Clint to go to the bonfire with them. Julian didn't know if he would have preferred her working tonight. If she were at the bar, she would be away from the bonfire and any potential danger. Then again, he would have spent the entire night thinking of her while he was staking out the bonfire without her.

At least now, he would be able to keep an eye on her as she mingled with the others at the party. The plan was for Quinn and Dani to attend the party at the fire, while the rest of them kept watch.

Julian shifted into first as Luther climbed in beside him; Chris and Melissa hopped into the back. Lou climbed into the backseat of Hawtie's Bronco. "Brace yourselves," Julian said and popped the clutch. He could practically hear Clint cursing him as he hit the gas and the Jeep launched forward.

Melissa and Chris grabbed the roll bar to keep from bouncing out of the vehicle; Luther remained composed beside him as they took off down the trail Quinn traversed. He'd relented to her being bait, but he refused to let her be out here on her own for any length of time. He drove for a couple of miles, keeping the dim glow of Quinn's taillights in view.

In the distance, he saw the growing flames of a bonfire above the sandy dunes. The sun had only set an hour ago, but the party had already started. "Quinn and Clint said they didn't get started until around nine," Luther said.

"Must have been a change of plans," Julian murmured,

not at all liking the fact they would be arriving late. He glanced at the nighttime sky; there had been plenty of time for other vampires to make it to the fire by now. Quinn could be walking into a trap.

His hand tightened on the wheel. *Stick with the plan. She's not that far ahead,* he told himself. Pulling to the side of the road, he jerked up the emergency brake and jumped out. "Be careful," Luther said and slid over to take his place.

"You too," he replied.

The sand slipped beneath his feet as he sprinted across the desert, taking a direct line toward the fire.

~

QUINN SLOWED as she neared the fire, her headlights bouncing over the sky and trail when the truck dipped into a hollow. They had no idea if this was the fire from Melissa's vision or not, but she still approached cautiously. "They started early," she murmured. "We may be too late."

"All other vamps would have had to wait for the sun to set too. That was only an hour ago," Dani replied, but Quinn still heard the note of concern in her voice.

"I hope you're right," she murmured.

"Me too."

The truck rose over the top of the dip. Before the fire came into sight, the smell of blood assaulted her senses. Her nose wrinkled against the coppery odor as her fangs pricked with hunger.

"We're too late," she said.

"How do you know?" Dani asked.

"I can smell blood already."

Dani paled visibly, but she thrust her shoulders back and pulled her stake from the holster at her side. Quinn had her normal arsenal strapped to her, but it didn't give her the same reassurance it normally did. "You should stay here," she said to Dani. "There's no reason for us to both see this if we don't have to."

"I told Julian I'd stick to you like white on rice, and I'm going to keep that promise. Besides, letting you go out there alone may be the thing he finally kills me over."

"He won't kill you," Quinn replied. Dani shot her a look that said she didn't agree.

Quinn focused on the trail before them as they drove closer to the flames dancing high in the air. The truck broke over the top of the last dune. The headlights flared over the fire before them. She managed to keep her mouth from falling open at the spectacle that greeted her, but her stomach turned and tears burned her eyes.

"Oh." Dani's hand flew to her mouth. "Horrible."

Horrible didn't began to describe the twisted scene before them. Quinn's eyes shot everywhere at once as she tried to take it all in, but there was no way to take all of this in.

About fifteen vehicles were parked around the fire; all of them had their grills facing the flames. Kegs of beer had been dragged out and set up before the vehicles. Coolers were neatly arranged, along with beach chairs and a volley-ball net. Laughter should have been filling the air; there should be people dancing to the music she could hear coming from one of the parked trucks.

Instead, blood splattered the sand, turning it from an orangey hue to a macabre painting of red death. Amongst the blood, bodies were sprawled across the sand. Some people remained sitting in the beach chairs; one was slumped over the keg with his cup still clenched in his hand.

The volleyball lying next to the keg had turned pink from

the blood covering it; white spots poked out from beneath the layer of blood. Someone's hand was tangled within the web of the volleyball net. Quinn's hand went to her mouth when she realized there was no body beneath the hand.

"Why would they mutilate them like this?" Dani whispered.

Quinn had no answer for her. This hadn't been a feeding but a bloodbath, a message perhaps, but what was the message, *I'm out of my mind?* Because that was all she could think about her stalker as she stared at the massacre before her. This was something beyond anything she could comprehend. Vampires could be brutal, this sick freak was no exception, but the savagery here made her skin feel like ice.

"They could still be here, so be careful," she said as she pulled a stake from the holster at her side.

She grabbed the door handle and pushed it open. Sliding from the truck, she kept her hand on the door as she continued to survey the carnage. Dani opened her door and climbed out to join her as Quinn walked closer to the fire.

Quinn moved cautiously through the bodies, listening for a heartbeat, though deep inside, she knew they were all dead. If the bodies hadn't had their throats slashed, they'd been torn out and spit on the ground. She could almost hear the echoes of the dying people's screams on the air, feel their pain and terror resonating from their broken bodies.

"We should have come here earlier," she murmured, trying not to shed the tears burning her eyes. "We didn't need the extra supplies."

"We couldn't have known they would start so early," Dani said.

Quinn lifted her head to look at her. She was about five shades paler than normal as she stared at Quinn from across the body of a young man. "Couldn't we have? Melissa had a vision."

"But we didn't know where or when, not even Melissa knew. We do the best we can with what we have. We *will* stop him so he can't keep doing this."

"I said the same thing after he slaughtered the Kemps, yet look." She waved her hand over the bodies sprawled around them. "There's at least twenty more dead here, and I can't help but feel it's my fault. He's here because of me. Maybe I should have left town."

"This is one twisted individual. If you'd left, he probably would have slaughtered the entire town before following after you."

Quinn glanced away. She knew Dani was most likely right, but she couldn't shake her sense of guilt. She scanned the night and kept her ears attuned to any sound other than the crackling fire as she walked.

Making her way around the flames, she stared at faces she recognized and those she didn't. Those two boys had gone to college in Yuma. That woman had worked in the hardware store. That man had always left good tips, and that one had never tipped. She drank wine. He drank gin. She drank beer.

About half the people here had wandered into Clint's at some point, or she'd run into them in town. If she'd been able to go out in the day, she was certain she would know everyone in town, but her knowledge didn't go far beyond the bar and her small apartment building. Now she wished she'd gotten a chance to know them all. To put a name with the faces screaming in endless horror and the eyes staring at the sky or at *her*.

She shuddered as she met the cloudy-blue eyes of a young woman who had her head turned toward her. From the truck, "Simple Man" began to play. The chill that caused goose bumps to break out on her flesh had nothing to do with the breeze blowing across the dunes and everything to do with those unseeing eyes.

She rubbed at her arms as she turned away from the woman and stepped over the arm of another young woman. The fire continued to burn beside her, but the heat of it did nothing to warm her as she stepped over the body of a young man who had once asked her for a date. Quinn froze, a single tear slipped free as she gazed at the next face before her.

"Oh, Dusty," she whispered. Her neighbor had never hurt a fly; he'd been one of the most easygoing men she'd ever encountered. He hadn't deserved this; none of the people here had. Kneeling beside him, Quinn's hand trembled when she went to close his eyelids. She jerked her hand back from the feel of his lifeless body beneath her fingers and hastily retreated.

Movement to her right drew her attention in that direction. Hope shot through her, a small cry escaped as she raced across the sand to the young woman she swore she'd seen move. Quinn fell beside the woman. Grabbing hold of her chin, she turned the woman's head in her direction. The vein in her neck had been torn out. The imprint of a vampire's fangs were clearly visible against her tanned skin. Blood coated her neck and pooled beneath her in the sand, but her hand twitched on the ground.

"Dani!" she shouted as a new set of headlights spilled over them. Glancing to the side, she spotted Clint's Jeep and Hawtie's Bronco pulling up beside the truck. "She's alive!"

Dani fell beside her. "How?" she asked.

"I don't know," Quinn replied. She ran her hands over the girl when her fingers twitched on the ground again.

Lifting her head, Quinn shadowed her eyes against the head-lights as doors opened and closed.

"My God," Hawtie breathed.

"This has nothing to do with God," Clint replied.

The girl's body jerked; her head turned to the side as she finally blinked. Quinn stretched her hand out to rest it against her cheek. Before she could touch the girl again, arms wrapped around her waist. They lifted her up as they pulled her away. A startled cry escaped her, and she instinctively fought against the powerful hold as she kicked herself for letting her guard down.

Turning, she almost smashed her fist into Julian's cheek. She managed to hold back her punch at the last second. "What are you doing?" she demanded as she squirmed in his hold, but he refused to let her go.

"Get away from her, Dani," he commanded brusquely.

"But…" Dani started to protest.

"Get away from her; she's turning."

Quinn gawked at the young woman as her body twitched on the ground again before going still once more. Memories of her own turning, the excruciating agony, the hideous panic and helplessness that had accompanied the change from human to vampire filled her. She so badly wanted to help the woman, but the damage had already been done.

To her left, she spotted someone else's hand jerking on the ground and then another. Julian's lips skimmed back to reveal his razor-sharp fangs. Her gaze slid around the circle as more of the bodies started to move.

"Get the supplies. We have to destroy them before they turn," he said.

He carried her briskly toward the vehicles with Dani close on his heels. The others were gathered before the head-lights, their faces ashen, and their eyes wide in disbelief.

"Wait, what if they still retain some sense of rationality after turning?" Quinn protested. "We can't kill them when we don't know if they could be good."

"They won't be." Julian placed her on the ground and raced over to the truck. He threw back the canvas before yanking supplies from the back. Pulling out two crossbows, he tossed one to Chris and the other to Melissa.

"You can't know that!" she protested.

He glanced at her before tugging another crossbow free and rising to his feet. He pressed the weapon against her chest. His eyes burned into hers as he spoke, "A vampire can keep control of the mind of the ones they change. They can warp them and bend them to their will. With everything you know about this vamp, do you think he would relinquish that kind of power over his offspring?"

"Oh," she breathed, her mind spinning at his words. That was a fate worse than death; one that could have been hers if the vamp who had attacked her hadn't believed she was dead after their first encounter. "No, he wouldn't, but he couldn't have killed all of these people on his own."

"He could have given them all his blood to turn them though. We can't risk letting even one of them rise, if they are going to do his bidding."

"Dusty," she whispered.

Julian's eyes softened, but his face remained inflexible in its resolve. "Stopped being Dusty the second he died. Don't let him be sentenced to a mindless existence now."

She closed her eyes before giving a brief nod. "You're right."

"I freaking hate this guy," Chris muttered as he loaded his crossbow.

"Get in the Bronco," Clint ordered Hawtie and shooed her back with his hands.

"Let's get this over with," Julian said crisply.

A muscle in his cheek twitched, but he strode forward. She didn't miss that he made his way directly to Dusty as his feet kicked on the ground. Quinn turned away.

People began to writhe and moan more loudly on the ground. During her change, she'd felt like every bone in her body was breaking, as if her muscles were trying to choke the life from her and were constricting until they would snap. She'd begged for death, but her body wouldn't let her die.

Someone screamed; another shook her head back and forth so forcefully that spittle flew from her lips. Taking aim, Quinn fired an arrow straight through the woman's heart, putting her out of her misery. She shut her mind down, refusing to acknowledge the faces of those she recognized as she made her way forward.

Already dead, she told herself.

She spun to put an arrow into a young man when something lurched at her from the side. Quinn swung the palm of her hand up, driving it up and into the nose of the man lunging at her. Blood sprayed over her, but starving and disoriented from the change, her blow didn't slow the new vampire. His hands wrapped around her arms as he propelled her backward toward the fire.

CHAPTER EIGHTEEN

QUINN SWUNG THE CROSSBOW UP, caving the man's cheek-bone with the force of her blow. His fangs continued to snap at her, slicing into his lower lip and shredding his flesh. Spittle and blood sprayed over her face as his fingers dug into her flesh and he tore at her arms.

"Quinn!" Julian yelled.

She felt the heat of the flames at her back, and the fire burned against her neck. The man tried to draw her closer as his momentum continued to push her toward the flames. A shout tore from her. Ever since Zach, she'd kept her power restrained, unwilling to risk using it again for anything.

Now, it burst from her, latching onto the man so fast she didn't have time to process it before she was drawing his life force into her in greedy gulps. Electric-blue sparks of light crackled from her fingertips, illuminating the death creeping over the man. His cheeks hollowed out as his skin became sallow and shrunken.

She tried to pull away from him, but her power wouldn't be sated until it had feasted and drained him entirely. Quinn started to shake and her muscles quivered, but somehow she managed to get her hand around her stake and jerk it from its holster. The power flowing into her and the enjoyment she took in draining him was so tempting, she hesitated with the stake pointed at his heart.

"No!" she screamed at herself. She forced herself to lunge forward. She slammed her stake into the man's chest and twisted it into his heart.

With the connection between them abruptly broken, her power shot into her so violently that she took a step back as she gasped for air. His life force kicked around her insides as it sought some sort of release, but there was no one to pour it into right now, and her body greedily absorbed its strength.

From the corner of her eye, another newly turned vampire launched at her. Her hand shot out to wrap around the woman's brutalized throat. Quinn met the vamp's reddened eyes as she lifted her easily off the ground. The woman's feet kicked in the air, and her hands tore at Quinn's. She swung the stake out, driving it into the vamp's heart before dropping her to the ground.

Turning, she spotted Julian by her side. Together, they carved their way methodically through the rest of the vampires until they stood near the volleyball net, surveying the bloodbath surrounding them. The others moved closer to them. Chris had a gash on the side of his head, Melissa was holding her arm, and it looked like Lou had a broken finger, but there were no major injuries.

Tears burned Quinn's eyes again as she wiped blood off her cheeks and flung it onto the red sand. She refused to shed them. These people deserved tears, and so much more, but she wouldn't give her stalker the satisfaction of seeing her cry if he was anywhere nearby.

"He didn't expect us to come here tonight," Julian said.

"These were supposed to be new recruits for his growing army."

"What do we do with the bodies?" Hawtie's lower lip trembled as she spoke. "Most of these people have families in town."

"We take them somewhere until the sun can come up and get rid of them for us," Julian replied.

"If they didn't complete the change, will they burn up?" Dani asked.

Julian rubbed at the stubble lining his jaw. "I don't know," he admitted.

"People with heartbeats will have to stay out here to make sure," Luther said. Blood splattered his face. He took the towel Melissa handed him and removed his glasses to wipe them clean. "And if they don't burn, we'll bury them."

"What about their families?" Hawtie demanded.

Clint rested his hand on her arm. "There's nothing we can do about that."

"Can't we leave them here? At least then their families will have them, and they'll have some sort of closure about their deaths."

"Not with the clear evidence of a vampire attack on them," Luther said. "And even if we did something to cover the marks up, they could burst into flames the minute the sun hits them. I don't think that will go over too well with the humans if they're here to see it."

"No, it won't," Julian replied.

Hawtie looked around the circle at all of them. Quinn found she couldn't meet her heartbroken gaze. "They'll never know what happened to their loved ones," Hawtie murmured.

"The blood will still be here. They may never know where their bodies are, but they'll know they were killed,"

Luther said quietly. "It may sound awful, but that's more information than some people have about their lost loved ones."

Hawtie shook her head and pulled a handkerchief from her pocket.

"We have to gather the bodies now," Julian said. "There could still be others coming to the party."

Quinn's eyes shot toward the trail. She scanned the night for any hint of another vehicle approaching the fire. They would be screwed if someone happened to stumble across them now.

"Let's get to work," Clint said.

Quinn kept her head bowed as she helped to gather the bodies and body parts. They had to use a couple of the trucks gathered around the fire in order to carry them all, but they were able to get everything cleaned up far faster than she'd expected.

They moved the bodies a mile away and dropped them off before returning the two borrowed trucks to the fire. Quinn refused to acknowledge the pictures on the sun visor above her head, or the Virgin Mary doll glued to the dashboard as she drove the borrowed truck. It smelled of beer and Old Spice, a combination more pleasing than she would have expected.

Julian stopped the other borrowed truck directly before her in the sand. She could see him searching the fire to make sure no one new had arrived while they'd been gone. He eased his foot off the brake and approached the fire. Quinn slid the truck back into its spot and clambered out as fast as she could.

Walking over, Julian wrapped his arms around her waist and pulled her close against him. Quinn savored his scent as she pressed closer, burying her face in his neck. "We're almost done," he whispered and kissed her temple.

She reluctantly stepped away from him and watched as he walked over to rip the lids off two coolers. "Your fingerprints may not be on file, but if they decide to fingerprint you at some point, they'll match with the ones on those coolers," she pointed out.

"No one's going to catch me, other than you, Dewdrop." Still, he picked up the coolers and heaved them into the fire. "We should burn anything any of us could have touched."

Together, they moved about the fire, tossing anything that might contain some kind of evidence into the flames. Quinn wiped down the inside of both trucks. When she was done, she accepted the cooler lid Julian handed her. Together, they worked to erase the tire tracks leading away from the fire and toward the makeshift burial place they'd picked. When driving out to the burial spot, they'd made sure to keep all three trucks on the same path. The tracks deviated in some areas, but for the most part, they only had the one set to cover.

When they reached where they'd left the bodies and the others, they discovered Chris and Lou already digging a grave with the two stolen shovels. They took turns digging until the grave was big enough to hold all of the bodies in case they didn't burn up.

Clint, Hawtie, Lou, and Luther took up a position on the rocks to see what would happen when the sun came up.

～

"ALL OF THEM BURNED UP," Luther said when he entered the apartment hours later.

Julian stretched his legs out before him as he leaned back

in the rickety chair. The subtle snores of the others in the living room drifted to him. Quinn had passed out almost as soon as they'd gotten home. He'd waited to speak with Luther before going to sleep.

"What he's doing now is reckless. He risks exposure for all of us, and he risks creating a bunch of monsters who will slaughter without hesitation. This vampire is insane."

Julian folded his hands and rested them on his stomach. "I know."

"No matter what it takes, he has to be stopped."

Lifting his eyes, he stared at Luther as he pulled out a chair and settled across from him. He may be human, but in his own way, Luther was as ruthless as any vampire. "You want to use Quinn as bait," Julian stated.

"I think we have to."

Julian had been thinking the same thing; he just couldn't admit it to himself, or anyone else. "And what if something goes wrong?" he inquired. "What if she's taken, and I can't get her back, or she gets killed? Who will be the one to destroy me?"

"You know I will if I must, but we'll make sure that doesn't happen."

Julian's fingers drummed on the table. "What this man has done to her..." His voice trailed off, and his fangs tingled as he contemplated what he would do to her killer when he got the chance.

"What he will do to *countless* others. If those people had turned tonight and come into town, it would have been devastating. That may have been exactly what he had planned for them too."

"I know, but the idea of using her—"

"I want to do it." Quinn had moved so quietly he hadn't heard her approach. She stood in the doorway, so fragile looking in her oversized t-shirt with the sleeve hanging off her slender shoulder. "This has to stop. I've lived in fear of this man, I've hunted him, I've planned to destroy him for six years now, and it has to end. I need to be out in the open for him, by myself."

"No," Julian said tersely. "Not by yourself."

"I won't risk anyone else's life. Not for this. I'll turn the tracking app on my phone on—"

"And if he takes you somewhere with no reception?" Julian demanded. "The desert isn't exactly cell service central."

She thrust her shoulders back as she gazed at him. "*You* will be able to find me. I have complete faith in that."

"Quinn—"

"We either do this together, or I do it alone. I've made my choice, Julian, get on board with it."

His fangs lengthened as his palm slammed against the table. Luther leaned slowly away from him. "*Get on* board *with it?*" he bit out.

"Yes. I will go into the desert and allow him to catch me. If I don't kill him, then you can come and find me. But I have every intention of killing him before that becomes necessary."

Julian kept his hand pressed against the table; he was half-afraid he'd throttle her if he moved it. "Do you now?" he murmured. "And what if he kills you before any of that can begin to happen?"

"He won't," Quinn said.

"You're so sure?"

"I'm his prize. He won't kill me."

"What if he rapes you?"

She waved her fingers at him. "He'll get to know the true meaning of shrinkage if he tries."

Despite his exasperation with her, he couldn't help but smile at that. He had no doubt she'd try to make it so, but there were so many things that could go wrong, and she was *his* light in a world of death. If he lost her because of this, or if something happened to her, he'd never forgive himself.

The idea of that man's hands on her made his fingers dig into the table. "Don't ruin my furniture," she scolded.

He bit back a comment about how he couldn't do anymore damage to it. She tended to get a little testy when he commented on her awful assortment of hand-me-downs she considered furniture.

"I can do this," she said.

"I know you can, but I can't stand the idea of purposely putting you in harm's way."

"We're all in harm's way while he's still walking around. None of us can sleep comfortably knowing one of us could be the enemy in disguise. If he dies, then all of that ends. We may get a little peace for a change," she said with a wan smile.

He rose to his feet and closed the short distance between them. Wrapping her in his arms, he pulled her against his chest and cradled her there. Over her shoulder, he saw that the others had woken and were watching them expectantly. Closing his eyes, he bowed his head and pressed his lips against her neck.

"I'd find you anywhere," he murmured.

She rested her hands on his chest and tilted her head back to look at him. "I know you would."

Brushing the hair back from her face, he memorized every one of her proud features as his fingers trailed over her skin. "Okay, we'll do it," he relented.

CHAPTER NINETEEN

QUINN STARED at the shifting sand of the desert as she tossed the trash bag into the dumpster behind the bar. She didn't sense anyone out there watching her, but somehow she knew he was. Now that she'd finally persuaded Julian to use her as bait, they had to figure out a way to lure her stalker out into the open. She didn't think the vamp would buy her wandering around alone in the desert all helpless.

She didn't do helpless well, and Julian had been stead-fastly by her side this entire time. No one would believe he'd left her to her own devices. The breeze blew her hair back from her face, the strands of it tickling her cheeks.

She could walk out into the desert right now. Glancing behind her, she stared at the open kitchen door before shaking her head and turning away. If she took off now, Julian would have her head. He'd agreed to let her be the bait, but it was supposed to be under controlled circum-stances, or at least as controlled as they could be.

She climbed the back steps and returned to the kitchen. Wiping the sweat from her brow, she nodded to the two cooks and washed her hands at the sink before entering the crowded bar. Julian stood at the end of the bar, his elbow leaning casually against it, but she sensed the tension in his rigid muscles.

Pausing beside him, she rose on her toes to give him a kiss on the cheek. "Don't worry so much."

"I think that's impossible not to do right now."

Quinn tied her apron around her waist before patting his cheek. "I'll be fine."

Before he could respond, she walked down the back of the bar to take the orders of the customers there. The hours passed in a blur of orders, drinks, and gossip about the people who had never returned from the bonfire last night. Talk of what the police were doing, at what was now a crime scene, ran rampant amongst the patrons.

Some whispered that the missing people had been taking part in some sort of satanic ritual that had gone wrong. Others believed a pack of rabid coyotes had taken them all, but the ones who believed that didn't have an explanation for how so many of their things had ended up in the fire. Still, others thought the party had been attacked by a gang as an initiation requirement. Very few assumed any of them were still alive.

Missing fliers were already going up all over town; a few of them decorated Clint's front window. The smiling people in those photos only served to reinforce her determination to stop this vamp no matter what it took.

About halfway through the night, Jeb, Ross, and Ernie came in again with a few other ranch hands. "What can I get you?" Quinn asked them.

"Beer please," Jeb replied before the others made their requests.

Quinn filled their orders and placed them on the bar. "I thought you weren't going back to the ranch?"

"Just stopped by to check on some things today," Jeb replied.

"You still having trouble out there?"

Jeb shook his head and took a swallow of his beer. "Checked the video but nothing new has been recorded in a few days. Whatever it was seems to have moved on."

"Probably coyotes," Ernie said.

"On speed," Ross muttered.

"I don't know what it was, but I'm glad they've moved on," Jeb said and pushed a ten across the bar toward Quinn. "Can we get some quarters for pool?"

Quinn grabbed the money and went to make change for them. "Thanks," Jeb said when she returned and handed him his quarters. She watched as they walked away before returning to work.

When the bar finally closed, she couldn't help but think that even though she was tired, now was the perfect time to tempt her stalker. "Maybe if you leave while I close up, he'll come around," she suggested to Julian when he remained sitting at the bar after the last person had left.

His jaw locked, a red ring encircled his pupil. "I don't think he'll buy that," he muttered.

"We don't know what he'll buy," she replied.

Julian rose stiffly and walked over to grasp her arms. "Turn your tracking app on, now."

She pulled her phone from her pocket and turned the app on. He stared at her phone before bending to kiss her forehead. She watched as he walked out of the bar with Chris, Lou, Luther, and Melissa. She looked over at Dani, Hawtie, and Clint, who were collecting the last of the glasses from the poolroom. It wouldn't look so obviously like they were trying to trap her stalker if she had some other people with her. She hoped, anyway.

She finished cleaning the bar and placed the rest of the glasses in the dishwasher. Her gaze repeatedly went to the window, but everything beyond remained hushed. The normal sounds of the ticking clock and the hum of the coolers had her on edge. Every noise made her feel as if she were going to jump out of her skin, but as time went on, nothing happened.

"It may take him a while to believe Julian isn't around," Dani said.

"Maybe," Quinn replied, but she couldn't tear her gaze away from the window.

CHAPTER TWENTY

FOR THE NEXT THREE NIGHTS, whenever Quinn would close the bar, he would go out to the desert and pace. The others would remain in the truck, watching him as he ran through the sand, trying to keep himself from going back to Quinn.

He would wait with his senses as attuned to Quinn as he could get them. He checked the tracking on his phone almost every minute to make sure she was still at the bar. At the end of the night, Quinn would call him to let him know she had returned home without incident. She'd begun making comments about ditching Dani, Hawtie, and Clint too, or at least Dani, but he'd adamantly refused.

On the fourth night, he couldn't take the idea of returning to the desert and the endless pacing anymore. "We're going to the ranch," he said brusquely to Luther who was sitting behind the wheel of the truck.

"What ranch?" Luther asked.

"The one where Jeb and his crew were having trouble."

"Do you know where it is?"

"Clint told me it's about five miles that way," he pointed down the road past Hawtie's and in the opposite direction of the ghost town where he and Quinn had killed the other vampires. "He said it's called *The Rising Moon Ranch.* We'll see the sign for it."

"You're willing to go that far away from her?"

Julian's teeth ground together; he glanced through the window of Clint's Bar. He could see Dani, Clint, and Quinn cleaning up. Hawtie sat at the end of the bar doing the books for her strip club. Quinn laughed at something Dani said and threw her rag at her. The smile on her face made his heart clench.

"We have to do something," he grated.

Luther shifted the truck into drive. Julian grabbed hold of the side and launched himself over and into the truck bed. He landed silently beside Melissa and Chris. Resting his hand on the roof, he kept himself braced as Luther pulled out of the parking lot and drove through the main road of the small town. His gaze remained latched on Quinn through the window of the bar until she faded from view.

The cool wind blew against his skin as he turned to face forward in the truck. He shivered against the cold. When this was over, he was taking Quinn somewhere near the equator for a relaxing vacation of endless nights and days with only each other.

He narrowed his eyes against the stinging wind as he watched the dark ribbon of road unfolding before them. In less than a mile, the businesses and homes comprising the main stretch of town faded away, and they were left with only the moon, stars, and headlights to guide them. The endless rise and fall of the dunes spread out all around. The stark beauty of it wasn't lost upon him, but the clawing sensation to return to Quinn made it difficult for him to focus on anything other than getting to the ranch.

After a few more minutes, Julian spotted a wooden sign on the side of the road with *The Rising Moon Ranch*, written on it. Kneeling, he knocked on the back window and pointed to it. "Stop at the edge of the drive!" he called to Luther.

Luther pulled onto the dirt drive and parked the truck.

"I know Jeb said they weren't having any more trouble, but I think it would be better if we go on foot from here," Julian said as he leapt out of the back of the truck. "Don't need to announce our presence with an engine, if we don't have to."

The others climbed out of the truck to join him. "I'll go ahead. If I see anything threatening, I'll come back and let you know. I'll also take care of the cameras as I go. Move the truck down the road and find a place to park it out of sight."

Before they could respond, he turned and loped down the drive, pouring on the speed as he raced toward the ranch. He'd remain undetected by the cameras he saw amongst the Joshua trees planted beside the drive, but the others wouldn't. Moving behind each camera, he leapt up or climbed the trees until he was high enough to tear the cameras from them. He ground each one beneath his boot before racing to the next one.

He listened for the small, tinging noise each camera made as he moved. No human would hear the noise, but it alerted him to a few well-hidden cameras he might have missed if he hadn't been searching for it.

Toward the end of the drive, another sign stretched from two wooden beams over the road. The name of the ranch was sprawled across the large board in the middle. Julian slowed when the massive main house came into view. It had been built to resemble a log cabin that could rival some of the ski lodges he'd seen in his lengthy life.

Cactuses and colorful rocks decorated the main landscape surrounding the wraparound porch. Lights shone in the lower windows, but he didn't detect any heartbeats, nor did he scent any life inside the home.

To the right of the house was a smaller building with glass windows all around it. As he neared it, he detected the scent of sawdust from recent construction work on the building. Glancing in one of the windows, he spotted a rolling chair set up before a large desk with TV monitors. The black TV screens shone in the light overhead.

He pulled his phone out to make sure Quinn was still at the bar before lifting his head to scan for more cameras in the few trees around him. Moving rapidly around the property, he tore down the rest of the cameras he heard and saw around the perimeter of the property. He smashed them all before returning to the security shack.

Circling toward the back of the main house, he slid down a small hill and stopped to take in the barns and pastures tucked behind the home. Acres of green land sprawled out as far as he could see. In the center of all the rolling pastures, fences, and wooden shelters for the animals, a lake shimmered in the moonlight. He didn't know if the lake was natural or if it had been dug to collect the scarce rainwater and more water was piped into the ranch from somewhere else.

His gaze scanned the horizon. His nostrils flared as he tried to detect any odor beside that of the animals and blood on the air. The stringent aroma of bleach made his lip curl. The humans must have used it to clean up after the animals were slaughtered.

He continued around the main house, his gaze raking

over the horizon, but nothing stirred in the night. There weren't even any desert animals creeping in to steal some water. *The vampires have decimated the wild animals in this area too,* he realized. His blood felt colder than the night air blowing around him.

How many of them are out there?

His hand twitched toward his phone; he fought the impulse to call Devon and tell him to bring an army here. *Cassie can't be here,* he reminded himself. He'd die for Quinn without thinking twice about it, but if Cassie ever fell into the wrong hands, it would be even more disastrous than having Quinn fall into the hands of someone who knew about the prophecy.

Over the years, he'd considered himself one of the most selfish bastards on the planet. At one time, he wouldn't have cared about what the consequences would be for others, but not anymore. He couldn't risk the lives of everyone he cared about and many other innocents by involving Cassie in this. His hand fell back to his side. He closed his eyes against the anger and frustration warring within him.

The smell of Chris and Melissa alerted him to their presence before he heard their footsteps on the hill behind him.

"Wow," Chris breathed, his eyes fixed on the lake and rolling green pastures. "It's like an oasis back here."

"Beautiful," Melissa murmured before turning to him. "Do you sense anything?"

Julian shook his head, his gaze raking the horizon again. "I sense *no* life out here."

"That just made my skin crawl," Chris muttered. "What does *that* mean?"

"I believe there's a lot of vampires," Julian murmured and ran his hand through his hair. "More than I'd anticipated, and they're feasting."

"But if he's changing vamps and turning them to his will, there would be more deaths reported in the area, not only the Kemps," Melissa said.

"The Kemps were a message to Quinn, to all of us," Julian muttered. "This isn't a message. This is a mission."

"The vamps that killed Angie were slaughtering illegal aliens in order to go undetected by law enforcement. Could he be doing the same, but turning them instead?" Chris asked.

"He could," Julian replied, "but I'm not sure he's created the vampires who are here. I think he may have brought them in or perhaps someone else has, and they're all working together to try and get at Quinn. When he goes to turn vamps again, he'll go after people Quinn will notice missing, like the ones at the bonfire. He's trying to make a point."

"That he's batshit crazy?" Chris asked.

"Yes, and he can get at people close to her, no matter what we do."

Turning away from them, Julian walked the rest of the way around the house. On the other side of the building were five smaller log cabins. Behind the cabins was another larger building. For the ranch hands, he realized. The full-time help had their own little homes in these smaller cabins, but when more help was required, the bigger building was also utilized.

He cautiously approached the smaller cabins to peer into one of the windows. Shadows danced across the walls of the small kitchen and living room, but the orderly home looked untouched. He climbed back down the stairs and around to the larger building as Luther and Lou descended the hill toward them.

"This place gives creepy a whole new meaning," Lou said as he joined them.

Julian pulled his phone out; Quinn was still at the bar. He hit her number as he walked up the steps of the porch. She picked up on the first ring.

"Still at Clint's. Everything okay?"

His shoulders relaxed at the sound of her voice. "Just checking in."

"Should be home in half an hour."

"Call me when you get there."

"Will do. Love you."

"Love you too."

He'd expected some wiseass comment from one of the others about his final words to her when he hung up, but they were all focused on the large building before them. Melissa's head fell back to peer at the roof above their heads. "I don't know why, but I don't like this place."

Julian slid his phone into his pocket and scented the air. Like the other, non-residential buildings on the property, it smelled strongly of bleach with an undercurrent of blood. Julian couldn't think of a good reason why the ranch hands would have scrubbed this place with bleach, or why it would stink so much of blood.

He grabbed hold of Chris's arm when he grabbed for the knob. "Something's not right in there."

Chris glanced between him and the door before pulling the crossbow off his back and raising it before him. The others all pulled their stakes and weapons free and braced themselves.

"What if there's an alarm?" Melissa inquired.

"If there is, we'll be out of here before the police arrive," Julian replied.

"Will you be able to enter?" Lou asked him.

"This place may have residents occasionally, but no one calls it home."

Julian nodded toward Luther then the door. Luther moved in between Chris and the building. Grabbing the door handle, he shoved the door open. A series of small beeps sounded, but no alarm blared as Julian swept inside.

"Why wasn't the door locked and the alarm on?" Lou asked.

"Whatever is in here, someone wants us to see it," Julian replied as he moved further into the building.

The scent of blood was more potent inside; it tickled his nostrils and pricked his fangs. Beneath the blood, he detected the stringent aroma of cleaning chemicals and sweaty men. The faint smell of livestock from the worker's clothing also lingered.

"Stay close to me," he commanded the others.

He walked through the kitchen and into what he assumed was the dining room because of the hutch and breakfast bar, but there was no table or chairs in the room. Instead, two twin beds were set up within. A chill slid down his back as he stared at the neatly made beds. He didn't think the beds had been placed here because the hands had required more sleeping space. He didn't know why they were in this room, but he was certain they'd find out before they left.

"What is going on here?" Melissa whispered.

"This is the part in the horror movie when you start screaming at the people in it to run," Chris replied. "And then call them idiots for staying."

"I think you're right," she said.

So did Julian, but he continued past the dining room and into the living room. It took up half of the building. Three large TVs, a pool table, foosball table, and a bar were set up within the room for the workers. His gaze swept over the paneled walls and wooden floors as he moved through the space, but he saw no evidence of blood anywhere.

Coming back around to the front door, he peered up the stairs to the second floor before jerking his head toward it. He kept his back pressed against the wall as he crept up the stairs. His ears strained to hear any noise other than the solid thumps of the hearts behind him. The wall across from him blocked his view of what lay beyond until he was nearly to the top of the stairs.

The scent of blood became more cloying here, but he still saw no sign of it. Two twin beds in the hall upstairs came into view. His hand wrapped around the banister as he continued upward. Chris's breath was warm against his neck, his breathing silent from all of his years of training to be a lethal killer of vampires. Melissa was just as quiet, and Luther and Lou wouldn't have been detected by anything other than their heartbeats to a vampire.

Julian rounded the corner upstairs and walked down the hall toward the room at the end. Turning the knob, he shoved the door open with the toe of his boot. The potent scent of blood hit him like a punch to the face. Staying low, he moved swiftly into the room, searching for a threat that he still couldn't see.

Rising to his full height, his eyes latched onto the macabre scene in the corner of the room. He assumed this had been a bedroom, but there were no beds within. Instead, there was only two dressers and the missing dining room table and chairs. Propped into the chairs surrounding the table, a family sat staring at the food before them.

Moving closer, Julian realized the mother and father had silverware clasped within their hands. The duct tape wrapped around them kept their fists closed around the forks and knives. The two young girls had their heads bent toward each other, but he couldn't see their faces as their backs were to him. The young boy across the table had his head propped up and turned toward the doorway.

"One minute Barry was opening the front door, and the next thing I knew they were on us," he remembered Quinn once saying to him. His gaze slid back toward the door through which he'd entered, past the others gawking at the scene before him.

He realized that Barry had been watching the door before the vampires had knocked on it. He'd been waiting for them to arrive, had known they were coming.

Quinn probably wouldn't have noticed such a detail at the time, but if her stalker had been watching them from outside, he would have seen Barry waiting. Disgust and unease twisted through him as he walked around the table to see the two girls. His eyes were drawn to the young girl wearing a golden locket that looked far too much like the one Quinn wore. He recalled that she hadn't worn the locket until after Betsy died; it had been her cousin's before then.

So that girl was supposed to be Betsy, he deduced, and the one next to her was supposed to be Quinn. He braced himself before he turned his gaze toward the other girl. Facial structure wise, she looked a little like Quinn with her high cheekbones and full lips, but her nose was larger and her cloudy eyes were blue. She had a jagged slice from her temple across to her right eyebrow; another one ran from her lip to under her chin. The well of blood from the gashes let him know they'd been inflicted while the girl was still alive.

Both of the girls appeared to be in their teens and looked as if they were talking in conspiring whispers as they leaned toward each other. Both of them were smiling. However, the smiles weren't real. They'd been carved into their faces, Joker style, to reveal the cheek muscle. Goose bumps broke out on his arms; he couldn't bring himself to tear his gaze away from the one who was supposed to be Quinn.

The others crept closer as he studied the scene. "Is their hair dyed?" Melissa asked in a harsh whisper.

Julian glanced at the head before him. The boy's body had been tied into the chair with a rope, as had all the others, but a nail had been driven through the back of his skull. A piece of rope ran from the nail to the chair in order to keep the head tilted back. Judging by the amount of blood it was another wound received while still alive.

Through all of the dark hair, he saw splotches of dye against the boy's skull and strands of gold that hadn't taken to the dye. He walked to the father and spotted the same thing amongst his hair. "It is," he confirmed.

Melissa rubbed her hands over her arms. "Why does that make this somehow worse?"

Julian didn't know the answer, but the exquisite attention to detail that monster had paid to this scene was something he understood. He'd once enjoyed taunting and torturing people too. Minus the children, this was something he would have done in the past in order to play with and torment someone.

Nothing drove a person madder than the loss of their loved ones in an atrocious way, and if he'd fixated on someone good and pure, he would do everything in his power to drive them mad before destroying them. He'd played the game often over the centuries.

This scene had been set up for Quinn, to unnerve her and upset her, but thankfully, she hadn't been here for it. It had been set for him too. He may not know who this vampire was, but the man was aware of who *he* was, and the vamp was letting him know that and reminding him of his past with this display. Julian's nails dug into his palms; they tore through his flesh to spill his blood.

He'd never felt sorry or guilty about his past; he couldn't change it, but for the first time, he wished he'd been someone better, someone good. He'd helped to bring this level of maliciousness and lunacy against them by the deeds he'd once committed. If this prick knew half of what Julian had done over the centuries and planned to use it to taunt him, then there were a lot more fun times ahead.

What the asshole didn't know was he'd picked the wrong vampire to screw with this time. He may have heard some of the things Julian had done over the years, but that was only the tip of the iceberg. This vampire would see the rest of that iceberg before Julian was done with him.

"Why would he put them in a bedroom and not in the dining room?" Melissa inquired.

"To build the suspense," Julian replied.

"The creepy beds in the dining room," Lou said.

"Exactly."

"Are they going to turn?" Lou asked nervously as he walked around to inspect the girls. "That's awful." His skin turned a pale shade of green as his hand went to his mouth, but he managed to keep himself from vomiting.

"They won't turn," Julian replied. "Judging by the smell, they've been here for at least a day."

"How did he know we would find them?" Chris asked as he walked around the table. "Wow, he turned them into the Joker. This guy is warped in a way I've never known before."

"If you'd known me a hundred years ago, you wouldn't say that," Julian replied. "Or ten years ago, or if you'd known what I really planned to do with Cassie." Their heads turned slowly toward him. He detected the increased beats of their hearts and the heightened smell of sweat on their bodies. "This is a message to me too. He knows who I am, and he's not afraid, but he should be. He should be *very* fucking afraid."

Melissa gulped. Beside him, Lou took a small step away.

"You did something like this before?" Chris inquired.

"Minus the children, yes, I've done something exactly like this, and worse."

"How could it be any worse?" Melissa whispered.

Julian met and held her frightened gaze. "It can always get worse, if your mind is twisted enough and you have no care for anything else."

An uncomfortable silence filled the room as they shifted nervously around him. Julian pulled his phone from his pocket and checked to make sure Quinn was still at the bar. Luther cleared his throat before speaking. "Do you think you could figure out his next move?"

"If it was me, and I still wasn't ready for Quinn, I'd go for one of you next, or someone else close to her."

"Crap." Chris's head fell into his hand. "And all the while he'll be growing an army of vamps."

"He may have pawns, but he'll be the one calling the shots," Julian said. "We have to get back to town, *now*."

"What about the bodies?" Lou inquired.

"Leave them," Julian replied briskly. "You've touched nothing and I took care of the cameras. We have to go."

"But who were they?" Lou demanded.

"The police will figure that out when they're discovered, or we'll discover it ourselves if we hear of a missing family from town. There is nothing we can do about it now."

He went to walk around the table, but froze when he spotted something clasped within the faux Quinn's hand.

Frowning, he grabbed hold of her cold hand and pried open her fingers.

"What are you doing?" Melissa gasped while Lou groaned loudly.

Julian tugged the piece of paper free and opened it. His blood ran cold when he read the words scrawled on it.

CHAPTER TWENTY-ONE

QUINN FINISHED WIPING the bar off and tossed her rag into the laundry bag at her feet. It had been a good night tip-wise, but she couldn't wait to go home and sleep. This limbo of not knowing who or what was going to come after her next had made her twitchy and she hated it.

"All set?" Clint asked as he spun the keys around his index finger.

"All set," she replied as she untied the strings of her apron and tossed it into the laundry bag. C.J. would pick it up in the morning and take it over to the laundromat to be cleaned. She turned off the bar lights as she moved toward the others standing by the door. Clint opened the door for them. They all hurried down the stairs and into the brisk night.

Clint locked the door behind them just as a set of headlights illuminated the road. Quinn shielded her sensitive eyes against the set of brights coming at them far faster than they should be. She took a step back as the truck skidded into the parking lot sideways. At first, she thought it was Julian and the others returning early, but then she realized the truck was red, instead of black.

"Is that Jeb?" Clint asked.

"It is," she confirmed.

Jeb jumped from the pickup and started across the lot toward them. His normal cowboy hat wasn't in place. His blond curls hung in tangled disarray around his face as he limped toward them. Blood smeared the right side of his face, and his hand kept hold of his right thigh as he dragged his foot behind him on the ground.

"Jeb! My God, what happened?" Hawtie demanded as she and Clint rushed toward him.

Quinn's eyes shot around the deserted parking lot and the night beyond. Nothing moved out there, but the hair on her nape rose. "Someone attacked me!" Jeb cried. "I was heading back north when I came on a broken-down car. I pulled over to see if the guy needed help. He jumped me, beat me, and stole my wallet. When I woke he was gone."

"Here, Quinn." Clint held the keys out to her. "Open the door. We'll get him inside and call the police."

She snatched the keys from Clint's hand before climbing the stairs. Unlocking the door, she flung it open and stepped aside for the others to enter. She shut and locked the door behind them. Hawtie settled Jeb onto one of the chairs at the bar. He winced and grabbed his thigh, his face twisting in pain as he rubbed at it.

"I'm so sorry, Jeb," Quinn said.

"You know the old saying, 'No good deed goes unpunished,'" he replied.

Something about those words made her adrenaline kick into hyper-drive; she spun back toward the window to keep watch. She half-expected to see a horde of vampires lining up across the street, but nothing stirred.

She tried to rid herself of the sense of impending doom as she looked at the others. Clint lifted the phone from the cradle and punched in numbers. He'd just put it to his ear when the first gunshot rang out. Quinn jumped, and a startled cry tore from her. A bullet couldn't kill her, but she almost threw herself to the floor out of reflex.

Her eyes shot around the room as the coppery scent of blood filled the air. A strangled cry escaped her when she spotted the red seeping across the front of Hawtie's body-hugging white shirt. Hawtie's red, full mouth parted as she gawked at the bloodstain growing across her chest. Her eyes flickered toward Jeb before they rolled up in her head and she slumped to the side.

"Chelsea!" Clint bellowed and leapt across the bar at her.

Breaking free of her paralysis, Quinn lurched toward Hawtie. Her arms wrapped around her friend, catching her before she could hit the floor.

What happened? I don't understand!

She fell to the ground with Hawtie. Blood seeped through Quinn's fingers, pooling beneath her. Memories of holding Julian like this and feeling his blood assailed her as she struggled to comprehend what had happened. Her head fell back when she realized who had fired the shot. She stared in dismay at Jeb's hazel eyes—so unseeing, so unaware of what he'd done.

"Chelsea!" Clint fell to the ground on the other side of her. "No! Oh no, no, no," he groaned as he grabbed hold of her chin and turned her head toward him. Tears rolled freely down his face to fall on Hawtie's cheek. "Don't you leave me!"

Quinn didn't know if she wanted to scream in rage or cry as she held her friend in her lap. She had saved Julian. Perhaps she could save Hawtie too, without killing Jeb.

Hawtie was still alive, and she was human. She wouldn't need the amount of life force Julian had required. She had to do something soon. With every slowing beat of Hawtie's heart, she pumped more blood onto the floor around them.

Quinn lurched for Jeb, attempting to grab him so she could yank him from the stool as he turned the gun toward his own temple. Hawtie's body in her lap caused her to miss his leg. "No!" she shrieked.

Beneath her knees, she felt a strange swelling within the earth. The jolt of electricity Dani unleashed shot Jeb straight out of his chair and onto his ass. Knocked from his hand, the gun clattered onto the ground and rattled as it spun across the floor. Quinn wrapped her arms protectively around Hawtie in case it went off.

Dani leapt at Jeb, grabbing hold of his legs when he began to crawl across the floor toward his gun. Quinn shifted Hawtie onto Clint's lap and jumped to her feet as Jeb's hand encircled the gun. He spun around and aimed the weapon directly at Dani's head.

She threw herself to the floor and screamed as the bullet sliced across her face, tearing away flesh and a piece of her ear before smashing into Quinn's shoulder. The force of the bullet knocked Quinn off her feet. A grunt escaped her when she crashed onto the floor. She heard a crack as one of her ribs gave way, but she couldn't be sure over the agony of the bullet searing into her arm.

Another gunshot caused her to flinch. She rolled to the side, determined to get to Jeb before he could inflict any more damage, but when she rose, she realized she was too late. There was nothing left of Jeb to stop. Tears burned her eyes at the sight of his bloody and mutilated body, but she had no time to grieve the loss. She had another friend who needed her now.

Falling beside Hawtie once more, she trembled as she rested her hands on Hawtie's chest. The only life she had to feed into Hawtie was her own. It would have to be enough. Lifting her good arm to her mouth, she bit deep into her wrist and pressed it against Hawtie's mouth.

"What are you doing?" Clint demanded.

"Keeping her alive, I hope."

She pressed the blood to Hawtie's mouth as Dani knelt beside her with unused rags from behind the bar. Dani pressed the towels against the bullet wound to staunch the blood flowing from Hawtie's chest.

"Use me to heal her," Clint said to her.

"I killed Zach. I won't take that chance with you," Quinn murmured.

"You were going to use Jeb, don't deny it."

"That was before I was injured too, and now I'm *hungry* in more ways than you can imagine."

Clint's eyes were unwavering as they held hers. "I'd rather be dead than live without her."

"I won't chose one of your lives over the other, and she already has my blood in her. That will at least help her heal faster and keep her alive longer. Now, let me do what I have to do."

Tears glistened in his eyes as he hovered anxiously by her side. She forced herself to tune him out as she focused on the pulse of life she felt emanating from Hawtie, calling to her. Quinn removed her wrist from Hawtie's mouth; she couldn't risk changing her if this didn't work.

Her hands shook when she placed them over Hawtie's wound. Focusing her attention on her friend, she let the flow of her life entwine with Hawtie's. The octopus tentacles she always imagined her power being like latched onto Hawtie, but instead of pulling the life from her, Quinn pushed her own life into her friend.

Her body shook as the life flowed outward; the skin on her hand wrinkled and shriveled before her eyes. The bones in the backs of her hands stood out as her skin became so white she could have given Casper a run for his money. Her forearms thinned to the point where the bones were evident, but she kept her hands pressed against Hawtie's chest. She'd give every drop of life she could if it meant saving her friend.

Her knees had begun to dig uncomfortably into the ground when Hawtie gasped and her eyes flew open. The warm brown of her eyes latched onto Quinn. Her hands grasped hold of Quinn's; her grip was stronger than she'd had expected it to be, or perhaps she'd just become that weak.

"Quinn?" Hawtie asked.

Quinn fell back, wincing as her tailbone made contact with the floor. She sat as her body shook and jerked on the floor. She tried desperately to get control of herself, but she felt like a fish out of water right then. Hunger burned through her body, searing her veins as her fangs slid free. But more than blood, she needed to *devour,* to feel the life of another flowing into her.

She threw her hands up to stop Clint from grabbing her arms. "No, don't. I don't know if I can control myself right now. Dani, we have to get out of here." In the distance, she heard the first wails of a siren echoing across the desert. "I need help," she murmured and held her arm up.

Dani rushed to her side and grasped hold of her. Quinn winced as the motion caused her bones to grate together. *Don't feed. Don't feed.* She told herself as she felt her power seeking out Dani. "Let go of me," she said to Dani who released her instantly.

Julian's blood and some coyote's blood and I'll be as good as new. I'll get some life from Julian; I won't kill him.

As she thought it, something bashed into the front door. Wood splinters flew inward and the door crashed into the wall with enough force to shake the building. Quinn's head shot up as the monster who had been destroying their town, and who had helped murder her family, strode into the bar.

A smile curved his mouth when his eyes latched onto her. "Not your best look, but just the way I wanted you."

Quinn's mouth fell open. Dani sucked in a loud breath beside her, and Clint lurched toward one of the stools. It clattered to the floor as he jerked on it and dragged it toward him. Taking his forearm, he smashed it on one of the legs. The leg broke off, and he snatched it up to use it as a stake before he positioned the stool protectively in front of Hawtie.

The monster's turquoise eyes, the only thing remotely attractive about him, slid toward Hawtie, and he released a snort of laughter. "That won't stop me, old man." His eyes came back to Quinn. "But your woman did drain her some."

Horror pooled through Quinn as she realized they'd been set up. The minute he'd sent Jeb in here, he'd intended for all of this to happen, or at least most of it. She was drained; she didn't know how Dani's power worked, but she knew a large blast often left Hunters and vampires depleted.

His eyes fixated on Quinn. The hideously awful hair curling out from the mole at the corner of his left eye actually seemed to wave or to be laughing at her. Quinn fought back a tremor as the man approached. He was as rail thin as she recalled and taller than Julian, perhaps six foot three or four. His arched cheekbones, flaring nostrils, and thin lips gave him a rat-like appearance.

Behind him, a dozen more vampires entered the bar. They fanned out around him to fill the room. "The police are coming," Quinn said.

"And we'll either slaughter them when they do, or you'll leave willingly," he replied.

"I'll never go anywhere with you."

His eyes raked over her disdainfully. "You don't have a choice. Either everyone in here dies, plus whoever else is coming, or you walk out the door with us now."

Quinn tried to feel the pulse of something within her, but most of her life force had flowed into Hawtie. If she could get her hands on someone...

Her eyes latched onto him, and she licked her lips as she felt the wash of power emanating from him. Beside her, she felt the pulse in the earth she'd experienced before Dani had released her blast of electricity.

"Bitch," Rat-Face sneered, his eyes shooting to Dani.

He lunged forward. His hand wrapped around Dani's throat as he lifted her off the ground. Quinn felt the electricity that shot out of Dani and toward him, but he'd interrupted her before she could get a big buildup going, and he'd been prepared for her jolt. His lip curled to reveal his fangs as his fingers dug into Dani's throat.

Before he could tear it out, Quinn lunged forward and grabbed hold of his arm. A low moan escaped her as life flowed back into her veins. Rat-Face threw Dani over the bar and into the shelves lining the backside of it. Bottles and shelves toppled over and broke. Alcohol poured over Dani as she slumped to the floor.

The man spun on Quinn. She tried to duck out of the way of the fist he swung toward her, but even with his life filling her, she was sluggish and awkward. His punch smashed into her temple, staggering her sideways. White stars burst before her eyes, and her grasp on his arm loosened enough that he was able to jerk it away from her.

Her hand flew to one of the stakes strapped at her side, and her fangs lengthened as a hiss escaped her. The wail of the sirens grew closer. Clint jumped to his feet and charged at another vampire coming toward her. He used the broken stool leg like a stake, but missed his intended target's heart when the man ducked. He plunged the stake into the vamp's shoulder instead.

Quinn managed to avoid Rat-Face's grasp, but the arms of another wrapped around her waist and hauled her up against a massive chest.

"Got her!" a man shouted triumphantly, then groaned in anguish when Quinn threw her head back and smashed it into his nose with a loud thwack.

The fresh scent of coppery blood filled the air as another vampire backhanded Clint and sent him flying across the room into the wall. Hawtie cried out when he slumped to the ground. Quinn drew on the life force of the vampire holding her as she thrashed to break free of his hold. He made strange, gurgling noises as his life force filled her cells with vitality once more.

Instead of growing tired from the repeated use of her ability, she felt invigorated as it greedily sought to replenish what it had lost. She suspected Julian's blood had helped to make her stronger, or perhaps her power was growing and changing. She'd only taken life or zapped people away from her before, but now she'd given life, twice—a sign her power had already begun to expand.

She bared her fangs, snapping as Rat-Face came closer to her. She jerked away from the vamp who had grabbed her and lunged toward Rat-Face again. Swinging her stake outward, she sliced open his shirt and chest. The smell of his blood filling the air caused bloodlust to surge within her.

She'd tear his throat open, sink her fangs deep into his vein, and drain him until he could barely move. Then she would take her time with him. She swung at him again, but though she'd managed to refill some of her life force, she was still underweight and moving at a slower pace than normal.

He managed to avoid a blow that would have spilled his intestines by jumping back at the last second. Quinn snarled and dove at him. Her hands grabbed hold of his chest when something hit her from behind with enough force to crack her skull. She cried out as pain exploded through her head. The stake clattered to the ground when her hands instinctively flew to the back of her caved in skull. It felt as if her brain was compressing, and she supposed it actually *was* compressed.

The world around her lurched, and she took a stumbling step to the side as the wooden floor of the bar became the sandy desert. Was she inside still? Was she outside? She couldn't bring anything into focus as the synapses in her squished brain misfired. Falling to the side, she hit something hard enough to break it. The world went dark.

CHAPTER TWENTY-TWO

JULIAN SHOVED dark sunglasses on to cover eyes he knew were red as he pushed his way through the crowd gathered outside the bar. A pudgy man tried to block him, but Julian shoved him out of the way as he climbed the steps.

"I'll arrest you for assaulting a police officer!" the man shouted at him.

Julian spun on him. "I'll tear your throat out if you try!"

The man took an awkward step back and bumped into the doorway of the building. Clint hurried forward; his hand wrapped around Julian's arm as he pulled him away. A large bruise in the shape of a hand covered the right side of Clint's face.

"Sorry about that, Ed," Clint apologized. "This is Quinn's boyfriend. He must have assumed she was still here. You know how it is to worry 'bout someone, I'm sure."

"Oh," Ed replied, but his hand still rested on the butt of his gun as he gave Julian a scathing glance. "You'd think he'd know where his girlfriend is."

Julian snarled at the reminder that he had absolutely no

idea where she was, and that was *his* fault. The tracking app said she was still here, but Clint had just said she wasn't. He didn't see her anywhere amongst the crowd, nor could he *feel* her close by.

"Easy," Clint murmured to him. "Killing him won't get us anywhere. Just walk away. It's the best thing you can do for Quinn right now."

"Where is she?" he hissed between his teeth.

Clint shook his head, drawing him aside as paramedics lifted a stretcher with Hawtie strapped to it. Her hand reached out to Clint, and he hurried to her side. He bent low so Hawtie could whisper in his ear. Clint nodded briskly and gave her a brief kiss before stepping away. Julian's eyes scanned the blood splattering the bar floor, the broken shelves, and mirror behind the bar.

"What did she say?" he demanded of Clint.

"To stay with you until we find Quinn. It's all she cares about right now."

Julian's eyes landed on the black body bag on the floor. It wasn't Quinn. He would know if it was. A piece of him would already be broken. He would be a monster, unstoppable in his determination to destroy anything that got in his way. Was it Dani?

Walking over, he grabbed the zipper and jerked it back to reveal the ruined remains of Jeb's head.

"Hey!" Ed shouted at him. "I don't care who you are! You touch one more thing in this room, and I'm throwing your ass in jail."

"What is wrong with you?" Clint demanded as he pulled him away.

"Where is she, Clint?"

"Not here. They took her." The entire bar became enshrouded in a haze of red so thick he imagined it was much like what Hell looked like. And that was exactly what he was in right now, Hell. They'd taken her, he had no idea where, and the sun was about to rise. "The police don't know that. I told them I'd sent her home early, and we need to keep up that appearance."

Julian barely heard Clint's words through the thrumming pulse of fury pounding in his head. "Her phone?"

"It fell out of her pocket when they carried her out."

His gaze slid over the bar again as he sniffed at the blood in the room. Some of it was Quinn's. The rest was human and...

His head turned as he caught a different scent. Hurrying over, he peered behind the bar to where two male paramedics knelt on either side of Dani. They were taking her pulse and blood pressure. She grabbed hold of one of their hands when they tried to put a neck brace on her and shoved them away.

"I told you, I'm fine," she said testily.

"You could have a concussion and you should be checked out," the other one argued.

"I'm fine," she insisted. "I'm not going to the hospital. Now leave me be."

"You have to sign paperwork saying you refuse."

"Yeah, whatever, just get away from me with that thing."

The other one shook his head and rolled his eyes. "Idiot," he muttered, earning him a wrathful glare from Dani.

Sensing his presence, Dani's head tilted back and her eyes widened on him. He could almost see her rethinking the hospital option, but in the end, she took a deep breath and pushed herself to her feet. She wobbled unsteadily for a minute, but managed to regain her balance before one of the paramedics grabbed hold of her arm.

"Miss, you really should be checked out. A concussion is nothing to mess around with," the man told her.

"Not the first, won't be the last," she muttered. "No sleep for this girl, I promise."

Finally giving up, the paramedics put away the last of their medical supplies and walked around the end of the bar. Dani rested her hands on the bar before him, her head bowed, but she finally forced it up. A long gouge had dug across her cheek toward her ear. The upper part of her right ear was a jagged mess as part of it had been torn away. The blood had been cleaned from the wounds and no longer flowed forth.

"I'm sorry. I tried." She shook her head, then winced and grabbed hold of it. "We'll find her, I swear it. I just don't remember…"

Julian could only stand and stare at her as her voice trailed off. He was scared if he moved even a millimeter, he would kill everyone and anyone standing nearby. He'd leave a trail of destruction wherever he went until he found her again.

When he did finally find her, would she even know who he was?

The possibility she wouldn't know him once he found her made the red haze intensify. Her captor could control minds; what would he do to her? What would he make her do? His fingers tore into the bar top, shredding the wood as his shoulders hunched up. His fangs sliced into his bottom lip.

"Everyone has to get out of here," Ed called from the front of the bar. "Even you, Clint. Hawtie's out now, you need to be too."

"We're going," Clint said.

Julian felt the man standing beside him before Clint's hand rested against his forearm. "You're a brave man," Julian grated.

"Perhaps, but we have to leave now. You have to get it together enough to get past the crowd out there."

Splinters dug beneath his fingernails. "He'll warp her mind—"

"Don't think of it. Keep it together. You'll find her, but if you spiral out of control now, it will never happen."

Julian reluctantly released his death grip on the bar and turned away from it. He kept his head down so he wouldn't be tempted by the pulsing heartbeats of those he passed as he made his way outside. Luther and the others fell in around him as they made their way to Quinn's apartment.

The first rays of the sun barely touched the horizon when he stepped inside the building. He stared at the rising ball of fire, despising it and his weakness to it.

"We need the RV," he said to Luther.

Luther nodded and hurried back out the front door. Julian remained unmoving, his gaze focusing on the sun as it crept higher into the sky to spill across his skin. His flesh began to sizzle and smoke curled around him. He welcomed the pain; he deserved it and more for allowing Quinn to be taken.

No, she had needed to draw her stalker out, and he understood her reasons for that. He'd wanted her far from here, but if their roles had been reversed, he wouldn't have left either, and he would have done everything he could to find and kill that bastard. The vamp had destroyed her family. Now he was tormenting her and menacing her town; she'd longed to make him pay.

"Julian, please," Melissa whispered. She rested her hand on his arm, trying to pull him back as blisters formed and burst on his flesh. "Someone could see, and you have to be at your strongest to look for her."

He hadn't felt the searing of the sun's warmth, and he didn't feel the coolness of the shadows when he stepped back into them. He leaned against the wall, his eyes fixed outside as he watched the RV approach. Luther hadn't come to a complete stop when Julian shoved open the door and strode over to the vehicle. He barely noticed the flames leaping to life on his fingertips as Luther shoved the door to the RV open.

He strode into the RV, the shadows smothering the flames from his body. "Hopefully no one saw that," Clint muttered as he climbed inside and settled at the table.

"Head toward the ranch," Julian commanded Luther as the others settled in around him. "The vampires were feeding there a lot. They may have a hideout nearby." Luther climbed into the driver's seat and shifted the engine into drive. Julian braced his hand against the ceiling as he focused on Dani and Clint. "Tell me exactly what happened."

Dani's head fell into her hands. "It's kind of a blur. I remember being outside and someone was attacked. Then we were inside and someone was shooting. Quinn, she became thinner?" The last statement was more of a question as she turned toward Clint.

Clint rested his hand on her arm. "That's the extremely shortened version. I'll tell them," he assured her.

Julian remained mute as he listened to Clint's retelling of everything that had occurred.

"He waited until you were both weaker before making his move," Chris said and pushed against Lou so he could slide into one of the bench seats around the table. Lou shot him a disgruntled look, but eventually slid over. "He purposely went for someone he *knew* Quinn would save."

"Yes," Julian rasped. His throat was parched from the fire and smoke that had drifted from him. His body had already begun to heal but hunger licked across his veins like lightning. "I need blood."

"There's some bags in the fridge," Luther replied and glanced at him in the rearview.

"I barely remember any of it," Dani muttered.

"It will come back to you," Melissa said. She opened the fridge and pulled out a half a dozen bags of blood before closing it again. "One good thing about being a Hunter, we heal fast. What happened to your ear?"

"My ear?" Dani reached up to touch her ears. She winced when her right hand made contact with the jagged wound. "What happened?"

"You were shot," Clint said. "But you're fine."

"Just missing a piece," she said.

"Yeah," Chris said.

"Quinn was shot too, in her shoulder," Dani recalled.

A sound he didn't recognize came from him at her words. Melissa kept her legs braced against the rocking of the RV as she made her way toward him. She handed the blood bags to him and rested her hand against the cabinets as he ripped the top off the first one and drained the contents in one swallow.

He tore into the next bag with the same enthusiasm, then the next until they were all gone. It did nothing to ease the bloodlust pulsating within him, but by the time he was finished, his skin had completely healed and he felt stronger.

Sliding past Melissa, he tossed the bags into the trash next to the sink and walked toward the front of the RV. Luther glanced at him as he rested his hand against the bed over Luther's head to brace himself. Tuning all of his senses to the world around him, he strained to catch any hint of Quinn's smell or presence amongst the endless desert.

CHAPTER TWENTY-THREE

QUINN WOKE SLOWLY. Her head throbbed like someone was beating on it with a hammer and her shoulder felt like a hot poker was digging into it. Her arms... why did they hurt so badly? They were above her head? What had happened?

Her eyes fluttered open before instantly closing again. The pain caused by just trying to look around was excruciating. She dimly recalled the last time she'd seen anything. It had felt like a bad acid trip as she hadn't been unable to figure out if she was inside or outside, and everything had seemed wrong. Someone had hit her with enough force to cave her skull in. She tried to move her hands so she could feel the back of her skull, but her fingers were numb and swollen.

Think. Feel your surroundings if you can't see them.

Taking a couple of seconds to gather her spinning mind, she gradually took stock of her body. She was standing, or at least it felt like she was in an upright position as she could feel air moving all around her body. There was no breeze; it was the simple ebb and flow of air currents as they traveled from one place to another.

Her arms *were* above her head. There was something cool and solid clasped around her wrists. *Chains*, she realized. She was chained with her hands above her head and... Yep, her ankles were chained too; she could feel the weight of the chains dragging against her legs when she tried to move them forward.

The metal clinked against something hard, concrete most likely. Lifting her head, she tried to open her eyes again. Blackness surrounded her, but for all she knew, it could be bright as day around her and her eyes still weren't working right from the blow she'd taken. She closed them again as the rest of the details of what had happened slowly came back to her.

They'd been set up, attacked, ambushed, and outmaneuvered. It had been a genius move to weaken her and Dani before coming for them. She wouldn't underestimate her opponent again. She'd also been shot. The burning in her shoulder was from the bullet making its way out of her body. She moved her feet, trying to turn on the chains she hung from. She was brought up short when they tightened to the point she couldn't move anymore.

If she were at full strength, or even at half her usual strength, she could've easily broken them. Right then, her muscles were cramped, her bones grated together in her shoulder blades, and she could feel her ribcage pressing against her skin.

When she'd been younger and still had pets, she'd once held her rabbit as it died after being attacked by the neighbor's cat. Beneath her hand, its coat had still been thick and fat still lined its body. However, a coldness she hadn't been able to understand at the time encompassed the animal.

Something had been broken within it, but her aunt and uncle hadn't been home to help her get it to the vet. So she'd held it, feeling the life fading from its tiny body until all that remained was the limp, lifeless shell.

She felt like that now, cold when she shouldn't be. Drained and fading. She wouldn't die, but if she didn't get blood and feed on someone's life force soon, she would be as helpless and weak as that rabbit against these vamps.

A creaking sound from her right caused her to go completely still. She kept her head bowed and unmoving as she listened to footsteps entering her place of imprisonment. There were at least three of them, she realized.

"Skinny thing. I can't see her being a menace to anyone," a woman's voice said.

"She's weakened right now, and we'll keep her that way until I can take control of her mind." *That* voice she recognized as Rat-Face. It took all she had to remain immobile and not fight against her chains until she tore free and beat him to death.

"I'm still not sure about that plan," the woman murmured.

"It's the only way we'll be able to keep her under control and make her do what we ask," Rat-Face replied.

"Hmm," the woman murmured. One of the footsteps approached her and began to circle. "But you could also make her do whatever you command against any of us."

"Come now, Helena, we must have trust between us."

"I trust no one," Helena replied, "especially not a man."

Quinn could feel the woman standing before her, staring at her. So not all of the vampires with Rat-Face were part of his burgeoning tribe. Judging by the vibe of power radiating from Helena, she was old. Older than Rat-Face, and Quinn craved her life force like a smoker craved nicotine.

"I must agree with Helena on this," another male said. "How are we to know you won't turn her against us?"

"I vow it," Rat-Face replied.

Helena released a bark of laughter. "I give more worth to fool's gold than your vow."

"Watch it," Rat-Face warned.

"Or you'll what, take control of my mind? Then everyone here would know you're not to be trusted."

"They wouldn't know if I did, and neither would you."

"Don't threaten me. *I'd* know, and I'd shred you before you could ever try and take control of me."

The other man snickered; Quinn could feel the tension in the room ratcheting up. She hoped the two of them tore each other to pieces and solved part of her problem, but neither of them made a move toward the other.

"What about Julian?" the other man asked.

"What about him?" Helena inquired.

"He'll come for her."

"Of course he will," Rat-Face replied. "And when he discovers his little girlfriend is under my control, we'll also have control of him. He'll do anything we say in order to ensure we don't hurt her."

"Are we sure she means so much to him?" Helena snorted. "Men tend to be fickle about women. He may move on; it's not like she's anything to look at."

Helena has a huge problem with men, Quinn decided.

"Maybe she's no beauty, but she's prettier when she's got some weight on her, and he'll come for her. I've seen the way he watches her, the way he treats her. She's special to him," Rat-Face replied.

"If they're mated we'll have him at our mercy," the other man said. "Did you check her neck for bite marks?"

"Any marks would have healed by now," Rat-Face replied.

"Perhaps, but if he's fed from her recently, they could still be on her body somewhere."

Quinn's stomach clenched. Julian had fed from her before she'd gone to work, but the bite mark was on her inner thigh. If they decided to strip her in order to look…

Don't move! She barked the order at herself, but it was taking everything she had not to squirm against the chains binding her when someone grabbed hold of her chin and turned her head back and forth.

"No marks," Rat-Face replied.

"Hmm. It would be a huge bonus for us if they were mates," the other man said. "We'd not only have control of the vampire of the prophecy, but also one of the remaining two Elders."

"Julian won't bow to our will, no matter whose mind we have under our control," Helena replied.

"How do you know?" Rat-Face demanded.

"I've met him, I know," Helena replied absently.

"We should strip her and see if there are any of his marks on her," the other male said. The eagerness of his voice made her already queasy stomach pitch and roll.

"And if there are, what would that prove? Have you never fed from another vampire in the throes of passion?" Helena asked.

"Perhaps, but I've never allowed another to feed from me."

"Well, aren't you special," Helena drawled. "I have." Another hand clasped hold of her chin. The tips of Helena's pointed fingernails dug into her skin as Helena lifted her chin and took a long, deep sniff of her neck. Seeming to find what she was looking for, Helena abruptly released Quinn.

Her chin slumped back to her chest. "There is another's blood in her, and it's powerful."

"Julian's?" Rat-Face asked.

"I can think of no one else's it would be," Helena replied.

"It's best if you let me at her mind," Rat-Face said. "If she's ours, we'll control them both."

"You're very eager for this, Earl," Helena replied. "Maybe too eager."

Earl! Quinn almost laughed at the innocuous name. Over the years, she'd imagined what his name would be, but could never come up with a name monstrous enough for the man who had laughed as he'd pinned her to the floor with his knives before draining her dry. Earl had never been one of the names to cross her mind. Satan or Lucifer had been her top two.

"I'm only eager to see us reclaim our rightful place, Helena. She could lead with me," Earl replied.

"Do you really think we would allow *you* to be our leader," the other man replied. "You're younger than either of us."

"I'm almost two centuries old," Earl replied.

"And we are nearing three hundred. You are still a teen in comparison."

"Fine," Earl relented, "but she could be my bride."

"If we agree to you taking control of her mind, I will not allow you to abuse her in such a way," Helena replied. "She is *not* to be touched by any man she does not give her willing consent to."

A man had once hurt her, Quinn realized and actually felt a stab of sorrow for the powerful woman standing next to her. The last thing Helena deserved was her pity, but she knew well what it was like to be at the mercy of others.

Quinn could practically feel Earl seething, but he didn't

argue with Helena. "Fine, she will simply do what she is told to do, when she is told to do it," he relented.

Quinn didn't buy that for one second, she doubted Helena did either, but the three of them finally stopped bickering. "When she wakes, we'll have her readied to be brought before the others. Perhaps we should get some weight back on her too," Helena murmured.

"If you're not going to let me control her, then keep her weak. She'll destroy anyone she gets her hands on otherwise."

"A weak vampire of prophecy is no good to us," the other man said. "If we're not able to use her to destroy our enemies, we might as well kill her now, so no one else can get their hands on her."

Apprehension slid down Quinn's spine. Helena's sharp tipped fingernails pinched her skin as she grabbed Quinn's chin once again. "You are right, what good is this pathetic creature to us? Earl, when she awakes take control of her mind."

No! The scream echoed within Quinn's head. Her heart twisted at the idea of this monster having control of her in such a way. If Helena thought Earl wouldn't use her in every way possible before turning her against anyone he deemed a threat to him, she was sadly mistaken.

"I have a feeling that won't be much longer," Earl replied.

Quinn heard a single footstep before a hand grasped her breast, twisting it cruelly as he fondled it. Instinct brought her instantly to life; she came up spitting at him as he laughed in her face. Quinn's fangs burst free of her mouth; rage poured through her body, replacing her physical weakness.

She swung her legs forward, jerking and twisting

violently against the chains binding her wrists and ankles in an attempt to break free. Earl released her breast and stepped away. Quinn lunged forward again, her fangs only inches from his face.

Something behind her gave a groaning creak. Metal bent and twisted as she swung her legs forward again. There was a lessening in the tightness of the chains as something gave way. She may not be at her strongest, but with her heritage and Julian's blood, she was still stronger than any normal vampire of her age would be.

"Guards!" Helena shouted.

Three vampires rushed into the room as Quinn swung her legs forward, dragging the heavy weight of the chain with her. She caught the first guard under the chin with the end of the chain. Blood burst from his mouth as he staggered into the wall. Twisting to the side, she smashed her feet into the chest of the next one who lunged at her. The force of her kick knocked him into the vampire behind him.

Swinging herself up, her feet hit the ceiling before she pushed herself down again. She landed on the shoulders of the third guard, causing him to grunt from the force of her weight. Her thighs clamped against the sides of the man's head. He howled and grabbed at her thighs as she began to compress his skull. Tentacles of power slithered out and latched onto the man's face. A groan of pleasure escaped her as more of his life seeped into her body, replenishing her strength.

Before she could feed from him too much, the chains clasped to her ankles were jerked down with enough force to knock her victim's feet out from under him. They toppled toward the ground together. A scream tore from Quinn when the chains binding her wrists abruptly stopped her fall. Her shoulders popped out of their joints with a resounding crack that reverberated within the small confines of the room.

Helena and the other man had scurried away from her, but Earl stood before her with a smug smile on his lips. He held up the chain he'd grabbed for her to see before slipping it over one of the massive metal hooks jutting from the wall. He turned to give a pointed look at Helena.

"Do you see why she must be kept under control?" he inquired.

"Yes," Helena murmured, her eyes filled with admiration and dread as they ran over Quinn.

Despite the excruciating pain it caused in her shoulders, Quinn strained against her bonds when Earl came at her with a malicious gleam in his eyes.

CHAPTER TWENTY-FOUR

JULIAN WOULD HAVE GIVEN anything to be able to get out of this RV and run through the desert in search of her. Being confined to this rolling tin can was making him edgier by the second. Turning away from where he stood by Luther, he paced to the back of the vehicle and through the doorway to the bedroom beyond. He caught a glimpse of his blazing red eyes and strained face when he walked past the bathroom. The thin thread holding the last of his control together felt about to fray.

Lou watched him warily when he walked back through, but the others kept their gazes focused outside. Chris turned toward him as Luther parked at the side of the road just past the driveway of The Rising Moon Ranch.

"Pull in there," Julian commanded.

"What if they've got the security system running again or if someone has shown up to watch the ranch?" Lou inquired.

"Then you'd better come up with some excuse for them," Julian said, "before I kill them."

Melissa rested her hand on Julian's arm, drawing his attention to her. She subtly shook her head as Lou nervously glanced away from him. Julian's teeth clamped together; he didn't have time to coddle a teenage Guardian right now. Every passing second was one more Quinn was in the hands of someone who would destroy her.

If they ever got out of this mess, he didn't care how badly it hurt, he would make his body able to withstand the sun. *Never* would he be this helpless again. *Never* would he be hindered in any way from getting to her.

Luther put the RV in drive and did a twenty point turn in the middle of the roadway. He'd finally gotten the RV turned around when a black car materialized on the horizon. It sped toward them, its illegally tinted windows making it impossible for him to see anyone inside it. Julian rested his hand on the back of the passenger seat where Clint sat.

Just as Luther was about to turn into the driveway, the car slid to a sideways stop before them, blocking their entrance to the road. "Who is that?" Clint muttered.

"I don't know, but they just signed their death certificate," Julian vowed.

Dani rose to her feet beside him. A new scent filled the air when the driver's side door of the car opened. Julian's deadened heart leapt hopefully in his chest at the same time he breathed, "No."

"Devon," Melissa whispered.

Devon slid from behind the wheel of the sleek new Challenger. Dark sunglasses shadowed his emerald eyes; his wavy black hair fell around his face. He turned back toward the car and said something before closing the door and walking toward the RV. He didn't get far before the passenger side door of the car opened.

"Get the door open!" Julian barked at Chris, but Chris was already scrambling toward the door.

Devon jumped over the hood of the car grabbing hold of Cassie as she stepped from the vehicle. Within seconds, the blanket covering her began to smoke from her burning skin. Devon pulled her against his chest and ran with her toward them. He tossed her through the door of the RV. He stormed up the stairs behind her, his eyes red behind his glasses.

Despite the turmoil rolling through him at losing Quinn and having Cassie here, Julian had to fight the urge to laugh. He understood Devon's frustration all too well now that Quinn had walked into his life. However, he still found it amusing to watch the normally composed Devon unravel in an instant.

Cassie tossed the blanket off her head. She scowled as she smoothed back her long, golden hair now standing in a million different directions from static electricity. Her violet-blue eyes flashed to Devon, and she frowned at him. A red burn on her cheek marred her otherwise perfect features and porcelain skin. She was as beautiful as he recalled, but looking at her now, he felt nothing other than friendship toward her as Quinn's striking, honeyed eyes floated across his mind.

"I still had some time," Cassie protested to Devon. "You didn't have to toss me inside."

"Seconds," he shot back. Devon showed no ill effect from the sun. After years of working to withstand its rays, Devon was the only vampire in existence who could tolerate it. "I told you to wait in the car."

"I don't like to wait."

Julian rested his hand on the cabinet over his head as she finally looked at him. "I see you've still got a death wish, Solar."

Her haughty expression softened to one of sorrow. His eyes widened at that look; his hand clamped on the cabinet door so forcefully he tore it from its hinges. Had she received a vision and knew something about Quinn he didn't?

"Julian, I'm so sorry," she said.

"What did you see?" he growled.

Devon stepped forward; he rested his hand against Julian's chest. "Easy," he urged.

Cassie shook off the last of the blanket and rose to her feet. "It's okay, Devon." She rested her hand on his arm, pulling him away as she focused on Julian again. "I only saw what she would become if she falls into the wrong hands. I convinced Devon to come here after he told me one of our own had staked you. Melissa filled us in on the events of last night."

Julian shot Melissa a look, but she shrugged negligently. "They were already on their way here," she replied nonchalantly. "They had to know what they were walking into."

"You could have told me they were coming," he grated.

"It wouldn't have made a difference. We need their help, and I wasn't going to turn it down."

"Is that really the only vision you've had of Quinn?" he demanded of Cassie.

"Yes." She looked away guiltily before focusing on him again. "If we can't save her, she has to be destroyed. I've seen the amount of good she will be capable of, but I've also seen the amount of destruction she could create, if she falls into the wrong hands."

The cabinet door snapped in half in his grasp. Devon stepped forward again, but this time he didn't bother to touch Julian; he only nudged Cassie back with his shoulder. *Such a foolish gesture,* Julian thought inanely. If Cassie decided to unleash the full force of her power, she was stronger than he and Devon combined.

Julian spun away, his shoulders heaving. He had to destroy something, had to sink his fangs into it and tear it to pieces. His gaze swung over the occupants of the RV as the beat of their hearts became as loud as drums in his head. He had to get out of here before he killed someone.

"Meet me at the ranch," he shot over his shoulder and leapt out of the RV and into the sun.

"Stop him!" Cassie shouted.

He barely felt the burning rays of the sun as he raced across the sand in massive leaps and bounds that ate away at the distance. The run didn't ease any of his hostility, but he was out of the RV, away from all the tempting heartbeats and pulsing blood.

His mind spun with the implications of what Cassie had told him. It didn't matter what Quinn did, he realized as flames danced from the tips of his fingers and up his arms. He'd love her no matter what she became. No matter what they did to her while they had her, she would always be the only woman he'd ever truly love. She would always be *his*.

If she had to be destroyed before she could be used for evil, he would do it. Then he would walk into the sun and welcome the rays that would sear away his flesh and bones. No matter how much he loved and needed her, he would never allow her to be used to hurt and destroy others. She would rather be dead before that ever happened, rather be dead than have her mind controlled by someone else; she'd said so herself.

He heard the loud rev of an engine and glimpsed the Challenger in the distance as Devon raced the car down the drive, almost keeping pace with him. "Get in!" Devon shouted at him, but Julian ignored him as he leapt over a large cactus. He darted to the side as flames began to consume his clothes and body.

Withstand it! he shouted to himself, even as he felt the skin melting from his bones.

The ranch came into view. Turning to the left, he raced toward the massive building used to house the temporary workers. He slid down the hill as his skin peeled away and his muscles started to feed the flames. The pain of the fire eating at his flesh had nothing on the pain twisting his heart and tearing at his soul.

He slammed into the door of the building, tearing it from its hinges as he staggered into the shadows. Falling to his knees, he rolled across the floor as something fell over the top of him. Hands rapidly ran over him, smothering the flames beneath their blanketing touch. With the flames smothered, Devon pulled whatever he'd draped over him away. He didn't scowl at Julian, didn't tell him he was an idiot; he simply tossed the ruined blanket aside and stepped away.

The charred muscles of his flesh cracked when Julian shoved himself to his feet. Fresh blood spilled from open wounds, but at least the flames had been doused. His clothes were nothing more than tatters sticking to his flesh as he moved through the building. Wordlessly, he led the way upstairs to the bedroom he'd discovered earlier.

The bottoms of his feet stuck to the floor as he walked. Charred bits of flaking muscle and skin fell on the ground behind him, but he could already see fresh veins and flesh beginning to form. He threw the door open to reveal the sickening display of the family gathered around the table and stepped back to let Devon enter first. It had only been a few hours since Julian was last here, but the stench of the rotting bodies was more potent than it had been before.

A low hiss escaped Devon when he took in the scene before them. Devon's shoulders thrust back as he circled the bodies surrounding the table. Julian knew Devon wouldn't recognize this scene for what it truly was, but he would recognize the drive of the twisted mind who had created it. He would recognize it as something he too may have done in the past, just as Julian had.

"What is this?" Devon demanded.

Before Julian could answer, he heard a set of nimble footsteps running up the stairs and turned as Cassie stalked down the hall toward him. "What were you thinking?" she shouted. "You could have gotten yourself killed, you stupid, foolish, idiot! Look at you! You look like a crisp fried corpse! What good is a crisp fried corpse to anyone? I knew you were reckless, but this…"

Her scolding tirade broke off when she spotted the decaying bodies positioned within the room. Her hand flew to her mouth as she took a step away from the scene. Devon stopped walking on the other side of the table. His eyes narrowed on the two girls.

At the end of the hall, the others appeared at the top of the stairs; they didn't come any closer. Seeing it once had been enough for them. Clint may not have seen it first hand, but he'd been informed about it and remained where he was. They probably didn't want to get anywhere near him right then either. He didn't blame them for that.

"I don't understand," Cassie whispered. "Why would someone *do* this?"

"Not someone," his voice actually sounded like a crisp fried corpse too, he realized. One who had been chewing on fire. "The man who took Quinn did this. It was a message to her, to me, to all of us."

"What's the message?" Devon demanded.

Julian's knees cracked and popped as he walked. The new cartilage forming made it difficult to get them to bend the way they were supposed to. Cassie followed behind him, staying as far from the table as she could.

"This is supposed to be Quinn's family," he croaked out. "Their hair has even been dyed to match them. I imagine this is exactly what they looked like before Barry," he gestured to the young boy he stood behind, "got up and let in their killers. Quinn didn't have any scars before that night, but what he did to that corpse matches the scars she has now."

"It's meant to unnerve her," Devon said as he rested his hands on the table to peer more closely at the scene.

"To let her know, to let *me* know, he's been watching her for a while," Julian said. "To let her know he is still watching her, or was, as he has her now. He may not have known she turned into a vampire when she did, but when he found her again, he remained in the shadows, biding his time before letting his presence be known here."

Devon stepped away from the table and slid a pointed look toward Julian. "He also knows who you are."

"Yes."

"How do you know that?" Cassie asked in a harsh whisper.

"Because this could have been some of my *own* handiwork not too long ago."

Cassie's already fair skin paled more. Her gaze shot to him before her eyes raked over them both. She wasn't naïve or one to live in denial; she realized it was something Devon would have done too. "I see."

Devon stepped back and stretched his hand out to her; she didn't hesitate before taking hold of it. "Do you think he suspects she's the vampire of the prophecy?" Devon inquired.

"I know he does." He reached for the pocket of his jeans before recalling his clothing had burned up. His hand fell back to his side. "He left a note in the hand of the girl meant to be Quinn."

"What did it say?" Cassie inquired.

Julian's teeth grated together as he recalled the words he would never forget. "You may not have been born of my blood, but I created you somehow, and I keep what is mine. P.S. Another one of your friends already belongs to me."

Cassie glanced at the others still watching from the end of the hall. "Do you think it's one of them?"

"Quinn's acquaintance, Jeb, is the one who helped lead to her capture," Julian replied. "I think it was referring to him, but it could still be one of them too."

Devon tilted his head to the side as he studied their friends. "We'll have to kill this asshole to make sure they're all safe."

"I'm going to," Julian growled.

Devon's gaze slid over him. "Not if you turn yourself into ash first." Julian gave him the best scowl he could muster with his barely there lips and cheek muscles just beginning to repair themselves. Devon gave Cassie a nudge toward the door. "Why don't you go downstairs with the others while we try to find some clothes for Julian?"

Cassie nodded and glanced back at Julian. "We'll get her back."

"You can't promise that."

"No, but I can promise we'll do everything we can to get her back, and I can make their lives *very* unhappy."

"I know you can, Solar."

"I hate when you call me that," she muttered as she walked toward the others. He knew that, but with her ability to absorb powers from others, she was like a solar panel and he'd always enjoyed needling her.

"You shouldn't have brought her here, not into this," he said to Devon. "There are a lot of vampires here."

Devon waited until Cassie was out of hearing before turning to him. "Do you think I could have stopped her from coming? She knew you needed us. *Nothing* was going to stop her. She would have come without me."

"What about the children?"

Devon ran a hand through his hair. "She trusts Liam and Annabelle to protect them if something were to happen to the rest of us."

"She has to be kept out of this as much as possible."

"Believe me, I intend to try and make that happen." Devon's emerald eyes focused on him. "I, more than anyone, know what you're going through. Remember, she was taken from me once too."

"I could never forget," Julian replied. "But this bastard has mind control, Devon. Quinn could already be lost to me, and the things he could make her do…"

Julian trailed off when fresh anger caused his shoulder muscles to bulge and his healing body to crack and bleed.

"My mind control is a lot stronger. I can take hold of his mind and make him release her. As of right now, he thinks he has only you and possibly some Hunters to deal with, but he's in for a rude awakening. We'll make sure you get the opportunity to kill him, but draining yourself unnecessarily isn't going to help. I know how difficult it is to maintain control right now, but you have to."

"I had to get out of that RV before I killed one of them."

"I know. Come on, let's get you something to cover yourself with so you can fill us in on the rest of what is going on. I know you probably don't care, but I think the others would prefer not to look at your burnt kibbles and bits. It's making *me* hurt."

"You're just jealous."

Devon released a small snort. "Not likely."

Julian closed the door on the display behind him. Before they left here, he would burn this building to the ground.

CHAPTER TWENTY-FIVE

No! No! No! Quinn's head whipped back and forth as she fought against the probing tendrils she felt trying to pierce her mind. She jerked her legs frantically, attempting to tear them free of the wall, but the motion only caused her shoulders to twist and grind together. A scream of rage tore from her throat as sweat poured down her face to drip on the cement floor beneath her.

Her eyes flew open and latched onto the woman across from her. "Don't let him do this!"

Helena's hazel eyes remained unsympathetic as Quinn jerked her feet again. Something clamped onto her mind. Her head jerked back as the sensation of fingers curling into her brain encompassed her. The fingers dug in deeper, holding her within their grasp as they slithered through her mind.

"Relax," Earl said.

Her body went limp within the chains at his word; she hung with her head dangling and her feet before her. *Fight!* She couldn't move though. Her body was no longer her own.

Her *mind* wasn't her own. Tears burned in her eyes and throat.

Earl walked over to stand before her. "Don't move. Don't speak."

This time when he grabbed her breast, she remained unmoving. A single tear slid free and trailed down her cheek. "Don't cry. It's beneath you and so unattractive."

The tears dried in her eyes, but on the inside, sobs wracked her body. In her mind, she screamed endless denials and curses at him; she tore at his face with her nails and fangs as she shredded him to pieces with her bare hands. She wouldn't use her power on this man; it would be too quick. No, what she would do to him would make the worst thing a vampire had ever done to another look like child's play.

"Stop touching her, Earl," Helena said briskly. "We get the point."

Disappointment slid over Earl's face, but he winked at her as he mouthed the word *later.* Revulsion curdled within Quinn's body. An endless scream sounded in her head. Inwardly, she continued to fight, but her body remained useless. Is this what Zach and Jeb had felt like? Were they aware of their actions and fighting them every step of the way? Had it somehow been different for them?

Why would it have been different for them and not you? She shuddered at the realization Zach and Jeb most likely had been fighting themselves the entire time, but unable to stop their actions.

Guilt ate at her, madness clawed at the edges of her mind. She had to keep it together, but all she wanted was to sink into oblivion, to get as far from this impossible situation and these monsters as she could.

Are you so different from them? Her mind tauntingly whispered at her. She was different; she had killed for love, not pleasure or power. However, she'd still taken a life. She'd still played God. When her time on this earth was over, she'd welcome Hell. She would deserve it, but she *was* different from them. She had to believe that.

Julian will find me. She knew it in every fiber of her being. If their roles were reversed, she would find him. There had to be some way to make it a lot easier for him to find her; she just didn't know how to do that when she had no control over herself.

She fell like a sack of potatoes to the floor when someone released the chains holding her up. A groan of bliss and anguish sounded in her head, but she remained mute, as she'd been commanded to do. The bullet in her shoulder succeeded in working its way out and clattered onto the concrete floor.

"We have to get her cleaned and fattened up before showing her to the others." Helena's black boots stopped inches from Quinn's nose. Quinn lifted her head to look at her. Helena had hair the color of midnight and narrow, aristocratic features. Her thigh-high boots clung to her shapely legs. The deep-red dress she wore matched the color of her nails and ended right below her ass. If she bent over, there would be no questions about what the dress barely covered.

Helena bent to place a hand on her shoulder, but Earl shouted, "Don't touch her!"

Helena recoiled as if Quinn were a crocodile ready to strike. *You have no idea what I plan for you.* Quinn watched as the boots stepped back. Her chain was jerked until she was lifted into a seated position. Her gaze slid around the space, noting the thick pipes running across the ceiling. It looked like she was in the small workroom of a basement.

Earl knelt before her, a smile curving his mouth. "I can make you do anything I command, but I can't take the fire from your eyes. Interesting mix of colors by the way, very fascinating. I can't wait to learn how you came to be. Now, dear, you're going to keep your power leashed. You're not to use it on anyone, unless I give you permission to."

Earl's hand wrapped around her bicep, and he hauled her to her feet, jerking on her dislocated shoulder. A rumble sounded in her chest as her eyes slid partially closed. That was the only reaction she revealed to the fiery needles stabbing deep into her flesh.

"We should learn how she was created before we take her before the others," the other man in the room said. "We can't take any chances she may not be who we're looking for."

"It's her," Earl insisted.

"Most likely, but the last thing we need is to be ripped to shreds by an angry mob because we didn't deliver on our promises."

Mob? Quinn's stomach plummeted.

Earl stepped before her and grabbed hold of her chin. "Whatever I ask of you, you must answer, and you must answer it *honestly*. Do you understand?"

Quinn tried to keep her mouth closed, but she felt the word sliding out from between her teeth. "Yes."

"Good." Releasing her chin, he stepped away from her. His eyes raked her from head-to-toe and back again. "I never gave you any blood so tell me how were you able to change?" Quinn's mind scrambled to come up with some answer that wouldn't be a lie, but not entirely the truth. "Answer right now."

"I was a Hunter," she blurted. "I already had vampire blood in me."

A cruel smile curved his mouth. "I know that but I've

killed Hunters before and none of them ever came back to life."

"Did you stick around after to find out?" she retorted.

A flash of red slid around his eyes. He stepped so close she could smell his rancid breath as it washed over her. She couldn't stop her nose from wrinkling. "They *never* come back. What else did you do that helped you stay alive? Answer truthfully, now."

She never had a chance to think of a lie before the words welled up inside her throat. She struggled to keep them back, but they burned within her.

"Answer now!" Earl commanded. A scream of frustration and suffering tore from her as the fingers in her head peeled through the layers of her brain. "It will only get worse until you answer."

"Vampire!" she gasped. "I was born part vampire."

The hand immediately retreated, leaving her shaken and weak on the floor.

"How is that possible?" Helena inquired.

"Answer her question," Earl ordered.

The crushing grip bore down on her mind again. It felt like a thousand wasps were stinging her brain over and over again. "My mother was a Hunter who was changed while pregnant with me. She gave birth to me and killed herself," she blurted.

The grip on her mind eased. Before she could stop herself, she vomited for the first time in her life. She had no idea what came out of her—bile, blood, or some combination of both. Her body jerked as she heaved repeatedly.

"What is wrong with her?" Helena demanded.

"She's fine. Her body's reacting to my digging through her brain," Earl answered. "I've been told it's far from a pleasant experience. She'll learn what resistance will earn her, and then she'll break."

The endless heaving finally stopped, leaving her with a bitter taste in her mouth. "What happened to my friend Zach?" Earl inquired.

Quinn lifted her head and tilted her chin up. "I killed him."

Earl grinned at her. "Wonderful news! Simply wonderful." Quinn didn't agree, but she remained unmoving before him. He clapped his hands eagerly. "Time to get cleaned up."

All of her power focused on the place where his hand wrapped around her arm as she fought to get it to latch onto him, but the tentacles remained leashed. Her teeth clamped so tightly together, she was sure they would shatter by the time this was done, if her mind didn't shatter first. Earl jerked her forward, leading her toward the door. Helena stepped in front of him before they could exit.

"I will see to her bathing and dressing," she said in a crisp tone.

Earl's hand dug into Quinn's flesh. The blood vessels beneath her skin burst under his punishing grip.

"Helena will take her," the other man said.

Reluctantly, Earl released her to Helena. "Tell her to truthfully answer any questions I have for her," Helena said.

Earl grabbed hold of Quinn's chin, his nails digging into her skin as he turned her head toward him. "Answer anything she asks with the truth. You cannot tell a lie, and you will do everything she commands you to do. You are not to hurt her in any way."

Earl released her and took a step away. Helena clasped hold of her arm and led her out of the room, up a set of stairs, and into a white hallway. Quinn was unsure if she could only speak when Helena told her she could. But then all she really had to say to her was how much she would enjoy watching Helena scream before she died.

She was led through a couple of hallways before they entered into a large room containing a small pool with beautiful green and gold tile lining the walls. Above her, the entire ceiling was made of arching glass. The sun beat upon the glass, but it wasn't unpleasantly warm in the room, and the thick tint over the windows kept the rays of the sun from causing all of them to burst into flames. Five other vampires stood in the room with their hands folded demurely before them.

She'd never seen anything this elegant before in her town. Had they taken her hundreds of miles away? How long had she been unconscious? Her mind spun at the hideous possibility of being in an entirely different state.

"We've had the water recently brought in." Helena's hazel eyes raked over Quinn; her upper lip curled in a sneer. "Hopefully, it will be enough to wash you."

Quinn smiled sweetly at her in response. *Hopefully, I will be feeling your heart in my hand soon.*

"Unchain her," Helena commanded. One of the vampires hurried forward to do as she bid. "You will not move," Helena said to Quinn.

Quinn's eyes slid to her, but it was the only motion she could make. "Your eyes truly are fascinating," Helena murmured.

Relief filled Quinn when the chains fell away from her bruised and chafed wrists. Dried blood cracked against her abused flesh as her hands fell before her.

"All of the men, out!" Helena commanded and waved toward the massive double doors they'd entered through only moments before. "And close the doors behind you."

Three women and Helena remained behind as the doors closed with a thud. "Strip her," Helena ordered.

Quinn's insides twisted at the command, but she remained unmoving as they cut her filthy clothing away from her body rather than trying to remove it in the usual way. When she was fully exposed, goose bumps broke out on her skin. She ached to be able to cover herself, but her hands remained unmoving, her body trapped in the cement of Earl's mind control.

"So skinny," Helena muttered and gave a disgusted shake of her head. An eyebrow quirked when her eyes latched onto the fading bite Julian had left on her thigh.

Quinn's eyes slid over her ravaged body. Her ribs and hips stood out in stark contrast to her pale skin. Her knees looked as if they were sticking out of her flesh. She felt like a skeleton as she stood there, but she wouldn't have it any other way. It was worth it to save Hawtie's life.

"Get in the pool," Helena commanded her.

Turning to the others, Helena ordered shampoo and soap to be brought forth, along with clothing, as Quinn stiffly made her way down the steps and into the small pool. She stood chest-deep in the water while she waited for her next command. The other vampires stripped before joining her. They scrubbed at her flesh with a look that made it clear they thought her less than a dog. They were either unaware or uncaring of the fact that her shoulders were still dislocated as they jerked and pulled on her arms.

The bullet wound had nearly healed, but Julian's mark was still on her flesh. She had to have only been unconscious for one night, she realized. The bullet would have worked its way out sooner if it had been a couple of days and Julian's bite would have healed, which meant she was most likely still in Arizona. That would make it a little easier for Julian to find her. She hoped.

"Is Julian your mate?" Helena inquired as Quinn was led from the water and wrapped in a plush, white towel. Her mouth remained closed, but she could feel the answer pressing against her lips, fighting to break free. "Answer me."

"Yes!" The word was painful as it tore from her throat.

A smile curved the edges of Helena's full mouth. "That means he'll come for you, and then we'll have an Elder too." She strolled around Quinn, her hand trailing over her shoulders before moving into her hair. "A mate will do anything for the other." Helena stopped before her again. "And while you are like this, he will have no choice but to fall in line and return to the vampire he once was. Our kind will rule again. There will be no hiding, no fear of the Hunters or Guardians. No more disarray and fighting each other."

Quinn would do everything she could to keep Julian from becoming a killer again, especially not because of *her*. Another vampire arrived with a goblet full of blood. Helena took it from her and held it out to Quinn. "Take it and drink."

Quinn's hands rose and clasped hold of the golden goblet. Lifting it to her mouth, her nose wrinkled when she realized it was human blood. *Warm* human blood. Her lips clamped shut against it. Her body burned with hunger, but she had a feeling this hadn't come from a willing victim.

"Open your mouth and drink it," Helena commanded.

Quinn's hands shook as she tried to keep her lips closed against the enticing liquid, but they skimmed back of their own accord and the blood spilled across her tongue. Even as her mind screamed against it, her body greedily gulped the empowering liquid. *So* much better than animal blood, sweeter and more tantalizing.

Inwardly, sobs wracked her body. Outwardly, she handed the goblet back to Helena, hungry for more, as she wiped the back of her hand across her mouth. Helena gave her a knowing smile and turned to accept another goblet of blood from one of the vampires. "You've been denying yourself the nectar of life, child. Drink," she commanded.

This time, Quinn didn't try to fight it; she needed the strength the blood gave her. She couldn't stop what was happening to her, but Helena had just secured her spot at number two on the list of vampires she was going to tear to shreds as soon as she had the chance. She smiled at Helena over the top of the goblet as she handed it back. Mistaking the purpose of her smile, Helena smiled back and took the goblet away.

"You're already looking much better. The others may actually believe you're a threat now."

You have no idea what kind of a threat I can be, but you'll find out. Quinn wiped the blood away from her mouth again and flicked the remaining drops onto the white marble beneath her feet.

"Dress her," Helena commanded the others.

The towel was torn away from her, leaving her bare body exposed to Helena's assessing gaze once more. One of her full lips curled when they fell upon the scar in the center of her sternum. Quinn turned her palms outward so Helena would be able to see the slices across both of them. She turned her hands to reveal identical scars running across the backs of her hands too.

"Disgusting," Helena murmured. Quinn lifted her chin at the woman; she didn't care what others thought of her scars. They were hers to bare, and she would do so for an eternity. "It must be your power that attracted Julian to you."

"Earl left these scars on me. This is what he did to me on

the night I turned." Apparently, she could talk to Helena without being commanded to do so, but that was all she had to say to the repulsive woman.

Helena's eyes widened briefly before narrowing on her. Without warning, Helena grabbed hold of her wrists and jerked her arms forward. Her shoulders slid back into place with an echoing crack. Helena's eyes were remorseless when they met hers.

"You will receive no pity from me," Helena said and stepped away.

"I want no pity from anyone," Quinn replied as she unflinchingly met Helena's gaze.

"Do not speak again."

Quinn glowered at Helena as her lips compressed. Having redressed themselves, the other vampires brought forth a small black dress and pulled it over her head. *Helena's*, she realized when the dress was snugged into place. She wanted to pull it up to cover the ample amount of cleavage the top of the dress exposed, but she was afraid she would bare her ass if she did.

Thankfully, they brought out a pair of underwear and tugged it up her legs. *Please let it be a new pair.* However, she didn't get the impression Helena bothered with underwear, ever.

The slinky, skin-hugging material of the dress felt out of place on her body. She would give anything for her pants and stakes. Her hoodies and tees. This dress wasn't her. They were trying to take everything she was away from her, and she *despised* them for it.

They could take her clothes and force her to do things she didn't want to, but they couldn't take who she *truly* was from her, she reminded herself. She'd never forget who she was, no matter what they did to her or made her do. Earl wouldn't be able to break her, not even if he was successful in the promise he'd mouthed to her earlier.

One of the vampires brushed her hair roughly out and left it to tumble around her shoulders. Helena grasped her chin as she stepped back to survey her again. "I think that's the best we're going to get with you," she muttered. "Bring her."

Quinn glared at Helena's back as she was led forward by two vampires who were holding her arms. The blood had helped to replenish her strength, but she still felt hollow and hungry for something more than blood. She attempted to latch onto the vampires holding her with her ability. Her power swelled against their hands but remained as caged as a bird.

CHAPTER TWENTY-SIX

"WHERE ARE JEB'S FRIENDS, Ross and what was the other one's name?" Julian demanded of Clint when he hung up the phone with Hawtie in the hospital.

Clint rubbed at his bloodshot eyes and slid his phone into his pocket. "Ernie. I don't know where they are, up north at their boss's other ranch, I 'spose."

Julian folded his arms over his chest, most of his flesh had healed by now, but his skin was still reddened and there were a few blisters covering his arms and face. Cassie had found a set of clippers and carefully buzzed his charred hair off, but his skull felt raw from them scraping against the burns. Stubble lined his head now, but a couple of burnt spots on his skull remained.

"How far away is that?" he asked.

"Three, four hours, I guess. Why?"

Julian spat out a curse as he turned on his heel. He stormed across the floor to the pool table before turning back. "They may have seen something helpful, or somehow know where the vamps are hiding."

He'd already gone through all of the buildings he was able to get into around the ranch and touched as many things as he could. The others brought out objects for him to touch from the few buildings he wasn't able to enter. All he'd learned was that some of the people who worked for the ranch held some secret addictions and odd fetishes. He'd discovered nothing sinister or useful to help him find Quinn.

"I know where Ross lives. He'll have gone home in-between staying at this ranch and the other one to see his wife and kids. If he does know something, would you be able to pick it up from his family or the things in his home?" Clint inquired.

"Maybe," Julian said. "Let's go."

It was the first lead they'd had to go on; he didn't intend to wait.

"I'll get the car," Devon said. "Both of you wait here." Devon shot him and Cassie a pointed look before running down the steps and into the sun dipping toward the horizon.

"I'll get the RV," Luther volunteered.

"The rest of you should go with him," Julian said. "I don't plan to leave this building standing."

He watched as the others hurried down the porch steps toward the drive. Turning away, Julian walked into the dining room, lifted the hutch, and smashed it onto the floor. He gathered the pieces and built a small pile on the floor of the kitchen before walking over to the gas stove. Turning it on, he held a small piece of the wood over the top of the flames until it caught fire.

He tossed it onto the pile of kindling and walked over to rejoin Cassie by the front door. "What about the bodies upstairs, their families?" Cassie inquired.

"They'll still find their bodies, but no one should discover their loved ones like that," he replied.

"You're right."

Devon brought the car down the gravel drive and parked it before the house. Julian turned to Cassie, making sure the blanket covered all of her flesh. Only her eyes could be seen beneath the swaddling of material covering her.

"Come on." He wrapped his hand around her head as Devon leapt out of the car and hurried around to get the door open and the passenger seat leaning forward so she could duck into the backseat.

Smoke drifted out the top of the blanket when Cassie dove into the car. Devon pushed the seat into place and closed the door after Julian climbed inside. Cassie tossed the blanket aside and sat up in the seat. Julian's still healing flesh had reddened and blistered again, but it was nothing compared to what he'd endured earlier in the day.

Devon climbed into the driver's seat. "You okay?" he asked Cassie.

"Fine."

Devon shifted into first before following the RV down the road. Smoke from the burning building billowed into the air by the time they were halfway back to town. This had to work; he had to discover something that would lead him to Quinn. Julian's hand gripped the armrest beside him as he fought the urge to tear it from the car in frustration.

Entering the town again, they made a right onto one of the backroads off the main street. The sun had slipped over the horizon before the RV stopped in front of a yellow house with a farmer's porch and cactuses lining the rails. A pretty blonde woman in her thirties was sitting on a porch swing, reading a book as she idly swung her feet back and forth.

She looked up when Clint emerged from the RV and waved to her. Julian opened his door as Clint called out a greeting, "Hey, Cathy!"

Cathy's brow furrowed as she placed her book down and rose to her feet. "Clint? What are you doing here?"

"I was looking for Ross," he said as he climbed the porch steps.

Her gaze drifted to Julian as he strode down the flagstone walkway to stand behind Clint. "What for?" she asked suspiciously. "He had nothing to do with what Jeb did."

"I know that," Clint assured her. "My friend here," he gestured back at Julian, "is looking for a job. I didn't know if they were hiring out at the ranch."

"Oh," she said and glanced at the screen door. "Probably. I can get his number for you. He's been spending more time up north lately."

"That would be great," Clint replied.

"Come on in," she said and nodded toward the door. "I'll get you both some iced tea."

Clint followed her through the door with Julian trailing behind. He slid his hands over the doorframe, picking up pleasant memories of laughter and children running in and out while playing cops and robbers. He felt the top of a table, picking up more laughter and some fights as was typical for any family.

"What are you doing in a RV?" she asked Clint.

"After everything that's been going on at the bar and in town, I've been thinking about buying one. Some old friends agreed to let me test-drive theirs. This here's their son. He's come into town with some of his friends."

"I'm so sorry about what happened last night. I can't believe Jeb would do such a thing. He was always so stable, so tenderhearted."

"He was," Clint agreed, "but I guess we never know what goes on in a person's mind. Is Ross coming back for the funeral?"

"I don't know. He was really upset when I talked to him earlier. He's pissed at Jeb. I think he's mad at the world right now."

"Understandable," Clint replied.

"You must be furious." They followed her into a small kitchen where she poured two glasses of iced tea and pushed them across the table. "How is Hawtie doing?"

"She's going to pull through," Clint said and took a sip of his drink. Julian wrapped his hand around the glass but didn't lift it.

"I'm surprised you're not with her."

"You know how Hawtie is; she won't let anyone fuss over her, and she hates being coddled."

Cathy released a snort of laughter. "That she does." She walked over to the counter and grabbed a pen and piece of paper. "Here's his cell," she said as she scribbled on the paper. She flipped through some papers in a phone book before tapping her finger against one. "And here's the number where he's staying now."

Walking over, she handed Julian the piece of paper. "You should probably wait a couple of days before calling. If they're looking for help, it's going to be to replace Jeb."

Reaching for the paper, Julian slid his fingers over hers. Images from her life unfolded like a flipbook through his mind. He saw her as a little girl with her puppy, a teen with a cigarette and leather jacket, a college student with her boyfriend, her wedding day, and the joy of the day she gave birth to her twin boys.

A tangled web of pictures from her life and the lives of those she'd encountered flooded him. Centuries of practice at dealing with the barrage of insight that came with his ability allowed him to sort through them rapidly.

One of her last memories caught his attention the most.

The image was from when her husband had been home a couple of days ago. It didn't fit into what he'd learned of the lives of the couple in this home. It didn't fit with what he'd come to know of the surrounding area either. Ross could have picked the image up from Jeb and transferred it to his wife, but just in case, Ross would be avoided until he succeeded in killing Quinn's captor.

Julian slid his hand away from Cathy's. "Thanks for the advice and the numbers."

"Best of luck to you." She turned to Clint. "Send my love to Hawtie, and tell her I'll be baking a peach cobbler for her."

Clint grinned as he slid his thumbs into his waistband. "That news will cheer her up."

Cathy smiled and followed them toward the door. Clint pulled out a piece of gum and stuck it in his mouth as they walked toward the vehicles. "Did you learn anything?" he inquired.

"There was a residual memory on her that wasn't her own and didn't fit with the rest of what I saw," Julian replied. "I'm not sure if it was Ross's memory, or something he may have picked up from touching Jeb and then left on his wife. Either way, tell the others Ross is to be taken down if he approaches them."

"Will do. What did you see?"

"A massive building, extremely luxurious in the front and surrounded by desert. It had a lot of windows, which wouldn't make sense for vamps, but they'd all been blacked out with paint or covered with thick drapes."

"Which would make sense for vamps." Clint chewed on his gum as he stopped walking and his gaze focused on the side of the RV.

"Does it sound like anything you know?" Julian asked.

"About five years back, some business men got together from New York or something like that and decided to build a luxurious hotel in the middle of the desert, turn it into a spa or something. Figured people would like to get away to an oasis of sorts. What they didn't figure was how much it would cost to keep their pools and green landscapes going, or that there were already plenty of spas near water that people liked to visit. The project was shut down before it was completed."

"But the building still stands?"

"As far as I know it does, and it had a ton of windows. It's about fifteen miles beyond the ranch."

Julian closed his eyes as he fought against the excitement and urgency pulsing through him. "Take us there."

Clint nodded and climbed into the RV. Julian walked over to the door of the vehicle and poked his head inside. "Is there any more blood?"

"There is," Melissa answered. "How much do you want?"

"All of it."

She came back with five more bags and handed them over.

CHAPTER TWENTY-SEVEN

Quinn felt like a show dog as she was paraded through hallways painted in desert tones of orange and yellow. The lack of imagination in the coloring grated on her nerves. It was such an odd thing to be bothered by, but considering all she could do right now was look around and think, noticing the colors was unavoidable. She expected bull skulls and wagon wheels to make an appearance at some point, but for now, the walls remained bare of décor.

Vampires stood in a few of the doorways lining the hall. They gazed at her curiously. Some licked their lips, and others grinned in a way that made her want to spit in their faces. She'd counted twenty of them so far, but there were at least thirty rooms along this hall, and there'd been another thirty lining the one before it.

It had to be some sort of a hotel, but one she'd never seen before. The room with the pool had been opulent. The halls held what looked like real brass sconces, and each one she'd traversed had a large chandelier hanging from the dome ceiling stretching over the hall.

For all of its grandness, there was still an air of disrepair and neglect about the building. Dust kicked up from the thick, red carpet beneath her feet. The glass of the chandelier didn't shine beneath the layer of dust coating it, and the brass was dingy and faded from lack of polishing. Burning lanterns hung from the bottom of the unlit sconces. Their flickering light danced over the walls and carpet.

She'd never seen anything like this place before. How far from home had they taken her? Apprehension burned like acid in her stomach. If she was hundreds of miles from her town, it may take Julian days to spread out that far in his search.

I will not panic. I will not panic.

No matter how many times she told herself this, she could feel the tide of fear rising within her. Closing her eyes —the only motion still her own—she struggled against the madness swirling at the edges of her mind. *You can survive days. You can survive weeks, if you must.*

Stepping from the hall, Quinn threw her shoulders back determinedly and opened her eyes. They became saucers as she took in more of the yellow and orange tones, but also the massive wooden desk across from her. There were no computers set up on it, but she knew immediately it was a check-in desk.

Her gaze slid to the front wall of glass, which had been painted black to block out the sun. Through some breaks in the paint, she could see the sprawling desert beyond. Three chandeliers hung above her, all of them would have cast a beautiful array of rainbow colors across the white marble floor, if they were clean. Now cobwebs covered them.

The walls remained clear of all decoration, but behind the reception desk was a large mural of an oasis in the desert. *Is that what this place was supposed to be?*

A jerk on her arm from one of her guards got her moving across the marble. Her bare feet didn't make a sound, but the heels of Helena's boots clicked against the floor. The sound grated on her nerves. She longed to clamp her hands over her ears, or break the woman's legs off. Yes, *that* would have been far preferable.

Dust swirled up around them as they walked past two elevators and what she assumed was an arboretum, but the trees within were dead. One of the benches had broken and fallen on the ground, and the elaborate fountain in the middle of the space had no water in it. The brown fencing surrounding it had one piece that had fallen over, and others were leaning precariously toward the ground.

Before her, thick wooden doors were pushed open. The vampires led her through another carpeted hall with only a few doors off the side of it. Each door was spaced about fifty feet from the other one. She had no idea what lay beyond them, but they had to be massive rooms. They emerged into another hall, this one all marble. At the end of it was a set of wooden doors with elaborate flower-etched designs around the edges.

She didn't know why, but a wedding was what came to mind when she looked at those doors. Then they opened to reveal a massive ballroom beyond, and she knew exactly why she'd been thinking wedding. Her mouth parted as she stared up at the dome-shaped ceiling with one of the largest chandeliers she'd ever seen hanging from the center of it. Around the edge of the entire room ran a second floor balcony with deep-red seats lining it.

Wedding or opera, she thought.

The floor beneath her feet would have been sparkling white marble if it had been cleaned and polished. At the end of the massive room was a stage with chairs set up on it. Earl and the other man from earlier were already sitting in the chairs. They both stopped speaking as she was led across the marble toward them. Earl and the other man rose. A lustful gleam came into Earl's eyes as they leisurely ran over her barely there dress.

"Well done, Helena. She is much improved," Earl murmured. Quinn forced her eyes away from the obvious arousal pressing against the front of his black pants. "Much improved and still helpless, I see."

The urge to vomit filled her again, but she kept her mouth clamped against it. *No more weakness.*

"She is," Helena said and climbed the steps to sit in one of the plush red chairs. Turning, she gestured to a spot behind her. "Put her on the floor."

"No," Earl said. "Bring her over here." *No!* Quinn shouted in her mind. "She'll be where it will be easier for me to command her."

Helena shrugged and folded her hands in her lap as Quinn was led over to Earl. His hands ran over the bare flesh of her arms as his gaze fell to her exposed cleavage. Goose bumps broke out on her flesh.

"No!" she managed to protest.

"Silence," he said as his fingers trailed toward her collarbone.

I'll kill you! she screamed in her mind, but her lips had been superglued together by his command. His fingers dipped, and a low moan escaped him when they brushed the top of her breast.

"Enough!" Helena commanded. "Leave her be, Earl."

He pouted like a child denied his toy, but stepped away from her. He settled into the chair, a spiteful smirk curving his mouth as he gestured to the space between his feet. "Sit."

Quinn fought against it, but her body moved toward him

of its own accord and sat in the space between his feet. He patted her head before settling back into his seat. Quinn's head bowed, her teeth grating together as her hands fisted.

"Are the others coming?" the other man inquired.

"They will be here shortly, Marvin," Helena replied.

Quinn lifted her head to take in Marvin. He appeared to have been turned in his mid-forties as he had lines around his eyes and mouth. The red hair of his sideburns had turned gray. His blue eyes slid to her; he studied her for a minute before turning away. He wasn't what she would consider handsome or ugly. She supposed average would have suited him best. He was one who would have blended into the crowd while alive and would only draw attention now because of the power he emitted as a vampire.

A muffled sound by the doors drew Quinn's attention back to them as the first of the vampires shuffled in. Curious murmurs went through the crowd as they studied her. Judging by the lack of power emanating from them, she didn't get the impression that these vamps were very old. A couple of them stood out as older than the others, but they weren't as old as the three on the stage with her. Still, even with their youthful ages, she would guess most of the vampires, except for maybe six or so, were older than she was.

In the beginning, she tried to keep track of their numbers, but she lost count at a hundred as the crowd continued to swell. She guessed there were nearly two hundred, if not more, in the room with her by the time they stopped coming forward.

If Julian did somehow manage to find her, he'd never be able to take on such a vast number, and she wouldn't want him to try. Hopelessness swirled through her, but she fought it back. Nothing was hopeless while she still lived. She'd find her way out of this mess, somehow.

If she could use her power, she'd destroy Earl and break his grasp on her. It was just figuring out how to do that. She'd been in bad situations in her life, and she'd managed to survive them. This may be the worst one so far, but where there was a will, there was a way, and she was determined to have that man dying in her hands.

She realized the eldest of the vampires, about twenty of them, stood the closest to the stage. Their power radiated from them and their eyes were assessing as they ran over her. Behind them, she picked out vampires with glassy, sightless eyes amongst the crowd. There were maybe a dozen of them, but she knew they were under Earl's control or he'd created them and kept their minds. She wondered if the others knew about them.

"Doesn't look like much," a brunette woman near the front commented.

"That's because I have her leashed." The prideful tone of Earl's voice caused her fingers to clench more as he patted her head again. "She's such an obedient little creature right now, but I assure you, she's lethal."

"Is she the one we're seeking?" another older vamp inquired.

"She is," Helena said and rose to her feet. "The girl's mother was a Hunter who was turned by a vampire while pregnant. She produced a half Hunter, half vampire offspring." Helena's red-tipped fingers briefly flashed toward her. "When Earl killed her, this combination allowed her to be reborn as one of us, with*out* his blood.

"As we all know, the prophecy states, 'A vampire, not born of vampire blood, will burn like the sun the life from anyone she touches. If used correctly, she will become our greatest ally, our savior.' This girl was not born of vampire blood, not as we all were."

All those eyes swung toward her once more. "Is this true?" the older vamp asked her.

Earl nudged her in the back. "You will answer all questions they have truthfully, now."

Quinn could feel the fire in her eyes burning brighter as she fought against the command. A few of the vamps closest to her gasped and pointed at her eyes; others nudged each other excitedly. "Her eyes. How strange. How fascinating." The agitated murmurs raced through the crowd. Their chatter grew, but the older vamps in the front remained concentrated on her as they awaited her answer.

"Yes," she finally said from between her teeth.

"What about the burn like the sun part? Does she wield fire? Is she our savior?" The questions were fired at her from all around the room.

"Better than fire," Earl said excitedly. "*Much* better."

With a wave of his hand, he gestured to someone beyond the red curtains lining the stage. Quinn frowned as two vampires emerged. They were holding the arms of a young girl as they dragged her forward. Quinn had never seen the human before, but with her dark hair, brown eyes, and gold locket around her neck, the girl reminded her of her cousin, Betsy. Something she knew had been intentional on Earl's part.

"Bring the girl here," Earl commanded. The girl's eyes swung wildly around the room; her frantic heartbeat pounded against her ribs. The cries escaping her reminded Quinn of a coyote with its leg caught in a trap. "Seat her beside our guest."

An uneasy feeling turned in Quinn's stomach as they sat the girl next to her. Earl cupped the young girl's chin within his hand as he lifted it. "Things are about to get a lot more fun, dear." He turned toward Quinn. "You are to use your ability to drain her. Not your fangs, just your ability."

"No." Quinn winced against the pain that lanced through her brain at the denial.

Earl leaned toward her. "Yes."

Quinn tried to move back, but her body remained pinned to the spot where Earl had told her to sit. He grabbed hold of her hands. "Open them." Her traitorous fingers sprang open at his command. Earl moved her hands toward the girl who tried to shrink away from Quinn, but the vampires holding her kept her in place. Earl rested one of Quinn's hands over the girl's heart and the other over the locket in the center of her chest bone. "She is the only one you can use your power on. Now, drain her."

Quinn shook her head, but she could feel those denied tentacles slipping forward, seeking out the life force they'd been so desperately seeking since Hawtie. A scream echoed in her head, despite his earlier command, tears sprang forth in her eyes and slid free as those tentacles latched onto the girl.

"Please no," she whimpered as she felt the girl's life flowing into her hands.

She'd lost control of her power before, but now she had absolutely *no* control over it as it fed. Not a Hunter or vampire, the girl would drain faster than any other Quinn had taken from before. The girl's rosebud mouth parted, and her deep-brown eyes were the size of an owl's as they rolled within her head.

"I'm so sorry," Quinn whispered.

The girl's cheekbones stood out more sharply and the color leached from her skin as Quinn feasted on her life. The weight slipped away from her victim's body. More whispered words of excitement and distress raced through the massive crowd. Tears streamed down Quinn's face as her malnourished cells were filled.

Then she realized something. Earl had said to drain her, but he hadn't said to drain her to the point of death, and he hadn't said she couldn't return the life back to her. The girl's heart gave a stuttering beat as her breath rattled out of her chest. The whites of her eyes had already turned a yellowish hue and were leaning toward brown now.

Gritting her teeth, Quinn forced her body to give up the life force it had been so desperately craving. Forced herself to give up the strength she needed. She'd survive this ordeal, but she wouldn't become like one of them in order to do so. She'd rather die.

Life flooded back into the girl. Like a balloon refilling, her face filled out again, and her eyes and skin returned to their normal hue. Her heart beat more solidly in her chest as she inhaled gulping breaths of air.

"What are you doing?" Earl snarled.

Quinn threw herself backward, tearing her hands away from the girl. Her body jerked to a halt when it came up against Earl's knee. Air didn't fill her deadened lungs, but she panted for it. She often had this kind of a reaction when she used her ability. She fought to regain what little control she still had over herself.

The girl gazed at her in awe, her eyes frightened and relieved as they met Quinn's. She felt almost a little guilty over the admiration in the girl's gaze. She'd kept a small piece of the girl's life for herself; she'd need the strength it would give to her.

Despite her guilt, she found her mouth curving into a smile at the girl. Their eyes met and held. They were prisoners together, and together they would escape this. Quinn would make sure of that.

Before she knew what he planned, Earl stretched over her and snapped the girl's neck. The sound of it echoed in the vast room.

A scream erupted from Quinn. She lurched forward as the girl's body slumped to the stage. Pain lanced through her brain as she broke free of her place on the floor. Her hands fell upon the girl's chest; she could fix her. She could fix her…

Earl grabbed hold of Quinn's arms, yanking her away before she could do anything to help. Another screamed escaped her as she thrashed against his hold. "Stop moving."

Her body instantly went limp. Her power surged toward him, but his command from earlier remained strong enough to keep it trapped within her body before it could take hold of him. "Stop crying."

The tears ceased their flow, and the ones on her cheeks dried against her skin. Misery and fury blended within her. All she could do was sit there staring at the girl.

"Next time, keep the life for yourself. I'm going to kill anyone you allow to live anyway," Earl told her.

He grabbed both of her arms and jerked them so they were half behind her back as he spun her to face the crowd. "Does that answer your question about what she can do?" he inquired.

The curiosity in the surrounding eyes told her the display had done more than that. It had also wet their appetite.

"She's young, and you see what she can already do," Earl continued. Quinn's head bowed, but she forced herself to lift it again to defiantly meet the eyes of all those gathered within the room. "Imagine what *years* of training and practice will bring to her ability; to *us*! We'll have one of the most powerful vampires on the planet under our control and she'll do whatever we want her to do. We will never have to run or hide from the Hunters, Elders, or humans again."

"What of the remaining Elders?" another vamp by the stage inquired. "They work with the Hunters now and will come after her and us."

"That's where it gets even better," Helena said. Quinn itched to claw the smile from her face. "The girl has confirmed the Elder, Julian, is her mate."

"What does that mean?" someone from the middle of the crowd called out.

"That means he'll do anything for her." Earl ran his hand over her face, under her chin, and back up again. "And right now, I have complete control over her. I can make her do anything we command, and he will do anything to keep her from being hurt or abused in any way."

Quinn barely managed to suppress a whimper; she closed her eyes against the eagerness those words caused to glow in some of the eyes in the crowd.

"Not only do we possess the vampire of the prophecy, but we will also possess one of the two remaining Elders when Julian comes for her, and he *will* come for her."

Quinn opened her eyes to take in the sea of faces. They all blurred before her, but she could see uneasiness growing amongst some in the crowd as they shifted and spoke with each other.

"I'm not so sure about this," one of the older ones near the stage said in a loud, clear voice.

"What is there to be unsure about?" Marvin demanded.

"First, as she grows older and her power grows, how can you be so sure you can keep her restrained?"

"I can keep her restrained until we have broken her to our way," Earl replied confidently.

The man's sympathetic gaze traveled over her. "I don't think she's going to be so easily broken."

"Everyone has their limits," Helena replied. "She's *more* of a vampire than any of us because of her unnatural birth. Her natural instincts to kill will eventually take control of her, and she will stop trying to fight us."

"It seems so wrong," another man standing to her right muttered.

"Does it?" Earl spat. "You knew what you were in for when you came here."

"No, we didn't," a woman replied crisply. "You said you had the vampire of the prophecy. That she would work with us. You said nothing about keeping her mentally chained like a dog, which is something you are enjoying far too much for my liking."

"Are you vampires or pussies?" Earl barked.

"Earl!" Helena snapped and lifted a hand to silence him. She turned toward the crowd and spread her hands out before her. "We must do what we must in order to survive. The Hunters and Guardians are growing stronger every day. Our only two remaining Elders work side by side with our enemies to help their numbers grow. They would slaughter any one of you if given the opportunity.

"*She* is the only advantage we have over them. I don't know about you, but I enjoy my life, and I will do whatever it takes to preserve it. Even if it means having to keep *one* vampire imprisoned until she realizes her true nature and how important she is to the survival of our kind. Julian was a killer for centuries; it won't take much for him to revert back to his old nature."

Heads bowed toward each other as they debated her words. Earl roughly threw Quinn to the ground as he strode toward the edge of the stage. Quinn glared at his back as she drew her brutalized arms forward. She really hoped Helena was wrong, but she knew Julian was capable of anything when it came to her.

"Julian is with Hunters and Guardians now," another vampire said. "What do we do with them if they come here too?"

"Kill them," Earl said flatly.

CHAPTER TWENTY-EIGHT

JULIAN KNEW they were in the right place the second he saw the hotel/spa. His fangs sprang free, they pressed against his lower lip as he surveyed the front doors. "This is it. Let's go," he said briskly.

Devon grabbed his arm, holding him back. "We have to get in there without them knowing."

Julian's lip curled into a snarl, but he knew Devon was right.

"How?" Cassie asked.

"Do you know anything more about the layout of this place?" Julian asked Clint.

"No, like I said, the project was abandoned years ago. I never came out here to see it. The kids didn't even come out here to party. It was too far away for them."

Julian's gaze slid over the building. He moved back to kneel behind a rocky outcropping. Dropping his head into his hands, he rubbed at his temples before turning to Devon. "We'll go around the back, see what we can find there. Stay here," he said to Cassie.

"No."

"Cassie—" Luther started.

"I can stay hidden and still be of help to you, and you all know it. Leaving your strongest asset behind is dumb, you macho butts."

"Butts?" Chris inquired with a look that said he didn't know if he wanted to laugh at her or slap her.

Cassie gave him a sheepish smile. "Trying not to swear as much, you know, because of the kids."

"Understandable, but please don't ever say that again. I'm not sure we can stay friends if you do."

"I think we're all going on this one," Melissa said. "You forget, all of our lives could hang in the balance, and Quinn has become our friend."

Julian turned away; he didn't have time to argue with them. The more help they had, the better, but if they lost Cassie too, all of their lives *would* hang in the balance. "Come on," he said and sprinted across the dark sand toward the back of the massive hotel.

One good thing about the painted windows was the vampires wouldn't be able to see out of them. Julian, Devon, and Cassie may be able to move faster than the vamps would be able to see, but Chris, Melissa, and Dani weren't as fast and would easily be detected. Dani still looked a little dazed, but her eyes were clearer than they had been a couple of hours ago. Luther, Lou, and Clint were a lot slower than the others were and would get everyone caught in a matter of seconds. With his big belly, Clint was panting heavily by the time they made their way around to the back of the building.

Julian's eyes constantly scanned for some sign of vulnerability in the building. His gaze slid up to a domed glass ceiling. "There," he said and pointed to the ceiling sticking out of a first floor room.

"How do we get up there?" Dani asked.

"We'll find a way," he replied.

He ran across the desert and toward a broken piece of wooden fencing. He ducked under the wood and into another garden area with more dead trees and a broken bench. The fountain in the center was filled with sand. His gaze scanned over the wall before landing on a wooden trellis leaning against it.

"You can climb up there," he said and pointed the trellis out to the others.

"Shit," Lou muttered, but he was the first one to grab hold of one of the railings and step onto the trellis.

Julian took a few steps back before running at full speed and leaping at the building. His momentum carried him ten feet into the air. He grabbed hold of the edge of the roof and effortlessly pulled himself over the top. Devon and Cassie followed behind him. Cassie moved to grab the top of the trellis while Lou swung himself over.

The others quickly followed behind Lou. Clint was huffing and puffing when he finally swung his leg over. "Good thing I quit smoking," he muttered.

Julian didn't look back at him as he knelt next to the tinted glass ceiling and narrowed his eyes to take in the small pool beneath them.

"What's in there?" Lou asked, unable to see beyond the tint.

"It looks like a spa pool or something," Cassie replied.

"Anyone in there?" Luther asked.

"Not that I can see," Julian answered.

"If we bust out these windows, the noise could announce our presence if anyone is near," Devon said.

"Would you prefer to walk through the front door?" Julian asked.

"No, but be prepared to fight once we're in there."

"I'm more than prepared for that."

The others pulled their crossbows from their backs and held them before them as Julian lifted his foot over the glass. "As soon as I break this, we're going in," Julian said. "You're staying here until we know it's safe," he said to Cassie. "We'll need someone on the outside if this goes bad."

She rose to press a kiss against Devon's cheek. "Be careful."

"Always," he replied.

Julian lifted his foot and smashed it into the glass. The first pane shattered beneath his boot; the second pane fractured in a jagged zigzag that raced all the way down the dome. Julian lifted his foot to break it, but the remaining glass gave way before he could kick it again. He leapt forward.

The glass fell on the tiled floor in a tinkling wave, just as he landed in a crouch. Spinning, his eyes scanned the shadows for any hint of danger lurking within. The room remained empty, but Quinn's crisp scent filled his nostrils.

She'd been in this room recently.

Excitement and bloodlust pulsed through him. "She was here," he said as he rose to his feet and stalked around the room. "I can smell her."

"We're getting closer," Devon said.

Julian spotted something in the shadows. Racing toward it, he snatched up the black shirt lying on the ground. He lifted it and inhaled deeply when he recognized one of Quinn's work shirts. It smelled of her sweat, blood, and fear.

"What is that?" Dani asked from behind him.

"Quinn's shirt," he growled.

What was she wearing now? Had they decided to parade

her around naked in order to humiliate and attempt to break her? The material tore in his hands.

"She's here. We'll find her," Devon said.

Cassie fell noiselessly into the room behind them and rose to her feet. "What?" she inquired innocently when Devon scowled at her. "It's safe."

Julian shook his head, but she'd stayed away for longer than he'd expected. Cassie's brow furrowed when her gaze drifted to the shirt in his hand. "Have you seen anything?" Julian demanded.

"Nothing I haven't told you," Cassie answered.

He looked pointedly toward Melissa.

"I haven't had a vision since the one about the bonfire," she said.

He forced himself to release the shirt as he walked over to the thick doors. Pressing his ear to one, he listened for anything beyond this room, but he heard no footsteps or voices. The breaking glass most likely would have brought them in here if there were vampires in the area anyway.

Opening the door, he poked his head out into a long, red-carpeted hall. He followed the faint trail of Quinn's scent down the hall before entering another one. They were almost to the end of that hall when he heard voices for the first time. The drive to kill shot through him as he listened to whomever it was talking quietly.

There were three of them from what he could tell. He flashed three fingers to Devon who nodded his agreement. *Taking them*, he mouthed.

He walked to the end of the hallway and flattened himself to the wall. Devon pressed himself against the wall across from him. "I don't know why we're sticking around here," a man muttered.

"They say she's the vampire from the prophecy," another said.

"Who cares about the prophecy? Most of those vamps are still living in the Middle Ages with all these stupid prophecies. They make her sound like she's the vampire's messiah."

"She may be."

"Or she could be the death of us all."

Quinn wouldn't be the death of them, but *he* would be. He burst out of the shadows and seized the first man by the throat. The man let out a squeal, his hands clawed at his throat as Julian slammed him into the ground. Jerking backward, Julian tore his throat out with his hand and threw it away. Blood shot up around him. The man's feet kicked on the floor before Julian thrust his hand into his chest and tore his heart free.

He squished it in his hand before tossing it aside and rising to his feet. Devon had taken care of the other one, but Chris, Melissa, and Dani had a third pressed against a wall. Julian stalked toward them, elbowing his way past Luther as he stepped in front of the vampire.

"Where is she?" Julian demanded. The vamp's eyes flickered toward him before nervously shooting away again. Julian grabbed hold of his chin, jerking his head toward him. "Where is she?"

"The ballroom," the vamp blurted. "Don't kill me. I didn't want to be here in the first place."

"But you are," Julian replied. The vamp whimpered and squirmed within Julian's grasp. "Where's the ballroom?"

The vamp lifted a shaky arm and pointed to another hall. "Down there. You can also enter the balcony if you go to the second floor. I'll show you if you like. I'll help you."

"No." Julian twisted his head to the side, breaking his

neck before he dropped the vamp onto the ground. Dani gave him a stake when he held his hand out to her. He drove it into the vamp's back and twisted it deep. The vampire went still beneath him.

"Let's go," he said to the others.

He walked swiftly, passing by the garden they'd run through to get to the trellis and the roof. They were almost to the end of the hall when he heard the timber of voices. He held his hand out, stopping everyone else as he crept forward and craned his head to look around the corner of the hall.

A wall of vampire backs greeted him. He pulled himself back as Devon stopped on the other side. Devon poked his head out before looking over at him. He would have to fight and destroy all of those vamps to get to her. He had no problem with that, but the others couldn't come with him. They had to stay free in case something went wrong.

"Tsss," the small hissing sound drew his attention to the others. Cassie stood by an open door. Chris slipped through it as she waved eagerly toward them.

Devon and Julian moved away from the end of the hall and back toward her. Julian peered into the stairwell the open door revealed before slipping inside. Cassie didn't make a noise as she closed the door behind them.

"We may be able to see more from the balcony," she whispered and gestured toward the stairs.

Julian glanced behind him. Quinn was in that room somewhere, he knew it. So close, he was so close, yet he found himself climbing the stairs with the others.

Keep your head; proceed cautiously. It's the only chance you've got to get her out.

Arriving at the next floor, Luther peered through the window of the stairwell door before pushing it open and sticking his head out. He stepped into the hall and the others followed behind him. Clint went to the left, sweeping down the hall with his crossbow raised. Dani and Lou followed him. Luther went to the right with Chris and Melissa.

Julian listened for anyone approaching, but he heard no voices or footsteps. At the end of the hall, Clint gave a low whistle and waved his arm at them. Julian ran toward him, then peered through the small window in the door Clint had indicated. Through it, he spotted the red seats lining a balcony.

Julian craned his head to each side, but he didn't see any vamps in the balcony area. Resting his hand on the knob, he turned it slowly and carefully pushed the door open before stepping into the small walkway running behind the rows of seats. He stayed low as he crept through the seats to kneel behind the waist-high wall running around the entire second floor.

Placing his hands against the inside of the wall, he rose a little to look below him. His deadened heart leapt in his chest when he spotted Quinn on a stage. Her eyes danced with fire as her chocolate hair tumbled in wet waves around her shoulders. The dress she wore could barely be called a dress, and he knew it had been chosen to make her feel vulnerable.

He didn't recognize the two men on the stage with her, but the woman at the end looked vaguely familiar. He searched his mind for how he knew her, and briefly recollected a party one night in London years ago. She'd been there with another vampire he barely recalled. It took a minute, but he remembered her name was Helena. They'd had little interaction that night, but she'd been more interested in the women at the party than in the men. Judging by Helena's lack of attire, he assumed it was her dress on Quinn.

Around Quinn stood a sea of vampires. All of them

watched her as she kept her hands pressed against a young girl whose face filled out before his eyes. His fangs sliced into his lower lip when he realized she was being made to exhibit her power.

"What are you doing?" the vamp he recognized as her stalker demanded.

Quinn threw herself away from the girl, but she came to an abrupt halt against her captor's knee. Her body shook on the floor, and her shoulders heaved as she labored for control. Anguish twisted Julian's heart as her distress radiated out from her. She turned her head toward the girl and met her gaze. Despite what she was enduring, a small smile curved the corner of Quinn's mouth.

Quinn's captor reached around her and broke the girl's neck. Dani ducked back; her hand flew to her mouth. Julian shot Dani a silencing look as a scream erupted from Quinn. She scrambled forward as the girl's lifeless body fell on the stage. Across from him, Cassie's eyes became entirely red as her fangs extended. Devon placed a soothing hand on her shoulder.

"He has to die," Cassie whispered.

"He will," Julian vowed.

He kept his eyes on Quinn, his chest aching with the pressure growing within it. It took all he had not to grab the wall and swing himself over and into the crowd below, but he couldn't reveal the presence of the others up here. His fingers tore into his palms when Quinn's captor grabbed hold of her arms and yanked her away from the girl before she could help her.

Quinn screamed again as she jerked against his hold on her. "Stop moving," the man commanded.

A rumble of fury slid up Julian's chest when her body went still. Tears streaked her face as she stared at the girl.

That bastard had taken control of her mind. He glanced over at Devon who met his gaze but didn't say anything.

Julian moved away from the wall and crept toward the others. All of their heads bent close together as they huddled around him. "I'm going down there. I want the rest of you to stay here," he said with a pointed look at Cassie. "If they don't know any of you are up here, we'll have the element of surprise on our side."

"We can try and get to her at another time," Lou suggested. "When there aren't so many vampires around her."

Julian shook his head. "No, we'll give them a show of power they'll never survive, if you're up for it, Solar?"

"You know I am."

"Julian—" Devon started in warning.

"She'll stay up here, away from all of them," Julian assured him. "No matter what," he added sternly to Cassie. It was probably useless, but maybe she would listen to him for once in her life. "Don't let them know you're up here. If this works right, they'll have no idea where anything is coming from."

"When should we make a move?" Cassie asked.

"You'll know when, and I'd prefer it if none of them walked out of there."

"We'll be fine, and I'll stay hidden," she promised before turning to Devon. "Go with him."

Devon hesitated before clasping her face and kissing her. Julian turned away and crept back through the rows, determined to get to Quinn before they could do anymore damage to her. Devon caught up with him in the hallway.

"If you can free her from his mind control, do it," Julian said as they stepped back into the stairwell.

"Should I keep her suppressed until you're ready to make a move?"

"No. If any of them somehow survive to walk out of here, and they think she's strong enough to break his mind control, they may think twice before messing with her again. I'd prefer them all dead."

"So would I. This is going to get ugly."

"I'm counting on it," Julian said.

He cracked his knuckles before opening the door at the bottom of the hall and stepping out. They crept to the end of the hall and poked their heads around the corner. Julian studied the backs of the vamps for a moment as he listened to the conversation within.

"Are you vampires or pussies?" someone barked; he recognized it as the voice of Quinn's captor.

"Earl," Helena said.

So that was the prick's name. Julian's mouth watered at the idea of sinking his fangs into his throat and tearing it out. Pulling back, he tilted his head up and closed his eyes as he fought to keep himself under control. He would need his bloodlust in that room, but he would also need to keep his head. Quinn's life depended on it.

Across from him, Devon frowned, his emerald eyes glinted with a murderous rage. Julian leaned back around the corner to listen to more of the conversation.

"Julian is with Hunters and Guardians now," another vampire said. "What do we do with them if they come here too?"

"Kill them," Earl said flatly.

There was more shuffling amongst the vamps. Julian nodded at Devon before stepping around the corner. He was as controlled as he was going to get until he had Quinn in his arms again.

"We are not the dead Elders," another vamp said. "Their battle with the Hunters and Guardians isn't ours. We want nothing to do with it."

"It will be your battle when they slaughter you without hesitation," Helena replied.

"What do we do when Julian comes here?"

"It will be a while before he finds us. We'll be prepared for him when he does," Helena assured them. "Even if he comes with the Hunters and Guardians, they will be no match for our numbers."

Idiot, Julian thought.

"Julian won't be so easy to control," another said.

Julian's mouth quirked in a smile as he leaned against the doorway of the room. "You've got that fucking right!" he announced.

Startled sounds accompanied his statement as vampires spun toward him. They pushed against the others as they stepped hurriedly away from him. Their eyes filled with fear as they gazed between him and Devon. Julian could feel the power within him pouring forth when the crowd parted enough to let him see Quinn on the stage again. A small noise escaped her and her fingers twitched on the floor of the stage, but she made no other movement as she remained mentally restrained. Julian's eyes never left hers as Earl began to laugh.

"Do you really think so?" Earl inquired. Quinn's eyes closed as he ran a hand over her cheek before cupping her chin. He squeezed hard enough that he drew blood and caused her to wince.

"Don't!" Julian barked and took a step forward.

"See, as long as we control her, we control him," Earl announced proudly to the room. "Take him," he commanded.

"You touch me and I'll tear your arms off and feed them

to you!" he snarled at the vampire who stepped toward him. The man took a hasty step away.

"Will you?" Earl grabbed hold of Quinn's arms, jerking her to her feet. He brushed the hair back from her face and neck to reveal her pale throat. "From what I understand, mates are extremely possessive of what is theirs."

Earl ran a finger down the side of Quinn's neck. His lips skimmed back to reveal his fangs. The fire in Quinn's eyes blazed brighter. Julian took an involuntary step toward her, torn between trying to keep his control and racing across the room to her.

"I'll tear her throat out if you take another step toward us. It may not kill her, but it will hurt like hell," Earl said, his finger dipping toward her cleavage. A bellow tore from Julian when Earl's finger trailed around the upper swell of her breast. "And then perhaps I'll let every man in this room take a turn with her. And you will watch, helplessly, if it means keeping her alive. But if you play nice, so will we."

CHAPTER TWENTY-NINE

QUINN REMAINED immobile in Earl's grasp, her gaze locked on Julian. She savored the sight of him, but she also wanted him to leave and never come back to this hideous place. These vampires couldn't have him too. He deserved to be free from this insanity, but she knew he would never walk away from here, not without her.

Looking at him, she believed he might be able to take on every vampire in this room. Barely leashed power oozed from his pores; his eyes were the color of rubies as they shone hotly in the torchlight of the room.

The jeans he wore hugged his powerful thighs. The black t-shirt was a little bigger on him than she was used to seeing. She didn't know what had happened, but his hair was now shaved into a buzz cut that emphasized his chiseled features. The black spots amongst the platinum of his hair looked like burn marks.

Dried blood clung to his right hand and streaked his cheek. The muscles in his arm stood out sharply. His fangs hung over his lip as he watched Earl with a look that would have many pissing themselves. She'd never seen anyone look so merciless before. If he got his chance, she had no doubt he'd tear everyone in this room apart.

Not so tough when you don't have control of someone, hey asshole? She thought as Earl's hand trembled against her throat.

More of the vampires fell back, eager to get out of the way as Julian took a step forward. A vampire she didn't recognize stood by his side. The vampire's black hair glimmered in the light; his emerald eyes surveyed the crowd with a dismissive air that would have made Quinn laugh at any other time. The vamp grabbed hold of Julian's arm, holding him back when Julian took another step forward.

The man's eyes focused on her before sliding to Earl. She didn't know how she knew, but she would bet money on the vamp holding him being Devon. Her gaze slid past him, but she saw no one else in the hall beyond. She'd never met them, but she knew Devon wouldn't be here without Cassie, and where were the others? There was no way they would have agreed to stay away. She may not have known them for long, but she knew they were loyal friends who didn't shy away from a battle. They wouldn't have left Julian and Devon to face this on their own. She glanced at the second floor balcony, but nothing moved up there.

"Seize him!" Earl ordered.

A few of the vampires exchanged nervous glances. Three of them stepped forward. Before she could blink, Julian lunged to the side and grabbed the arm of the one who had made a move toward him before. Quinn's stomach turned as a sickly wet, tearing sound filled the air. The vampire screamed as blood sprayed from his now empty shoulder socket.

Julian spun the arm he'd torn from the man around. He shoved the man's hand into his mouth and down his throat, muffling his screams. With barely a glance at the floundering man, Julian placed his foot in his stomach and shoved him back. The crowd flowed away from him as the vampire fell to the floor, writhing in agony as blood continued to pulse from his missing arm socket.

"Classy," Devon commented dryly.

"I warned him," Julian replied flippantly.

Julian's face was as chilly as the arctic ice his eyes normally mirrored when his gaze came back to Earl. Blood streaked his short, white-blond hair. He took another step toward them but stopped when Earl wrapped his hand around her throat and lifted her so her toes barely touched the ground. His fingers dug into her throat, drawing blood as he tore into her flesh.

"Did she tell you how I pinned her to the ground the first time we met?" Earl inquired as his index finger stroked Quinn's neck. "That was just the beginning of what I'll do to her if you take another step."

A few of the vampires started to edge toward the doors. "Shut the doors!" Julian bellowed.

She didn't know whom he yelled at, but the doors banged closed. Everyone within the room jumped, including Quinn. Whispers of alarm washed through the crowd. A few of them took a menacing step toward Julian.

"You can't take us all down," one of them growled at him.

"If you behave, you may walk out of this alive," Julian replied without looking at the man. "We're not here for you."

"Is that Devon?" Helena asked Marvin in a whisper that didn't carry beyond the stage.

Earl's hand squeezed Quinn's throat. A small whimper

escaped her before she could bite it back. Beneath his hand, her windpipe began to collapse as he dug deeper into her flesh. Julian's nostrils flared; he took two more steps toward them. When blood spilled freely down her skin, he halted abruptly.

Devon walked forward behind him, his eyes turning crimson in color as his gaze bored into Earl.

"Earl," Helena said as she spun toward him. "You need to take her and get out of here, *right* now."

Quinn didn't understand the note of panic in Helena's voice, but Earl took a step back with her. Her heels dragged across the stage when he took three more steps before stopping.

"I don't run," Earl growled. "They are greatly outnumbered."

Some of the vampires closed in on Julian and Devon. Others moved back further as they tried to stay out of the way of the impending battle. The power radiating from Julian and Devon caused the hair on her arms to stand up as they remained standing side by side.

They looked completely different from each other, Devon so dark and Julian so fair, but they'd hunted, killed, and fought together for centuries, and it showed in the way they moved simultaneously without saying a word to each other.

Devon's eyes continued to bore into Earl.

"Earl, take her out of here *now*!" Helena snapped.

Earl kept her pinned against his chest as he reluctantly took another step back. Quinn's foot brushed against the girl's unmoving body on the stage when Earl came to an abrupt halt.

"Earl!" Helena spat. "Go!"

The invisible grip that had kept rigid control over her mind suddenly eased and retreated. Stunned, Quinn remained unmoving as the pain of Earl's mental hold on her vanished. It couldn't be, but when she commanded her fingers to move, they *did*.

Free! She was free. Devon had mind control, she recalled dazedly. No wonder Helena had been so adamant that Earl take her out of here, but it was too late now. Devon had sprung her free, and now he had a hold on Earl's mind.

She almost laughed aloud, almost shouted with glee, but her momentary elation was buried beneath her fury. She threw up her arm, knocking Earl's grip on her free before she snatched him by the throat. The tentacles of her power whipped free and tore into him. He bellowed and tried to jerk away from her, but she kept a stronger hold on him than an octopus on a fish.

She'd never unleashed her ability with such wrath before, but years of pent-up hatred for this man burst free. She would make him feel vulnerable in the same way he'd repeatedly made her feel vulnerable. They fell onto the stage together. The fingers of her free hand curled into his throat as she pinned him beneath her.

She dug in deeply and tore backward, ripping his throat out. She barely felt the warm blood spraying over her as she clawed and tore at him with her hands. In places where her hands didn't touch, his skin sliced open like she'd taken a whip to him beneath the lashing assault of her ability. He'd destroyed her family, he'd had Julian killed, he'd killed her friends, and he'd used her as if she were nothing more than garbage. She would make him pay for *every* one of those acts.

Blood coated her and the stage as she continued to

pummel and tear at him while savaging his body with the full force of her power. This release was unlike anything she'd ever experienced. She *loved* the feeling of finally allowing her power to have free rein. Earl's body took on the appearance of a year-old corpse as it shrank inward. His graying skin flaked and fell off as she gorged on his life force.

~

JULIAN'S HEART leapt into his throat when Quinn spun and threw herself on Earl. Cries of rage emanated from her as she tore at him with a savagery Julian had never expected of her. He'd always known she was lethal, but Earl had pushed her to a breaking point, and now she looked like one of the furies of legend as his blood splattered over her.

"Quinn!" he shouted, but she didn't hesitate in her attack.

Vampires swelled around them; their fear made them braver than they'd been before. Julian punched one in the nose before kicking another in the stomach. He kept his back pressed against Devon's as they fought to make their way toward Quinn.

A vampire grabbed hold of his arm, trying to jerk him back as another sank their fangs into his arm. He smashed his fist so violently into the man's forehead that the vamp's fangs were still embedded in his muscle when the vamp fell away. Julian yanked the fangs free and threw them away as he grabbed hold of another vamp and twisted her head around.

For every vampire they took out, five more rose around them. Someone landed a blow against the side of his head that caused blood to trickle into his eye. He lashed out, tearing the man's throat away and flinging it across the room. He lurched toward another vampire, but she was flung across the room before Julian could get his hands on her.

Cassie, he realized as more vampires were thrown aside by her telekinetic ability. Some of the other vampires screamed as they scrambled to get away from their unseen foe. Julian leapt forward, racing toward the stage while they were briefly distracted. A vamp seized hold of his ankle, snatching him back and nearly causing him to fall on the floor.

Spinning around, he drew his foot back and smashed it into the vamp's face until it was nothing but mush beneath his boot. The vamp released him, but ten more jumped on top of him, burying him beneath the pig pile of their bodies. He punched and kicked at them as they clawed at his face and belly. The weight of them caused his knees to give out.

One scrambled over his chest, seeking to find his heart as its fingers tore into his flesh. He grabbed hold of the hand, snapping it back. One of the other vamps was lifted off him and tossed aside. Through the hole the vampire's missing body created, he spotted Devon as he pulled some of the other vampires away. Over Devon's shoulder, Julian saw Luther rising on the opposite side of the balcony from where they'd left him. He lifted his crossbow and took aim at the crowd. Chris rose up ten feet to Luther's left and Dani ten feet to his right.

Dani didn't have anything in her hands, but he felt a change in the pulse of the earth as she drew electricity from it. She released the wave of electricity in a rush that bowled over the vamps at the back of the room. From the other side of Chris, Melissa rose and fired arrows into the crowd. On the opposite side of the balcony, Clint and Lou emerged about fifty feet away from where they'd left them with Cassie.

Cassie's head popped up above the wall for a second before she disappeared behind it again. Devon grabbed for a vamp; it was lifted and thrown out of the way before he could touch it. Devon blinked at the empty space before turning toward the next vampire. Julian lifted his elbow and smashed it into the cheek of another vamp, finally freeing himself from the bottom of the pile.

Howls erupted from the vamps as arrows continued to rain down on them. Some of them leapt at the balconies and grabbed hold of the red material dangling beneath the seats. They used the material to climb upward. Another draw of power shook the earth beneath his feet, but this one wasn't coming from Dani.

"Watch out!" Dani shouted as an electrical blast erupted from a female vamp climbing one of the thick red drapes.

Dani remained the only one standing as the force of the electrical current threw the others back. Cassie's hand shot up, a pulse of power erupting from her. The world seemed to tilt on its axis, becoming distorted and blurry as she used her Spinner ability to warp the room.

The vamps who had been climbing toward the balcony lost their grip on the material. They screamed as they toppled to the ground. Cassie could have probably burnt them all, but there was a chance she'd set the whole place on fire if she released a fireball, and he still hadn't seen any of the others pop up again after that last electrical current.

Julian grabbed hold of another vamp and heaved him away. The man flew across the room and smashed against the back wall. Vampires scattered, running toward the doors that remained closed by Cassie's power. Bangs resonated through the hall as the vampires beat on the doors and howled for release. Some of the others came back at him and

Devon; their fangs exposed and their eyes a shining crimson color.

Julian rolled to the side and shoved himself to his feet. Quinn shouted and released Earl. She sprinted across the stage to where Helena was heading toward the back of it. Julian jumped toward the stage, but the heavy weight of a vampire slamming against his waist knocked him to the side.

CHAPTER THIRTY

HELENA STUMBLED BACK before turning to run. "No!" Quinn shouted.

She leapt off Earl and pounced on the woman before she could escape. Helena toppled beneath her weight when Quinn landed on her back. Grabbing hold of her hair, Quinn smashed her head into the floor. Helena's movements slowed, and Quinn delved into her and latched onto her life force.

A sigh of pleasure escaped her when she felt the rush of Helena's power filling her. There was so much of it. She'd been denied for too long, and now she had the opportunity to feast on those who had imprisoned and humiliated her. Helena's hands shriveled on the ground; her skin turned gray and peeled back from her muscle. Her red nails sparkled in the light as a few of them fell off her brittle fingertips.

Around her, Quinn could hear shouts and the smell of blood intensified, but she continued to devour the woman beneath her. Unlike Earl, whose death she planned to savor for hours, she didn't care if Helena died now.

Helena's body shriveled until nothing remained of her. The dress she'd worn lay flat on the ground with her ashes around it. Quinn flicked Helena's ashes off the tips of her fingers as she fell away from the remains.

She staggered to her feet and nearly fell over as power surged through her body and into her head. She stumbled to the side and fell beside Earl, who was trying to drag his useless legs across the stage away from her. "No!" she yelled.

Arms wrapped around her, pulling her against a solid chest. Unable to control it, she felt the tentacles slithering out again, seeking the vast amounts of power and life she sensed in the arms embracing her.

"I've got you, Dewdrop," Julian whispered against her ear. "I'm here."

She shuddered against him. The tentacles instantly retreated as love and warmth flooded her body. "It's okay," he whispered, his lips brushing over her forehead. "Feed from me if you must. Take whatever you need from me."

Helena and Earl's life force flitted through her like a ghost trapped in a house. Julian's life slipped in and out too, flowing to mingle within her as she returned what she'd taken from him, plus some. There was too much in her, she couldn't handle it, but Julian was older and stronger, he could. She had used him before to fuel her power and as a source to funnel it into.

"Quinn," he breathed. His arms clenched around her when she continued to feed life and power into him.

He launched to his feet and spun her out of the way when Marvin leapt at them with his fangs snapping. One of Julian's arms remained latched around her waist; his other hand shot out to take hold of Marvin's throat. The flood of life continued to flow from Quinn and into Julian. At the same time, she kept her eyes narrowed on Marvin as she began to draw from him again.

"Shit," Julian breathed against her ear when Marvin withered and shrank within his grasp.

Julian's heart gave a mighty kick. It pumped for fifteen beats before stopping once more. Those beats hadn't gone unnoticed by the vampires within the room. They'd all frozen at the booming sound of life pumping within a dead man's chest.

Quinn continued to use Julian as a conductor to drain Marvin. She relied on his vast strength to curb the rush of power and the feeling of being out of control as her body craved more and more life.

It would be so easy for her to give in, to leave a trail of death behind her, but locked within Julian's arms, she knew she could withstand the temptation. Knew he would be there to bring her back when she felt the unraveling within her. Marvin's sneakers fell to the floor with a thud as the gray husk of the vampire shriveled further within Julian's grasp. His ashes crumpled to the floor with his clothes falling on top of them.

Julian shook his hand to free it of the rest of the ash before wrapping his hand around Quinn and pressing her against his chest. She could feel the tremor in his muscles, feel the increase of his power as Marvin's life fueled him. He cradled her closer when he turned to face the unmoving, dumbfounded crowd.

Devon stood at the front of the crowd, an eyebrow raised as his gaze slid between the two of them. Blood dripped from his face and clothes; his shirt was torn and gashes marred his chest, but he appeared otherwise unharmed. Behind him, Quinn saw the trail of bodies he and Julian had left in the room.

"Burn like the sun," someone near the front whispered.

The impulse to slaughter anyone who said that hated prophecy again shot through her.

"No!" Julian snarled. "She is not yours to use. She is *not* your savior. She is *my* mate, and I can assure you that what you just witnessed is only the beginning. You think about touching her, and I will drain *every* one of you in this room. She may keep her power leashed; I will set it free. Stand down, or face the consequences."

Talk ran through the crowd. Devon climbed the steps of the stage, his gaze still assessing on Quinn as he stepped next to Julian.

"Can you drain them without her?" he asked in a low tone of voice.

"No," Julian replied in a whisper. "But these sheep don't know that. They have no idea what we're capable of."

Earl moaned and rose up as he attempted to crawl away again. Without looking at him, Julian smashed his foot into his back and snapped his spine with a loud crack. Earl cried out, his fingers scrabbled at the wood, but all motion stopped when Julian dug the toe of his boot into his back.

Near the back of the room, a couple of vampires ran for the doors again. Before they could reach them, a ball of fire shot from the balcony to encompass them. They shrieked as flames burst over them, consuming their clothing and flesh as they raced around the room. The other vampires rushed away, cries of distress and alarm radiated from them as they tried to escape the balls of fire running toward them.

After a few minutes, the flaming vampires mercifully fell silent as they collapsed beneath the weight of the fire devouring them. Quinn gulped, but she tilted her chin as she met the hostile and frightened eyes of the vampires in the room. Julian grinned cockily back at them, and Devon rubbed at the bridge of his nose. Quinn remained immobile as she waited to see what would happen now.

"Get them!" someone in the crowd shouted.

Julian pushed her behind him. As the first wave of the crowd rushed toward the stage, another ball of fire swooped down, knocking the vampires back. The flames formed a wall between them and their would-be attackers.

"I'm going to kill her," Devon muttered.

"They don't know it's her," Julian reminded him. "Or where she is, and most of these vamps aren't making it out of here alive."

Devon's gaze slid to the balcony, Quinn followed it, but she still didn't see anyone up there. "We have to get out of here," Devon said.

"I want one or two of them," Julian replied.

"Why?"

"I have my reasons."

Julian bent to grab Earl by the neck and lifted him effortlessly off the ground. Quinn barely glanced at Earl dangling within his grasp as she lifted her eyes to scan the vampires blocked by the fire across from them. "What will happen to them?" she inquired. "They didn't all approve of what was being done here."

A muscle in Julian's jaw ticked as he surveyed them. "We don't know which ones didn't, and it will take too much time to figure it out. They're going to die."

Quinn shuddered, but she couldn't feel overly bad when a good chunk of them had been quite content to watch her be Earl's lapdog.

Julian's gaze slid over the crowd again. It landed on two vampires off to the side, clutching each other. "Those two," he said to Devon and pointed at the couple. "Can you bring them here? We'll take them with us."

Devon shot him a questioning look, but didn't argue as he focused his attention on the couple. Quinn watched in amazement as their heads turned toward them, their eyes taking on that glassy look she'd seen in Zach and Jeb. She would never forget the helpless feeling that had assailed her when Earl had taken control of her.

"Don't," she whispered.

Devon glanced at her as the couple moved toward them. "I'll let them go soon," he promised.

"You don't... you can't know what it's like."

Julian's arm tightened around her. He pressed her against his chest as the couple climbed the steps of the stage. "They're coming with us," he said. "But we have to make sure they're not a threat. They won't be hurt."

"Why are they coming with us?" she inquired, unable to watch as Devon directed them to the edge of the flames.

A small break appeared in the wall of fire, allowing the couple to step through. A vamp rushed at the opening and burst through it before the wall flowed up to block the gap. The vampire didn't run at them; instead, he tried to flee toward the back of the stage. Julian released her and Earl to chase after the vamp. He brought the man down beneath him and banged his head against the floor before he twisted it around and tore it from the man's shoulders.

Turning away, he took the head and carelessly tossed it into the crowd. Quinn couldn't shake the image of a bouncing ball from her head as it thudded across the floor before coming to a halt against a woman's legs. The woman gawked at the spectacle as she did an odd, lurching dance away from it. Julian wiped the blood from his face before returning to her and grabbing hold of Earl again.

"Let's go," he said.

He drew her against his side and kept her locked there as

they made their way behind the curtains. "Hope there's a back door," Devon said.

"There will be," Julian replied with the confidence only he could muster.

Quinn's gaze fell to Earl's unmoving body as Julian dragged him across the ground. His crazed eyes spun in his head, his booted toes thudded as they descended a set of stairs and made their way into the shadows behind the stage. The roar of the flames grew larger as they greedily consumed the ballroom and those within. Screams resonated around them as they walked through some band equipment before coming across an emergency door.

Devon pushed into the bar, shoving it open and holding it for them as they stepped into another white hall. The couple followed obediently behind them. Quinn chanced a glance back at the orange glow spreading across the stage. The acrid scent of smoke and burning wood filled the air as the screams increased in fervor and intensity. Smoke curled through the shadows, its tendrils stretching toward them.

Julian nudged her forward through the stark, white hall with white tile flooring. The doors along the hall were all open, and as they hurried down it, she realized it was a service hallway as she spotted a couple of laundry carts and empty metal shelves that had probably once held linens.

Devon moved faster when smoke slid out from beneath the door. They were all running by the time they made it to the doors at the end. Quinn pressed her face against Julian's chest, savoring his spicy scent beneath the aromas of smoke, blood, and sweat. His fingers slid over her face as they ran down another hall and toward the main entrance.

"Cassie!" Devon shouted.

Quinn lifted her head as a beautiful blonde woman broke away from the group clustered by the front doors. She ran across the marble floor and flung herself into Devon's arms. He embraced her before turning her toward the doors. Cassie's gaze slid curiously toward her, but she allowed Devon to push her forward.

"What do we do about this place?" Cassie asked.

"Burn it all," Julian replied when they reached the main doors.

Cassie nodded and turned back to the hotel. She released a wall of fire that caused the desk to burst into flames. Ignoring the blood coating her, Clint grabbed hold of Quinn and gave her a bear hug. His bushy gray hair stood strangely on end, and there were burn marks on the tip of his nose and cheeks.

It took her a minute to realize one of the vamps must have sent out an electrical jolt as she now saw all the others had their hair standing on end too. Quinn hugged Clint back; a tremor shook her as they stumbled outside together.

They ran across the sand toward a rocky outcropping. When they made it to the rocks, Julian dropped Earl and spun toward her. Dragging her against his chest, his hand snaked into her hair, pulling her head back as he took possession of her lips. A feeling of rightness slid through Quinn as his tongue swept headily into her mouth.

A low moan sounded in the back of her throat as she eagerly met each of his hungry, driving thrusts. He held her up when her knees gave out, but he didn't relent as his lips moved greedily over hers. Tears of love burned her eyes, but she kept them restrained when his fangs scraped over her bottom lip before biting down.

Quinn whimpered at the wash of relief and love pouring out of him. Through their bond, she could feel the terror and fury that had driven him since she'd been taken. Now he was unraveling as his hands ran over her back, drawing her closer. He continued to feed on her, drinking her in, in a rush that made her body quiver.

He released his hold on her lip. She clamped onto his, needing to taste and feel the connection between them more than anything right now. His blood flowed into her, filling and strengthening her as it seeped into her cells. Releasing her hold on him, her head fell against his chest as she struggled to control the desire clamoring through her body.

"My Dewdrop," he whispered lovingly against her ear. She lifted her head to look at him; he gently smoothed the hair back from her face as his ice-blue eyes searched her face. "It's over."

She closed her eyes. She'd spent the past six years of her life hunting for Earl and living with him hanging over her head. He was all she'd thought about for so long now; her need to get revenge on him had consumed her life. And now, it was… "Over," she breathed. "Free."

For the first time in years, she felt *free*. She didn't have to worry about never finding him and getting her revenge, didn't have to wake up every morning with the knowledge he was still out there, most likely destroying other families. He may still be alive right now, but it wouldn't be for long, and he was no threat to her or anyone else anymore. Now, she was free to do whatever she wanted, with Julian.

"You'll never have to fear him again," he whispered in her ear.

Her fingers dug into his back as she tried to pull herself closer, but she'd never be able to get close enough. He embraced her as he rocked her back and forth. She opened her eyes to look at the others, but they'd slipped away into the desert, leaving her and Julian to each other and taking Earl and the couple with them.

Quinn turned her head as flames leapt high into the sky.

Their crackling noise drowned out any other sounds. "What was this place?" she asked.

"A hotel, or it was supposed to be," Julian answered. "Clint said the project was abandoned five years ago."

"Before I came to town."

He pressed a kiss against the top of her head. "Are you okay?"

She tilted her head back to look at him. The concern in his eyes tugged at her heart. She smiled at him as she placed a hand against his beautiful face. "Yes, but I'd really like to get out of this hideous dress."

His overconfident grin spread across his lips as his gaze raked over her. The arrogant look that made her want to kick him in the shins most of the time was a welcome sight. "I don't know, I kind of like you in it," he said as his eyes lingered on her barely covered breasts.

"If that's the case, maybe I'll wear it to work from now on. It will probably help increase my tips."

The smile slipped from his face. "Not gonna happen."

Now it was her turn to smile at him. "But if you like it so much—"

Before she could finish her statement, he jerked his shirt off and slipped it over her head. He tugged it down to mid-thigh, which was longer than the dress itself had been. "Much better."

Quinn stared at his bare chest, not so certain she agreed, but thankfully, right then she didn't have to worry about other women looking at her vampire. The sound of engines rumbling drew her attention to the RV and a black sports car driving toward them.

"Now what?" she asked.

"Now, we enjoy each other, a *lot*." The promise of his words made her quiver. "Then we put an end to the vampires clinging to this prophecy and we make some changes with the vampires, Hunters, and Guardians."

"And how are we going to do that?"

He grinned at her as he bent to place a kiss against her nose. "I have a plan."

One of her eyebrows shot up, but she couldn't resist his smile or the warmth of his lips as they slid over her flesh. "A plan?"

"Yes."

She shivered when he nibbled at her earlobe. "What about Earl?"

"He's part of the plan."

"Julian…"

"We can discuss it later," he said as he brushed back a strand of her hair. "Just let me look at you and feel you now."

There was no way she could argue with that when it was all she wanted to do too. She ran her fingers over his shortened hair and the black patches marring the platinum color. "What happened to your hair?"

"I had an incident with the sun."

Her eyes narrowed on him. "What kind of an incident?"

"That can also wait for later," he whispered against her ear.

The black Challenger pulled up beside them. Before she knew what he intended, Julian bent and swooped her into his arms. She pressed her palm flat against his chest and tucked her head beneath his chin as she relished the strength and love radiating from him.

Safe. She was finally safe, for now. There may still be other vampires out there hunting for the vampire of the prophecy, but Julian had a plan and she trusted him completely.

"I love you," she whispered.

"You're my everything," he told her as he brushed a kiss over her forehead. "From now until eternity."

"That won't be long enough."

"No, it won't."

He adjusted his hold on her as he opened the passenger door and slid inside with her against his chest. Quinn's head fell into the hollow of his neck as she pressed her lips against his flesh. She couldn't wait to hear what his plan was, but for tonight, the only plan she had was to stay in his arms, tasting and feeling him until long after the sun had risen and set again.

The End.

**The final book in the series, *Scorched Ice*,
is now available!**
***Scorched Ice* on Amazon:** http://bit.ly/ScIcAmz

**If you haven't read it yet, you can get more of Julian in
The Kindred Series.**
***Kindred* on Amazon:** http://bit.ly/KinrdAm

Stay in touch on updates and new releases from the author
by joining the mailing list!
**Mailing list for Erica Stevens & Brenda K. Davies
Updates:** http://bit.ly/ESBKDNews

FIND THE AUTHOR

Erica Stevens/Brenda K. Davies Mailing List:
http://bit.ly/ESBKDNews

Facebook page: http://bit.ly/ESFBpage
Facebook friend: http://bit.ly/EASFrd

Erica Stevens/Brenda K. Davies Book Club:
http://bit.ly/ESBDbc

Instagram: http://bit.ly/ErStInsta
Twitter: http://bit.ly/ErStTw
Website: http://bit.ly/ESWbst
Blog: http://bit.ly/ErStBl

ABOUT THE AUTHOR

Erica Stevens is the author of the Captive Series, Kindred Series, Fire & Ice Series, Ravening Series, and the Survivor Chronicles. She enjoys writing young adult, new adult, romance, horror, and science fiction. She also writes adult paranormal romance and historical romance under the pen name, Brenda K. Davies. When not out with friends and family, she is at home with her husband, dog, and horse.

Made in the USA
San Bernardino, CA
04 June 2018